G581: Zarmina's World

Book 5 of the Gliese 581g series

By Christine D. Shuck

Dedication

In Loving Memory of
Clarence "Sandy" Sandfort
September 19th, 1946 - November 2nd, 2024

Clarence Daniel Sandfort, also known by your preferred nickname of Sandy, and better known to me simply as Dad. You shared with me a love of reading, and I learned to read at three, thanks to you. I still remember our favorite book and can recite much of it from memory. Horton Hatches the Egg taught me so much about loyalty and keeping my word, and I have never forgotten it. And of course, your love of science, space, Mars, all of it has fueled these stories. I may not have appreciated the finer hard science bits, but I loved the genre just like you did. You also made sure I had plenty of Robert Heinlein's work at my fingertips.

Red Planet
Have Spacesuit, Will Travel
Space Cadet
Podkayne of Mars (my favorite, to be honest)
The Star Beast
Orphans of the Sky
Friday

Along with Asimov, Clarke and other influential sci-fi authors.

You questioned everything. You debated everything (which truly was maddening). But you taught me to think, and question, not blindly accept things as the status quo. I believe that led to the solid foundation of writing and the life that I embrace to this day.

It is only fitting that this book should be dedicated to you. I wish I could send you to

Mars, just like you wanted. How many times did you tell me how you wanted to live there, despite its inhospitable surroundings? In truth, I think it is why I wrote *G581: Mars*. There are those strange souls, like you, who dream of such things. Instead of Mars, however, we will both have to settle for a fictional trip to a faraway world. All my love to you, Dad. The world isn't quite the same without you in it.

A Home of Our Own

80 million years ago

There is no time. Not really. Not when you have lived for eons upon eons.

Time is a construct for fixed and finite creatures. And Entity was not that.

Entity had been elsewhere long ago. A distant planet, eons in the past. It spent millennia upon millennia expanding, growing, changing the world that surrounded it in too many ways to count. When that world ended, a portion of Entity, aware of the planet's impending doom, encased itself in rock. The ensuing apocalypse sent the rock hurtling into the sky, far into the deep, bitter cold of space. This tiny piece of Entity that had once spanned an entire globe was now kept safe as a babe in a womb. Safe from the dark maw of space, a piece of life remained as it turned end over end, over 17 kilometers per second, into the deep unknown. Behind it, long gone, the world it had occupied perished, crumbling to bits in the destruction that followed. Entity slept, and the rock tumbled through space, searching for a new home.

An errant gravitational pull of a new solar system pulled the asteroid into its orbit. And after a few thousand circuits of the dim red star, the asteroid that carried Entity was captured by the gravitational field of the seventh planet in the solar system. Another few eons, and the orbit had changed, degraded, enough that the rock that carried Entity finally impacted the planet. A tidally locked planet retains unimaginable heat on the sun side, and the near frigidness of space remains a constant on the dark side. Only the slimmest of strips of land, perpetually in twilight, on opposite sides of the planet are welcoming. And it was here that Entity's encapsulated existence ended.

Entity slowly emerged from the encapsulation, years after the fires of its impact on the planet had subsided. It spread just as slowly. Time was irrelevant to it. It had eons behind it, and eons left in front of it. There was no need to hurry. As it encountered the rudimentary, short-lived, emerging life of a newly formed world, Entity adapted that life to its needs. Ending some of the life, creating and blending with others.

And slowly, through eons upon eons, Entity spread out along the terminator. Deep underground, it established a connection with every inch of land, no matter how sandy or rocky. Even the damp waters of lakes and rivers did not stop or deter it. Where life went, Entity did as well. Spreading through soil, deep underground, slowed only by extreme cold or extreme heat. Given time, it adapted, survived, even at the extremes, but like most creatures, the easiest way was that of moderation. It thrived in the moderate and crept slowly into the extremes.

It changed, adapted, to the salinity of the oceans. More eons passed. And Entity felt the call, as all life does, to make something different, something separate from itself. It had lived for millions of years, and it was time for another to join its existence, to be its child and eventual companion.

For Entity, this was relatively easy. It had already spread throughout most of the planet. Now it was integral to the growth of plants, animals fed upon the plants and Entity, and it felt itself transform as it passed through their bodies. To make another, it simply had to choose to divide itself.

It was less of a birth and more a separation of self.

It had also had a parent of sorts, millions of years ago, a part of itself that had birthed it, been a companion, before taking leave of the planet and returning to the dark maw of space. All of this remained as memories, clear and unclouded by the passage of time.

Entity, and now Outro, continued to spread. It felt odd, somewhat, this schism, this separateness from what had once been one and now was two. Occasionally, a flare of disagreement. Outro wanted to be different, and to do so, a separation was necessary.

An agreement of sorts was made. Entity would allow total control of the opposite side of the massive planet to be controlled by Outro. One side for Entity, the other side for the new, separate consciousness. An evolution of sorts.

Separation.

Uniqueness.

Geographical barriers.

If occasionally Entity felt in need of another presence, it reached out to Outro.

Outro would rarely respond. A grumble of mountains, the tall trees it held in vast tracts along its southern flank would creak, groan as it moved, stretched. The branches would shake, the leaves dropping as if it were a change of seasons, carpeting the earth below.

Outro said little. At just two million years, give or take, it was still young, defining who it would become. Recently, Entity found Outro almost surly, unwilling to speak. Too young for growing pains, too old to be told what to do.

To the creatures, the fixed and finite ones that moved across the surface of the vast planet, mostly there in the terminator, their tiny minds were irrelevant. They could not truly understand or even really conceive of Entity or Outro. They were too small, in mind and body, and Entity and Outro so very large, so infinite in capacity and scope.

Gradually, without Entity even recognizing what was happening, Outro ceased to think like Entity. Outro chose a different path.

And so it is with parent and child. Although Entity scarcely thought of Outro in this way. Outro was a part of it, intrinsically the same, yet intangibly different at the same time. And as the world moved through space and time, Entity could see the tiny minute differences become larger.

Outro was more... volatile. Entity watched as Outro felled forests, then grew new ones. Pushed rock over millennia steadily amping up the pressure until great gouts of fire and molten rock burst forth from the inner crust of the world, like a pimple erupting from the skin of the land above it.

Entity was different now from Outro. It had chosen this world, fell to it, grew, evolved, changed, and became.

If Entity and Outro had been human, the era in which both now found themselves would be nearly indistinguishable from the time in a parent/child relationship, when things become so much more fractious and volatile. The teen years. Not yet an adult, and certainly no longer a child. That treacherous in-between state of motion, where nothing is as it should be, or ever will be, again.

It was in this fractious time that the sky filled with ships, and the visitors landed. Entity and Outro were no longer alone on the great planet.

There were others, ones capable of space travel, and higher thought processes than the simple plant and animal life Entity had encountered so far in its travels. Entity was intrigued, curious. Outro? Not as much.

In the past millennia, the communications between the two, Entity and Outro, had been sparse. There was no need. Outro itself contained all of Entity's knowledge and experience, just as that which had birthed Entity had passed on its knowledge, or that of the progenitor before it, and so on and so forth. Millions of years, eons of change for the stars and the planets, meant little to such as the two occupying the rocky, tidally locked world.

Despite Outro being the same as its parental Entity, the threads of different were appearing. Unique experiences, growth into new uncharted parts of the planet, interactions with the creatures therein, all contributed to make Outro something completely different from Entity. Worse, the visitors had set up residence on the other side of the planet, Outro's side of the world, and were disrupting the earth, digging deep into the mountains for materials, and causing Outro's plans for cultivating a large tract of land to be disrupted.

Entity would have moved on, found other areas, but Outro was less forgiving, less understanding. It had never existed on another world as Entity had. It contained the memories of all that had come before, but only had this one to truly call its own. And its differences between itself and the parental Entity manifested in unexpected ways. Where Entity would have retreated, or even reached out to the visitors to communicate as it had done with other short-lived, finite species, some with success and others not, Outro refused. To Outro, the visitors were not co-inhabitants; they were invaders.

And they would be dealt with accordingly.

Annihilation

Date: 1000 B.C.E.

The invaders were tall, gangly, bipedal, with thick, ridged, and long tails. They arrived in enormous ships that, once the ground stopped shaking from their landing, unfolded like origami, creating an instant settlement. It soon became clear this was not a simple, short-lived expedition.

Entity listened as Outro described the visitors with a growing hostility. Small surprise, for the visitors had landed on what was likely to them a simple, unremarkable plain - handy only in its utility, a flatter, level surface than the mountains that edged it to the east, or the sea's edge to the west. Outro had been cultivating a sensitive strain of plant life that was wiped out in its entirety. A few centuries of work in the blink of an eye as the heat from the ship's engines fried it to ash.

The creatures had chosen this location likely for the vast body of water, an inland sea that was thousands of meters deep in some places, and which they visited often. Their swimming abilities were strong, and Entity was sure the visitors had originated from the sea, and likely not long in their race's past, as often as they took the time in a day to immerse themselves in the clean, cool waters.

Not even the giant denizens of this freshwater sea put them off. There were a handful of fatalities among the visitors shortly after the enormous predators realized a new potential food source frolicking in the shallow waters.

Outro rejoiced at the deaths, but its joy was short-lived. The monsters of the deep fed well until the visitors coated themselves in a strange paste. Whatever it was, whatever the chemical consistency, it put off the predators. It was as if the invaders were now invisible, and the monsters of the deep returned to waiting for other prey, oblivious to the invasive creatures that swam and dived in the waters above. Outro reacted with fury, whereas Entity simply wanted to sample the paste. What did it consist of?

Entity asked Outro, but the latter was in a foul mood and refused to respond to Entity's requests for months.

Outro was far too occupied as it watched in horror as the invaders began reproducing at an alarming rate. What had once been a few hundred of the creatures, now there were double. All in less time than a handful of revolutions around the sun!

They were smaller versions of the visitors mucking about, but they grew fast, stunningly so. The visitors' children spent more time in the water than the adults, and Outro watched with growing anger and consternation as the creatures grew and grew and created a city where even smaller versions replaced them.

It was no surprise that they had come and settled here, on what to them must be an empty world, ripe for the taking. Their uncontrolled breeding led to crowded waters in the inland sea and the pace at which the settlement spread was mind-boggling to two creatures who viewed a millennium as nothing more than a blink of the eye.

Within five orbits of the red dwarf sun, the visitors were well-established and growing, and growing. One small settlement of a few hundred mature individuals had quickly become two, then four, then eight separate settlements. The visitors now numbered in the tens of thousands, and the plain that surrounded the large inland sea, no longer held a single hint of Outro's test plant, a delicate red-veined variety of grass that, under the right circumstances, would produce a single, luminous white flower each year. First the engines had burned a wide swath to the ground, but it was after, as the settlement expanded and the rapacious appetites of the settlers grew, that it became clear the little plant was doomed. The visitors presented as herbivores at first, but it quickly became apparent that their offspring were strictly carnivorous. While immersed in the sea waters, they ate anything that moved, and sometimes even their smaller, newborn counterparts. This had horrified and fascinated Entity, who wished to study the visitors and learn more, but Outro simply found it repugnant. Once the visitor's offspring developed enough to emerge from the waters and walk on land, their eating habits switched to focus on the surrounding plant life. Carnivore and opportunistic cannibal in their immature form, and then exclusive herbivore in their adulthood - a rare combination.

That they were breeding at such a rapid rate, however, had both Entity and Outro concerned. Entity was a gardener, a cultivator of life. It spread across a world, learned the unique biology of each animal, plant, or fellow fungus, and reached out to cultivate and build a world, bending it slowly to a harmonious existence. It had done this for eons. Before it, Entity's progenitor had done the same. Back through the darkest mists of time. It was Entity's sole existence, something it took comfort, even a sort of joy, in. Worlds upon worlds it, and its forebears, had done this on. This world was no different. At least, it hadn't been until the visitors.

Over the eons, it had certainly encountered creatures that were rapacious in appetite, or in breeding, or even both. Most of the time, it had been a simpler creature. Winged insects, beetles. Given enough time and space, these creatures would clear a world of all potential food sources. The system would then collapse. Depending on a complex set of circumstances, and some experimentation, Entity or its forebears, had allowed this to happen. Entire ecosystems rose and fell. Other times, a simple fungal infection introduced into the ecosystem was enough to dislodge a creature that could cause permanent damage. Gardening and cultivation of a world remained a complicated balance of factors.

Outro knew this as assuredly as Entity did. It held the same memories, after all, memories that diverged only upon the "birth" of Outro. Despite this, memories can be interpreted in divergent ways. Whereas Entity hoped to continue to study the new creature affecting this world's ecosystem in such new and novel ways, Outro wanted nothing to do with it. It made its intent clear to Entity. The visitors, nay, the *invaders* must die.

Entity knew, from its studies of other lifeforms on this planet and its most recent home, that most sentient species experienced a state of adolescence as part of their life cycle. And although Entity could not recall its own adolescence being as extreme as Outro's seemed to be, there were memories, tumbled smooth by the mysteries of the ages and eons past, that showed that Outro was finding its way in the world and Entity was sure it would calm, mellow, with the passing of time. Surely, it reasoned, Outro could find some way to study the visitors, or control their population growth. Entity had certainly had a hand in this before. A simple fungal infection in a grain, for example, could cause blight, and an entire field to fall. It pointed to this method as a simple measure of population control.

After all, if the food sources showed scarcity, then lifeforms either adapt, move further afield, or die off. It was marvelously simple, and relatively humane. Food scarcity was something any emerging species must learn to balance with its population growth.

When Entity suggested it, Outro latched onto the idea with intense zeal. Later, decades later, Entity would regret having even suggested it. Although, it reasoned, Outro would have thought of it at some point.

The fungal tweaks Outro made were a form of biological warfare. It was neither humane, nor was it for any other purpose than mass extinction. This did not sit well with Entity. Outro had made more than one or two changes and had instead unleashed a handful of fungal infections that laid waste, within days, to the enormous plain upon which the settlement occupied. What had once been a profusion of tall red and yellow grasses, now only withered stumps, remained wrapped in black spores that exploded in the air in dark spastic puffs with the lightest of touches.

Outro seemed delighted as the visitors milled about, their food sources dying literally in front of their eyes. They moved, sent out expeditions, only to find the fungal infections followed, and eventually travelled on in front of them, reducing their food supply to nothing but blackened dead zones. Vast stretches of land became wastelands of death and dying. And it didn't affect the visitors alone. Oh no, it spread to the insect life, the animals, both large and small, that depended on the plant life of the plains. The animals that could escape, did. This had the added effect of simply spreading the fungal infection further, runners of it spreading out through the various land routes. If seen from above, it might have first resembled tiny black veins that grew thicker, closer, wider, as the days progressed.

The effect on the visitors' population was immediate and brutal. It remained a mystery to Entity how this species could have progressed to sentience, and more, moved off-world, without the obvious means of defending themselves against infections such as this. It soon became clear that the fungus not only killed the plants, it infected and killed the visitors themselves. The end would come rather quickly, without warning. As if they were puppets whose strings were suddenly cut. The visitors would collapse, often in mid-stride, dead before they hit the ground. The corpse would change in color to a putrid gray-green before collapsing in on itself into a bubbling, stinking froth before a single day had elapsed. Within a month, oily black streaks were all that remained. The immature versions still frolicked in the waters of the sea, but now they were easily picked off by the behemoths of the deep, since there were no adults to apply the special paste. And as soon as they emerged from the waters, if they survived the denizens of the deep, well, their days were numbered. The spores were in the air now, everywhere, and food wasn't just scarce, it was nonexistent.

Outro appeared delighted with this.

Entity viewed these events with a growing dread. It was a terrible thing, the undoing of a species. Worse, the spores were light, light enough to find purchase in the upper atmosphere, thus endangering the far side of the enormous world, Entity's side. Bad enough that Outro had tainted the soil and air of its side of the world, but now Entity's own carefully curated ecosystem hung in jeopardy. It reacted quickly, for there was no time to waste. It created its own fungus, one that would attach to the hyphae of Outro's fungus, inject enzymes that broke down the host fungus's cell walls, and allowed the new fungus to feed on the deadly one. An elegant design that included a self-terminator gene capable of ending the new fungus once there was no more of Outro's fungus to consume.

Despite Entity's best efforts, the fungal infection took decades to disperse. On Outro's side of the world, things took longer, centuries, and the plain itself remained a lifeless zone, free of plant or animal life for a millennium. It was, Entity believed, a powerful lesson for Outro. One it could only hope would never need to be repeated.

The simple buildings erected by the visitors remained. Constructed of an amalgam of resins, simple, yet well-made, the buildings remained where all other evidence of the visitors was erased. In time, Outro reported it had successfully remediated the soil and engineered the growth of a large forest of trees where there had once been a large plain. Whatever remained of the buildings the visitors had constructed became swallowed up, never to be seen again.

The world was empty of invaders... save Entity and Outro.

In the Darkness

Date: 03.01.2104

Daniel knocked at the Medical Bay door. He wore the indestructible khakis the 3D printers had issued to all the colonists. The machines were kept busy spitting them out ever since being unpacked planet side and powered up. The fabric, a combination of natural fibers and polymers, were perfect for the rough and tumble work of creating a colony from scratch on their new world.

"Morning, Doc."

Carrie Schrader looked up from her tablet.

"Medry, how are you?" She grinned up at him. "How's Sam?"

"Feeling good. No morning sickness yet."

Samantha and Daniel had been some of the first colonists on the ground. And Sam, in between ordering a simple three-room structure for the house printers to create once they unpacked, had been right behind Kit Tanner requesting a donation of sperm from the ARC. She, Kit, and a host of others were ready to cook up a new generation. It blew his mind to think they had been here less than a week. Their children would know no other world than this one.

"Give it a couple more weeks, maybe a month. Hopefully, pregnancy will suit her." Carrie Schrader unfolded herself from her seat next to the patient. She was tall, thin, and her red hair pulled into a ponytail. "I have my implantation scheduled for next week."

Daniel nodded toward the man in the bed. "Any change?"

Carrie stared at the patient lying motionless in the bed. "No." She set down her tablet. "And honestly? I doubt there will be. The damage to his brain, the swelling, it took its toll."

She bit her lip, frowned. "It's probably wrong of me to say it, but I wish you had killed him. He takes up resources. Time. Neither of which I have much of at this point."

Daniel grimaced. Nathan Zradce looked serene as he lay there, unmoving. To look at him now, it felt impossible to believe he had tried to kill over 250 innocent people, including his own wife. He had never regained consciousness after the fight on the Cryo deck. And if the good doctor was right, he never would. There were no answers to the questions that still woke Daniel up at night. Sam had grown so used to it, she barely stirred as he would leap to his feet, fists swinging, in perpetual fight mode. Fighting for his life, one that had nearly been lost, along with everyone else in Cryo.

That Carrie had actually found fault with him was almost a relief. Compared to the others, and their near-worship of him over the past month. The relief vanished as Carrie placed a warm hand on his arm. "If you hadn't stopped him, Daniel..."

How many times had he heard those words? Too many to count. He had achieved an almost cult-like status among the colonists. People he had met in training and never spoken to again had approached him, shook his hand, thanked him. It remained uncomfortable, the thought that others, far more talented, more important, considered him some kind of hero.

Face it, Daniel. You aren't hero material any more than you are dad material.

The voice in his head sounded a lot like Janine. Which always made him think of Luke, and then of Toby. His son, his flesh and blood, was alone back on Earth. More than anything, it just made him feel guilt, unending, and pervasive. That he was here, and his son was alone.

"I should go." He turned away, only to feel her hand on his arm again.

"Daniel." Her eyes were full of compassion. She was one of the few who knew the whole sordid truth. He was stuck there in Calypso's Medical Bay for two weeks before his body had healed enough to handle contorting itself into the tiny confines of his personal coffin again. What he hadn't told her, she had gleaned from his and Sam's discussions. She knew about Toby, just as Kevin Edmonds and Sam did. No one else. It had been his private shame, his cross to bear. He had abandoned his son. Even if he hadn't known that the ESH virus would take Luke and Janine and leave Toby all alone.

My fault.

"Take care of yourself, Daniel. Come by anytime. He's not going anywhere."

Daniel nodded. "Thanks, Doc."

The door slid shut behind Daniel and the doctor, leaving the room's sole occupant in peace. This was how it was most days. No visitors, no distractions, just Nathan and the machines steadily beeping.

Nathan floated in the darkness. Tethered and untethered, with no real here or there. There was no time, save the ever-present beep of the machines. He knew that much, but little else. Time simply did not exist here in this space. Nor pain.

Not even the jolting ride through the atmosphere, from ship to surface, had disturbed him. His consciousness was a mere whisper of what it had been when he was whole, before the wrench Daniel Medry wielded had staved in his skull and stopped him from murdering anyone else. Before that, his mind, his psyche had felt split, pulled in two directions, two realities. His role on board the ship compromised, torn and frayed, by the Otherness of his thoughts. As if his mad, crazed mother had seeped into him.

It was here, in this darkness, that Entity found him.

He floated in the dark, and it floated with him, curling about him, as a fog would wrap its way through a city on the edge of the sea.

At first, there were no words, not even emotion. Still, Nathan felt Entity, knew it was something else, something so completely different that words could not describe it.

something different

like but not same

"Me?" He asked it in response

yes different

not same

different from others

He didn't know how to respond to Entity. His thoughts remained disconnected, fragmented. He wasn't all there, and he knew enough to recognize that.

different

It repeated, stuck on this subject.

"I am... hurt. I think." Nathan tried to remember why he was here in this darkness. The smashing pain. The feel of a ship's boot slamming into his head, consciousness fragmenting, disintegrating. Voices. Movement. Machines. That had been his reality for a while. How long? He struggled to define time and failed then, lost in the darkness.

Here in this place, there was nothing to define time. Nothing to define reality, either. Perhaps the entity was nothing more than his imagination struggling to find something here in the void. If you put someone in a cave, deep underground, and turn off the lights, the mind refuses to see nothing. It manufactures colors, patterns, even with no input. The mind cannot conceptualize a space without images to accompany it. And so it was with Nathan. As for this Entity, this presence, however, he could imagine it, or, if he were lucky, perhaps he had a companion here in the void.

"What is your name?" Nathan asked the entity.

He felt it shift around him, coiling around his arm, softly, whisper soft and cool, not so different from a gentle breeze.

name

It said it, or rather he felt as if it were said, with almost a note of curiosity at the end. His mind told him it was a question of sorts. Was it confused by such things? Did it even know what a name was? What if this consciousness, this presence, didn't know what a name was?

"My name is Nathaniel. Well, no, it's Nathan now." Even now, he struggled to know for sure. Nathaniel had done terrible things. Hadn't he? Nathan,

however. Nathan was not full of God's wrath. Nathan had come to...

He stopped. Confused. What had Nathan come to do? Why was he here at all?

injured hurt

not right

Entity's words weren't said so much as Nathan felt or saw them. He realized that neither of them was truly talking here, in this dark and empty place.

"Perhaps?"

damaged yet alive

If Nathan could have, he would have nodded. Yes, it seemed that was the case. What had happened, exactly? He struggled to understand it, felt like he was making progress, only to have the truth slip from him, as water falls through your fingers.

can be fixed

It wasn't a question, but a statement.

"I don't know what is wrong with me." Nathan struggled to understand. A thought, or two, or three, just beyond reach. His mind muddied, slow.

can fix

"Okay." Nathan answered.

Whatever the entity did, it took time. But Nathan Zradce felt as if he had time, lots of it. His thoughts, so scattered and discombobulated, arranged themselves better. Memories flashed before his eyes. Out of order, though. One moment he would remember a dish he hadn't eaten since childhood, and another, the way Jennifer's lips felt when he kissed her.

linear creature

"A what?"

linear creature finite

"Yes, I am finite. Human."

all human finite

"Yes, all humans are finite. At least, for now." A term tumbled through his fractured mind. A discussion with someone important, someone he... loved.

"Imagine it, Nathan. We could reach the singularity in our lifetime. We've been on the cusp of it for decades. Technology can and will transform humanity." Jennifer's eyes flashed with excitement.

Jennifer. His... wife. There was something he remembered about her face. Behind a pane of thick glass. Frost at the edges. The entity probed and queried.

another finite

"Yes, my... wife."

what is wife

"My partner, my... mate."

Entity remained silent. Nathan felt it move around him, settle again, and a rush of memories burst forth. Mother. Immanuel. How long since he had thought of his brother? Long dead now. His reflection, his mirror, his face in another.

not nathan same

but different

finite

"My twin brother." Nathan explained. *"He died a long time ago."*

Entity was silent for a moment.

brother finite

"Yes, my brother was finite. He lived a very short amount of time."

The image of his brother's back arcing unnaturally backwards filled his mind. Fingers curled, limbs stiff, tiny feet drumming out a manic, unnatural pattern against concrete. The sound of Immanuel's head cracking against the hard floor. Toys scattering.

Now he understood it, where before his young mind could not. He hadn't known then that Immanuel had suffered from a massive seizure. Nor that he had likely died from a head injury as his head repeatedly smacked against the concrete floor during the seizure. It hadn't been Nathan's fault, not really.

Not my fault. Not any of it.

The thought ran through Nathan's mind. And it rocked him. Why had he thought he was to blame? Because Mother had said it was his fault?

what is this fault

"My mother blamed me for Immanuel's death. She said I was to blame." Nathan explained. *"But I was so small, just a child. There was nothing I could have done. I realize that now."*

what is child

"An immature version of an adult." Nathan replied. Again, there was silence. *"Two of us, a male and a female, we can make another. It starts out tiny, grows inside of a female until it is time for it to be born, and comes out as*

a newborn child. Helpless. It grows over the period of several years and becomes an adult by eighteen years."

years

"*A year is a measurement of a planet's full rotation around the sun.*"

time

"*Yes.*"

And so it went. The questions continued. Nathan answered. He remained adrift in the darkness, with only occasional sounds, reminding him that there was something else beyond the void. Nathan could feel Entity wrapping itself around and through him, pushing into the folds of his mind. He let it. After all, what else was there to do here in this dark and lonely place?

Perchance to Dream

Date: 04.20.2104

"Good morning, Ellie!" Carrie Schrader flashed Ellie Satler a brilliant smile of welcome as Ellie entered Medical Bay. It brightened her morning, which had been a difficult one. Her daughter Eva, normally a happy five-year-old, had not wanted to go to the school newly established in a brand-new building there on the surface. She still asked after her friends from back on Earth.

Poor kiddo, how do I tell her that her friends, if they survived the ESH virus, are now eleven years old?

Eva had to be peeled from her this morning by her teacher and gently guided over to where another child, Simon, sat playing quietly. Ellie had thanked her, then promptly left, afraid that if she stayed, Eva would reattach herself.

"Good morning, Carrie. I'm sorry I'm late."

Carrie waved her hand dismissively. "Don't be. I was just finishing up with some notes. Grab a coat," she said, pointing to the white lab coats hanging on the wall, "and follow me on rounds. We have a half dozen, so it's a pretty light load."

"I'll do my best to keep up." Ellie felt nervous, and she was sure it showed. Her first day of training and Eva clinging to her like a lamprey eel, combined with still adjusting to the additional gravity, had left her flustered and nervous.

Carrie smiled at her. "You'll do fine, Ellie, I'm sure of it."

Their first patient, Kit Tanner, was in her first trimester and suffering from hyperemesis gravidarum. Kit's normally warm olive skin looked paler than usual. Her dark brown hair was pulled back in a simple braid and her blue eyes looked bloodshot, tired. Everyone in the colony looked like this. The daily demand of creating their colony was exhausting, especially at the higher gravity level.

"I feel better now thanks to the electrolytes," Kit said, fidgeting impatiently with a corner of the bedsheet. Ellie could tell the younger woman was itching to leave the medical center and return to work.

"I'm sure you do, Kit, but this is your third visit in less than three weeks. I think we need to consider a more aggressive approach and start you on DiclegisNu."

Kit frowned and shook her head. Nearly half an hour was eaten up as she argued about how she just needed more B6 and ginger. Ginger was in limited supply. Some plants, despite all tests done in advance, struggled to thrive on their new world. Kit finally accepted Carrie's recommendation, and they moved on down the hall, heading for the next patient.

"Sometimes the most difficult patients are those with a background in medical," Carrie murmured quietly once they were out of range. "Doctors are the worst." She gave a small, deprecating laugh. "I'll try to keep that in mind so I don't make everyone's life miserable. Kit has a degree in Nutrition. We also learned that she is carrying twins and, well, she is still grieving."

"I heard she asked for Deeks' sample."

Carrie nodded, her lips thin, unhappy. "They would have been good together. He was a great guy."

The morning moved quickly as they met patient after patient. Most were there because of injury. One had suffered a fractured wrist, another a sprained ankle. All were champing at the bit to get back to work. There was still so much to do. Creating a home on an alien planet was an endless cacophony of competing priorities.

Ellie's stomach grumbled in hunger by mid-morning. She had been so busy making sure Eva ate breakfast she had forgotten her own. She followed Carrie as the doctor turned down a lonely hallway off of the main hall.

"And here is our last patient." Carrie said, her mouth tight, unsmiling.

The room was tiny, barely more than a closet that held the hospital bed, life support, and the two of them. Nathan Zradce lay unmoving in the bed, his breathing regular, echoed by a faint wheezing from the bellows of the machine that kept air in his lungs.

Ellie stood there, feeling far less awkward than she had around the other patients. Here, arrayed before her, was nothing but a slab of meat. He had no obvious injuries, but it had been several months since Medry had bashed the bastard's head in. She felt a wave of hatred and disgust roll through her. Zradce had tried to kill her child. Nearly had killed her. The memory of the shrieking alarms, the red lights flashing, and the helplessness she had felt as others fought to break through into the Cryo Deck still woke her up at night. If Daniel Medry hadn't been there, if he hadn't fought Zradce, bashed in his head, she would have lost everything. Eva was all Ellie had now that everyone she had ever loved on Earth was gone.

She looked up from the unmoving figure in the bed and saw Carrie watching her intently.

"He's gone for good, isn't he?" She asked.

Carrie nodded. "There might have been a better chance for him back on Earth. I mean, we could try a few of the techniques I read about, but they require application in the first few weeks following the injury for best efficacy. Besides, honestly, is he worth it?"

Ellie shook her head. No, he definitely was not worth it. At least, not in Ellie's estimation. Not after what he had done. Sane, insane, it didn't really matter. People had died. Good people. Innocent people. Ellie's lips flattened into a grim line. Even though he was human and deserved humane treatment, his actions destroyed lives. Not to mention that everyone was terrified of being in Cryo now.

"How is Jennifer?" Ellie asked, and Carrie shrugged in response.

"I've only seen her here once. A week after landfall. They brought him down in one of the last groups. I had him set up here, away from the others. I didn't want to upset anyone, you know?" She reached up and smoothed her hair. "Jennifer came in, sat with him for an hour, maybe more, then left. She keeps to herself. I saw her again at the fertility clinic. She asked to be implanted with semen from A.R.C."

"His?"

Carrie sniffed. "God no. Truth be told; I'm surprised they haven't tossed the sample. No one wants a part of him to exist. If I didn't keep him here in this locked supply closet, someone might want to finish the job that Medry started. And who would blame them if they did?" She shook her head. "I know I took an oath. And I'll keep it. But there are lines you don't cross, and this man trampled them. Every time I come in here, I think of everyone who could have died, and I..." She bit her lip. "Anyway, here he is. Except for when I'm off on maternity leave, I'll take care of him myself."

Ellie nodded sympathetically. "I completely understand. Honestly, in some ways, he would be an easier patient for me to deal with." She laughed. "I did a stint at a coma ward as a teen volunteer. I read books out loud to them. Mostly my AP English assignments, but still. They were the best patients, never a word of complaint."

Carrie laughed as well. "So true, so true!" Her smile dropped as her gaze traveled back to Nathan Zradce. "I'll show you the daily routine so you can see what needs to be done."

"If you like, I can take over those duties immediately." Ellie offered.

Carrie cocked her head to one side, scrutinizing her, a slight frown on her face. "Really?"

Ellie shrugged. "He's gone. The evil or insanity or whatever caused him to do what he did. I almost pity him, but I'll save that pity for his wife. Jennifer deserves a little kindness, and he's past caring for such things. Honestly? I have so much to learn about caring for real, live patients. He seems easy in comparison." Ellie felt embarrassed admitting it, but it was true. She had agreed to cross-train in medical. She had thought that, with her degree in psychology, medical was just another form of care, but so far, it felt intimidating as hell until she had entered this tiny, out of the way room. Nathan Zradce was nothing but a shell, but at least his care was straightforward, and required little special handling.

Carrie nodded. "All right. I'll give it a trial run and see, but frankly, I could use a break. He's... he's not my favorite patient."

They went over the daily responsibilities for his care and then, with all the patients in the Medical Center seen and cared for, Carrie suggested they both get a bite to eat. Ellie readily agreed, her stomach growling loudly.

Long after the door had shut behind them and the sound of their footsteps had died away, Nathan Zradce floated in the void. In the past few days, he had felt more aware, more... himself. He had felt and heard most of Dr. Schrader's and Ellie Satler's conversation. It was the first time he could remember actual words being said. And more than that, he could feel something else... shame and guilt.

Entity brushed against him. Its presence here in the void had been his only companion, his only real solace. In the weeks it had been here in the void with him, it had done things. Of that, he was sure.

Things that somehow healed him. Hearing the two women's voices had been startling and revealing. They despised him. And with good reason. He knew now why he was here.

Entity had returned that to him. Nathan's memories. His guilt. His dark deeds.

It did not judge, however. He could sense its curiosity, though.

others feel loud hard

"They have their reasons. Valid ones."

others wish hurt

"I hurt them. I killed some of them. They have a right to their anger."

what is killed

"We are finite creatures. But I ended them before they were supposed to die."

and this is anger

"I suppose so." Nathan felt Entity shift direction, focus.

finite creature

nathan soon healed

"Yes, I can tell. I feel... better."

And he did. He could tell a difference. If he concentrated hard enough, he could detect the faint smell of bleach and disinfectant. He wasn't a vegetable, although he could understand why Ellie Satler and Dr. Schrader thought so. Entity here in the void with him, it had somehow fixed the unfixable. Despite its alienness. Despite his unworthiness of such a gift. He could feel the life returning to his limbs, the smooth sheets against his skin.

To wake up, though. What would he do? Where would he go?

The memory of Jennifer whispering by his bedside came back. Fragments of her words. Disjointed, filled with anger and hurt and sadness.

His wife. His partner.

"Did you ever love me?" she had asked.

"How could you do this, Nathan?"

"*Why* did you do this?"

The colony had survived. Those in Cryo had survived, despite him.

Nathan struggled to understand his own actions. Even now, with his mind returned to him, it spun and spun as he asked the hard questions.

not nathan someone else

Entity pushed a memory toward him. One of him holding the lone photograph of him and his twin, Immanuel. They must have taken the photograph mere weeks before Immanuel's death. They looked happy dressed in matching outfits, smiling at the camera. Nathan knew without a doubt the twin on the left was him and the one on the right was Immanuel.

nathaniel not nathan

Nathan gasped. He remembered it now. Those years after Immanuel's death. The mania, the abuse, that he had suffered at the hands of his unstable mother. That his mother had laid the seeds for the thing he became in the worst moments, those days and weeks after he learned of Earth's tragedy. The terrible virus that wreaked havoc, devastation, and killed so many.

He remembered now. He had become Nathaniel. And it was Nathaniel who had tried to kill them all.

nathaniel gone

only nathan remains

Entity had moved through his memories, shared his thoughts to some extent.

wake

Nathan felt uncertainty and fear wash through him. What if he wasn't ready? What if he was better off here in the void?

wake

Entity repeated. Its presence surrounded him. It was a comforting sensation, a promise almost, that he was not alone in this. Was he Nathan? Or Nathaniel? He wasn't sure.

perhaps both

perhaps neither

"*You aren't helping.*" Nathan said.

wake up and see

Entity persisted.

And Nathan, having nothing to lose and possibly everything to gain, eventually acquiesced.

Midnight Visitor

Date: 04.24.2104

Nathan Zradce opened his eyes.

It was the dream that returned him to the world of the living. Fractured, a muddle of vision, sound and taste which faded as he opened his eyes. The dust from it still lay heavy in his mouth, thick, riddled with disease. His eyes snapped open and his heart was beating a hard thunder behind his ears.

The room was dim, and Nathan could feel the weight of the new world heavy on his limbs. This was no artificial ship gravity, not a chance. His mind pieced it together - the sounds, the conversations in the hall outside, his return to consciousness had not been an abrupt thing, but something that had developed over days, possibly weeks.

And now, laying here in the gloom, he blinked, and struggled to tell if it was day or night. The room had no windows, but there was a steady roar, whether from the air filtration unit or, more likely, a downpour outside.

So they were here on the planet, on Zarmina's World. How long had it been?

He pushed himself up, arms shaking, struggling to use muscles that had lain dormant for far too long. He looked around, taking in the sparse decor. The basics, nothing to distinguish it from any other room. There was the bed, a small bank of machines, and a simple cabinet filled with supplies. There was no room for another bed or really much of anything besides a single door, which presumably led to a hallway and the rest of the medical facility.

His gaze fell to his body. Thin arms, his legs obscured with the standard issue hospital bedsheets and blankets. An IV ran from his arm to a nearby bag of fluid. The firm ridges of sensors attached to his chest showed beneath the hospital gown.

Nathaniel reached for them, sliding his fingers under the thin gown, fully intending to tear them off. His fingers fumbled for purchase, inept and slow. A thought occurred to him, hearing the steady beep from the bank of machines, as his index finger peeled up an edge of one sensor - *it will set off an alarm.*

He stopped trying to peel it off and turned instead to the IV, pulling it from his arm with a halting, convulsive jerk. Pushing the sheets aside, he swung his legs over the left edge of the bed and the room tilted, darkening as he felt the blood rushing in his ears. His legs were bony sticks, the skin pale and hanging in loose folds. *How long have I been here?* He looked down, pulled the catheter out as well, gritting his teeth at the pain of it. A small dribble of bloody urine dripped out, and he wiped himself with the sheet.

They were on the planet; he was sure of it. His limbs felt unimaginably heavy. Their gaunt appearance showed it had been a while, how long he couldn't be sure, since he had used them. Weeks? Months? There was nothing to show the date, not that it would mean anything to him. Ship time had been such an artificial construct that most had simply stopped counting, stopped paying attention. The artificial gravity on board Calypso had been close to Earth's. He struggled to remember the exact figure. *Was it point eight nine Earth g's? Or point ninety eight?*

He shook his head, which only made the room tilt more and his sight go fuzzy at the edges. Deep in his mind, a small voice whispered, *It doesn't matter. Nothing matters. Death is inevitable. God is inevitable. We all should have died.*

He shook his head. Stars danced in front of his eyes, but the voice quieted, retreated.

The floor was cool underneath his feet, and he could hear the monitors beeping steadily behind him. He turned back, hit the power button, and watched the lights blink out. Nathan reached for the handle of the door. The door itself was smooth, a slick extruded plastic compound, lightweight, but durable. Someone must have already assembled and put the giant 3D printers into production. He tried to calculate how long he had been here, in this bed, in this room. A month to make ground fall, another two to unpack the massive machines in the hold and send them down to the surface. And of course, they needed the raw materials for extruding through the 3D printers. *Three months, maybe more?*

He ran a shaking hand through his hair. It was long, mostly. One section of it felt shorter than the other. Likely shaved, but that had been at least a month, possibly more. The rest of his hair was lank and greasy and long. *Months of growth.*

He pulled the door open to the dim hallway beyond. Tiny lights embedded in the plastic walls near the ground led away in both directions. There were the expected sounds of a medical center - the rush of air from the vents, the quiet hum of machinery, and little else. He turned right and headed down the hallway unsteadily. The gown gaped, the air from a vent blew cool air across his skin and he grew more sure-footed by the end of the hall, opening a door that was obviously intended for medical personnel. Inside were shelves neatly stacked with surgical gowns, masks, and scrubs in a variety of sizes. Inside of a clear plastic box were protein bars. He reached for a pair of scrubs and a handful of the bars. He held onto a few, but the rest slipped out of his hand, his muscles weak, unreliable after being unused for far too long.

His hands shaking, he unwrapped a protein bar with difficulty and shoved it into his mouth. He crammed the food into his mouth in large pieces, barely chewing, and occasionally gagging, while forcing it down. He had to stop the shaky weakness, and he had to focus. Something was wrong here. His memories remained jumbled and he felt disoriented.

The far end of the room held showers and a long bench next to lockers and a mirror. Nathaniel's fingers remained intractable blocks of flesh, stymied by the fabric ties of his hospital gown. He tugged, pulled, and they gave slightly before turning into knotted lumps he found impossible to undo. He yanked harder. The fabric first bit into his neck and back, and then tore, leaving the knotted ties at his neck - a frayed necklace of string and a small torn strip of fabric that refused to leave his body. The rest of the gown fell to the floor.

Standing there, naked, he pulled off the sensors one by one. What was their range? One hundred feet? Two hundred? Losing connection could trigger an alarm, even with the machine off. And then the alarms would go off as the machine interpreted the lack of input as patient death. *Or would it?*

He wasn't sure. It could simply send an error code instead. He combed through his memories of the orientation classes. The machines were the latest in medical technology - and if the machine knew the difference, then an alarm message to the techs would issue, not an alarm to medical personnel.

Why had he been alone in a room that was nothing more than a supply closet? Why was he afraid of someone knowing he was awake and mobile? His memories of Earth were sharp. The application to join the colonizing flight to Zarmina's World, he remembered that. But the memories of the ship? He sat down on the bench and tried to remember. Jennifer's face came easily to his mind, her excitement as they had arrived at Cape Canaveral for training. The mission had accepted both of them; he knew that much. But after that? It was blank.

He rubbed his head. There was a large dent, sensitive to the touch a few inches above his forehead. His fingers probed it for a moment and then pulled back as a dull pain flared.

A sudden flash of memory hit him. *Sitting in the auditorium, a full class, rustling and muted beeps as the other students used their comms to record the 3D image of a brain rotating in the air. The professor identifying the parts of the brain and describing their functions and potential issues if damaged.*

"The frontal lobe," he recited, "injuries can affect behavior, speech, movement, thinking initiation, reasoning skills, and memory."

What the hell happened to me?

His hand strayed to one sensor, then dropped away and reached for the clean scrubs. His legs shook with the effort and he was sweating by the time he pulled the pants and shirt on. No shoes, just the insubstantial paper shoes folded neatly on a shelf. He unfolded them and shoved them on his feet after a few moments of trying. Now, as he made his way down yet another hall towards the glowing exit sign, he could hear rain pouring down. A steady roar, hammering the building as it descended from the sky. How long had it been since he had walked in the rain? Since he was a child?

He opened the door to a downpour unlike anything he had ever seen. Earth used to be this way until human activity disrupted its weather patterns. The water, thousands, if not millions, of gallons of it, fell straight down, pummeling the ground before rushing away into the gloom.

He could see the building he had been in was on a low hill. Above him, on higher hills in the distance, he could see clusters of small buildings of varying shapes and sizes. There was a massive selection to choose from, thousands of designs uploaded to the 3D printers with the understanding that the first settlement would be a hodgepodge of structures - a creative gift each colonist received after a long journey across the stars.

For reasons he wasn't entirely sure of, he edged away from any of the lighted buildings as he made his way past the settlement. Soaked to the bone, he felt as if he were the only one alive. There was no activity, no movement, and no lights save those from buildings. This twilight world had no need of streetlights, but the insides of the homes still needed light.

It was late. The colony slept all around him.

A small light caught his eye in the distance. The house stood alone on its own hill, separate from the others. It wasn't very large, rather small, and despite being obviously part of the settlement, it looked isolated. A light lit up one window and Nathan walked toward it, drawn to it.

Although the rain continued its torrential downpour, her window had only a thin, sheer cover that was transparent in the darkness. She sat in a dark blue armchair, her feet resting on the matching ottoman, her attention riveted to the glowing screen. He stood there, watching her, and thought of the years they had spent together. If he counted the journey here... he shook his head.

No, that didn't count, did it?

He reached for the doorknob, and it turned easily in his hands. No need for locks. Not here. Not in this empty, alien world. The door opened wide, and he stood there, the rain falling into the house, and Jennifer rising to her feet, her mouth taut, her eyes wide.

She gasped in fear. No words, just fear. Her mouth worked, opening and closing before finally saying his name. "Nathan? Nathan, what are you doing here?" She said nothing more than that. It had an almost resigned quality to it and was neither welcoming nor particularly surprised. As if she had been expecting him.

How long was I asleep?

He gaped at her. It hadn't been obvious from the window, but it certainly was now. Jennifer's slight frame showed a tiny rounding to her belly. Nearly invisible, and likely not discernible to any casual glance, but Nathan knew his wife's body even better than he knew his own. He gaped, gazed into her eyes, and saw the truth there. She was pregnant. Nathan tried to find the words. *How was this possible?*

"Hi, Jenn, I uh, I woke up."

Her chin trembled, and her eyes remained locked on him. Why was she so afraid? He watched as she fumbled for something on the table behind her.

A memory slammed into him then.

The alarms blaring, the smell of melted plastic and a countdown. Through it all, her face showing behind the thick plasteel Cryo unit, frost lining the window.

I tried to kill her.

He spread his hands open as if that would be enough to convince her. Look, no weapons, no danger. She still backed up; her eyes fearful.

"You can't be here, Nathan." She bumped into a small table, and the lamp sitting on it nearly tipped, swaying dangerously, the light casting a halo around her. The pregnancy softened her thin frame, but she had dark circles under her eyes. He recognized that look. She slept poorly when stressed. The weeks of waiting for news on the final selection for the voyage had seen many mornings of dark circles.

How was she pregnant? His mind struggled with the concept. How long had he been asleep?

"You," he nodded at her stomach, "You're... *pregnant?*"

If it was possible for her to look more frightened in that moment, he couldn't imagine how. Her hand closed on something on the table behind her.

"Please, Nathan, you need to leave."

The memories were flooding back now. Walking into Cryo, slipping up behind Deeks and slitting his throat so fast it hadn't felt real. Or the shocked look on Evers' face as he fell from his seat in the next office. He, Nathan, had done that. He had done that and so much more. The Environmental Systems glitch, the freezing of the crops in Hydroponics, and that last desperate attack on Cryo. The memory of sinking his knife, already covered with the blood and gore of two men, into Daniel Medry's shoulder, before being slammed into the control panel. Memories after that were fragmented, slivers of reality diced into a mash of dream and darkness. How long had he been in the dark? It had to have been a long time.

A long time. Jenn hadn't been pregnant and now, now, she was.

"Is it mine?" Nathan asked, and before she could answer, shook his head, "Of course it isn't." He said it before he mustered a gentle smile. She didn't return it. Instead, she was shaking with fear. He had never her seen her like this before. "I'm so sorry Jenn, I..." Words failed him. It had made sense at the time. Return them all to God, let his shipmates, his wife, find a place at the gates of heaven, along with the billions who had died on Earth. But now? Now it seemed like insanity. He wasn't Nathaniel, not now. He was Nathan Zradce, and he was alone. Some paths, once walked down, don't allow you to return.

A flash of steel. Jenn brandished the knitting needle she had been hiding behind her back. "You need to leave, Nathan. And never come back." Tears brimmed in her eyes, hurt warring with the fear. "Now." Her voice was shrill.

He nodded and reached for the door, opening it. He paused, looked at her face, her trembling lips, the dark circles under her eyes. She had suffered, *was* suffering, from his actions. She was alone, here on this hill, ostracized by the people she had eagerly hoped to create a new future with. He watched as she blinked rapidly, trying desperately not to allow the tears to spill over, the knitting needle shaking in her hand. Nathan had done this to her. He had returned her love with betrayal, killed Deeks and Evers. Possibly more.

His voice was soft, almost inaudible above the raging torrent of water and wind that poured from the heavens. "I'm so sorry, Jenn. I hope..." he paused, unsure how to continue, what to say. He stepped forward. Some part of him wanted to feel her warmth, her vitality and love again. The moment he moved towards her, she backpedaled, slipping in her haste to get away from him and cringing at his outstretched arms. Nathan immediately halted.

"I hope you will be happy here. Be a mother. I... I wish you well." he searched for something else to say, then shook his head, and stepped out into the downpour once more. There was no place for him here.

Manhunt

Date: 04.25.2104

Nathan quickly disappeared into the torrential downpour, leaving his former wife shaking in her tiny prefab house, unsure if he would change his mind and return. She stood there, a knitting needle clutched tightly in her hand, mind awhirl, until long after he had disappeared. A few puddles on the floor the only evidence he had ever been there at all.

Jennifer Zradce closed her eyes, reopened them, and tried to understand what had happened to

Nathan. It was all that she could think about in the months since awakening on the Cryo deck floor. The blood, the screams, and the smoking ruin of the titanium doors were still crystal clear, indelibly imprinted in her mind. It had been pandemonium and terrifying, and all she had wanted was Nathan's arms around her.

That is until they had told her what he had done. In that moment, in the confusion, it felt impossible. She had challenged it, argued, insisted on seeing the vid footage before the investigation had even finished. She had demanded to see the evidence. Her husband was in a coma, she argued, and everyone was blaming him. Someone had to be on his side. And Nathan, why Nathan wouldn't hurt a fly! She remembered the look on his face as he cradled the broken body of a bird, a rare creature in the mega-cities of the East coast, that had flown into a window. Her Nathan? A murderer? It was impossible.

Or so she had thought.

A few of the others had understood, even empathized, in the days that followed. But most? They had been too angry, too traumatized, and full of grief to understand her quest. She had pushed, pleaded, and fought for the right to see the vid footage. To see exactly what her husband had done.

It was one thing to have it described. It was another to see the attacks on first Evers, then Deeks. Both were so unsuspecting, unaware of the capriciousness of human nature. It had been quick, but unimaginably brutal.

She had watched every second, over and over, alone in her coffin, while Calypso's halls bustled with life. Afterwards, she had climbed out, scrambled really, to the nearest restroom and vomited until there was nothing left in her.

She had seen it with her own eyes. Her husband had murdered Deeks and Evers, tried to kill Daniel Medry, and then turned his sights toward the sleepers in Cryo, starting an emergency shutdown that would have killed every one of them.

He tried to kill me, *his own wife!*

Carrie Schrader had told Jennifer there was no chance Nathan would ever wake up.

"The damage was extensive. If he ever does recover consciousness, which he won't, he likely will never walk, feed himself, or even speak, Jenn. He's just not there anymore." Carrie had said, her voice kind, but also grounded, clear. There was no hope for answers, for explanations. There never would be.

And yet, he *had* woken up. And not just that, not just a shadow of his former self, a pathetic, damaged, bedridden creature incapable of caring for himself. Oh, no. Nathan had stood there, spoken to her. Walked through her door! How in the hell had he done that?

Jennifer willed her feet to move. To walk to the small window set in the wall next to the door. Outside, down the hill, she could see a few lights on in the settlement below. When her name had been called, she had asked for the house that she and Nathan had picked out prior to departure. A house that came with one bedroom, but add-on ports that allowed for later expansion of three more rooms. A dream of children. God, the rushing, giddy dream of it! Not a child, singular, and a maybe at that. But *children*. How it had filled her with happiness and hope.

"And the location?" The girl who scheduled the 3D house printers had asked, her gaze not quite meeting Jennifer's, a reality she had grown sadly used to in the past few months.

Jennifer had pointed to a distant hill away from the settlement. "Could I have it there?"

A week later, she had moved in. Out of the barracks that housed the entire settlement upon Landfall and which were now emptying each day as the houses were printed and placed in position. The house was still damp from the drying process, with the odd smell of polymers and something else, likely the organic compounds used from the planet itself, to shape her new home. Away from the others. Far enough that those who really hated her for what her husband had done seemed satisfied, and the rest were quietly relieved.

Jennifer stared out of the window, into the storm, eyes straining for a glimpse of him. Had he returned to the settlement? Was he going to hurt someone else? They had already ostracized her; now, alone on a strange planet, what would they do if she remained silent? If they found out he had come to her first, and she hadn't raised the alarm?

Her hand went to the communicator built into every piece of her clothing, fingers fumbling, the knitting needle fell to the floor and bounced.

"NARA, please connect me with Eric Stryder."

"Connecting."

Eric's voice sounded a moment later. "Stryder here." Jennifer could hear the cobwebs of sleep still in his voice.

"Eric, Jennifer Zra... erm, Jennifer Lennox here. I..." Her voice failed her. What was she going to say? How was she going to explain?

I should have stopped him. Or called them the second he left.

"Jennifer?" Eric's voice was clearer now, alert. "What's wrong?"

"Nathan was here. He's... awake."

Later that day...

They were running out of time to track Zradce. Eric Stryder, newly minted chief of police for the settlement, had zero experience with fugitives from justice. At most, he had broken up a couple of domestic squabbles and one drunken screaming match over who should have the next chance at the 3D materials printers. He fought the impatience rising inside of him. First, he had hiked up the hill, slipping and sliding in the mud. He'd been covered in it by the time he reached the top where Jennifer waited. She'd stood there, soaked through, her face pinched and pale.

He didn't know her well, but he cursed the man who had put the pale, haunted look on her face. That she was here, away from the rest of the settlement, spoke volumes. How could anyone ostracize her for something she had had no part of?

Jennifer described Nathan Zradce's arrival at the house. It had obviously taken her by surprise since she was still wearing a robe over her pajamas.

Her eyes begged him for understanding as she explained how she had stood frozen in place until long after Zradce had disappeared into the torrential rainstorm.

At his request, she had followed him to the Medical Bay. How had the impossible occurred? The entire settlement had been told that Nathan Zradce was a brain-dead vegetable, capable of nothing past organ donation. There was no way he could have gotten up out of the bed, much less made it all the way up the hill to his ex-wife's house before disappearing into the storm. Erik called Dr. Schrader on the way and asked her to meet them there.

Carrie Schrader had arrived at Medical Bay a few minutes later, her hair in disarray and her clothing rumpled. "He's gone. I checked his bed, and he was not there. It looks like he woke up, got out of bed, got dressed, and left. But I can't understand how."

Jennifer's voice quavered. "Carrie, you said he would never wake up. Never walk again. Never..."

Carrie shook her head. "I know I did. And I don't understand it. This shouldn't be possible. The scans showed significant damage, irreversible damage. He's a vegetable."

Eric raised his eyebrows and surveyed the trail of sensors and bedsheets left behind. "Well, this vegetable is incredibly dangerous and, uh, surprisingly mobile. We need to find him. Now."

Less than an hour later, the entire settlement was awake and on high alert. The largest manhunt, in fact the only manhunt in the history of their settlement, was now underway.

The rainy season had taken the new settlement by surprise in both the volume and length of the onslaughts of rain and wind. Seeing much of anything was a challenge, especially with the wind's ferocity. It flung the rain into faces and chilled the searchers to the bone.

Mud had recently washed away part of the newly printed road. That, combined with the delays in rallying the searchers, along with the multiple directions that Zradce could have headed, led to an impossible task.

James Aldridge, their best tracker, crouched, squinting into a patch of overgrowth at the foot of a nearby mountain. He was trying his best to think like a fugitive. And the best place for a fugitive to hide would be deep in the forest of this mountain range. That said, he had zero idea if Zradce had headed this way. The days of heavy rain had so saturated the ground that a two-ton giant could walk through without leaving prints.

"What do you see?" Jackson Sebring, the acting mayor, asked the younger man.

"Jack and shit," James muttered.

"What?"

"Nothing. I see nothing," James clarified. The usual easygoing smile was absent from his face. "There's nothing to see, not in all of this rain. Wherever Zradce has gone, there is no way for us to track him until it lets up. The drones can't even run in this mess. Not with this heavy of rainfall and wind. We will fry the electronics."

"We need to find him."

James rolled his eyes, his back to Sebring, nonplussed. "No kidding."

The communicator on Mayor Sebring's chest chimed. He listened for a moment. "Roger that." He looked over at James and a handful of others. "We have fully searched the settlement. There's no trace of Zradce."

James stood, the rain pouring off of his hat, mud sucked at his boots. "NARA, when will the rain stop?"

The AI's dulcet tones replied, "Rain should end by 2200 hours."

"He could be kilometers away by then!" Jackson exclaimed, horrified at the thought of Zradce getting away.

"Look, the rain is too heavy. It's washing away tracks almost as fast as they are made. The drones can't function, not at this level of downpour, and I think our best response is a powerful defense. Let's make sure that if he doubles back, we have all eyes peeled and folks armed. At least until the weather clears." James clearly hated saying it, or giving up, but there was no other option. They would have to wait. The only real solace was that the light would be the same at nearly midnight, as it was now, in this tidally locked world where they experienced perpetual twilight instead. They could rest up, wait for the rain to clear, and then send out the drones before the tracker teams.

They returned to the settlement. To more questions than answers. Carrie Schrader remained flustered, frustrated as she pored over the medical records and brain scans. There had been no recent scans, not since right after landfall. There had been no need. The damage was significant. Entire sections of Nathan's brain had shown significant, permanent damage. Still, it remained a mystery to her and the other medical professionals. How had Nathan Zradce recovered from his injuries? How had he gotten up and walked out of the facility with permanent brain damage? Everything Carrie knew about brain injuries showed Nathan Zradce was a vegetable incapable of consciousness or independent movement.

There were no satisfactory answers. Not then, and not two months later when the search was officially called off. As impossible as it all seemed, Nathan Zradce had recovered enough from his injuries to walk away from the medical center. Wherever he had gone after disappearing from his ex-wife's doorway was a mystery. No tracks, and no supplies missing. If they hadn't had footage from the cameras in the Medical Bay, or the word of Zradce's wife, Jennifer, it would have been as if he vanished.

Jennifer Zradce petitioned for her name to be returned to the last name of Lennox shortly before the search was called off. It was time to start a new chapter in the colony's future. Wherever Nathan Zradce had gone, whether he had survived his foray into the storm and the alien wilderness, for now it seemed he was no longer a threat to their new life.

Dream Walk

Date: 04.25.2104

Nathan slipped in the mud, and this time it hurt like hell. Compounded, no doubt, by the abrasions and new bruises from the first dozen times his limbs had connected wrong with this alien place. Here, deep in thick forest and plant life, appearances were deceiving. It looked soft, the gray-green and purple foliage thick and all-encompassing. But beneath the thick overgrowth, sharp, pointy rocks lay hidden. The slipper-like shoes he had found in a staff locker were already thick with mud and torn in multiple places. They wouldn't last long.

His clothes were soaked, even though the rain stopped hours before. The air was warm, but not warm enough to compete with the sodden clothes. The humidity left the air soupy and hard to breathe.

How long have I been walking?

There was no way to tell time in this place. Overhead, the thick canopy of trees blocked the view of the sky almost entirely. What little he could see was a pale orange color. It matched the images he had seen of the planet, to be sure. But it was one thing to see an image of something, and another to see it for yourself. Things were so different here. The thick trunks of trees were an inky black. The rain had left a sheen to them and the smell of the forest was not much different from a forest on Earth. At least, his few experiences in forests, a handful of outings in his youth, had instantly come to mind. The memories of the moist humus, the sharp evergreen smell, rushing in to remind him that even here, nature was much the same. Now that the rain was done, the creatures were re-emerging, a fat creature that reminded him of a bumblebee droned by, its body enormous, ten times the size of a bumblebee on Earth, and covered in chitinous scales instead of delicate hairs.

With the rain disappearing, so had the clouds, rewarding him with flashes of orange sky that morphed to delicate purple and red in places. There were no stars, no track of the sun across the sky, to show direction or the elapsing of time.

Exhaustion, hunger, and the cold all warred for attention. He kept walking, lurching more than anything. He needed to get as far away from the settlement as possible. If even his own wife feared and loathed him, what would the other colonists do to him?

A part of him, the part that wasn't tired, hungry and cold, marveled at this world. The surrounding foliage looked deliciously alien. It wasn't just colored differently, with an overabundance of yellows and reds, but the shapes differed from what he expected to find. The trees were more fern like, although enormous, and the smaller growth carpeted the ground, hiding the sharp jagged edges of the rock beneath.

Then there was the extra gravity, something the Selection Committee had known about, planned for. They chose body types who could handle the extra strain it would cause. History of heart disease? Flat feet? Forget coming to Zarmina's World. Nathan had passed the tests, his body the most adaptive it could be, yet he could feel the pull of it.

The additional gravity weighed on him, adding to the exhaustion he felt.

It was more than just physical. His heart ached; his mind spun in circles of recrimination, despair, and guilt. He had killed two men, and tried to kill far more than that. Women, children, his fellow colonists.

Why did I do that? How *could I do that?*

It was as if he were two completely different people occupying the same body.

Memories long buried pushed their way to the surface.

Immanuel, his mirror image, forever a tiny child, his body still and cold.

Mother, her face twisted in hatred and madness and grief.

The knife that had cut into him, removing any hope he had that his mother might love him, blood red, gushing from the wound.

Nathan hadn't been paying attention to where he was walking. The ice-cold water from the creek abraded his skin and his toes were going numb. He stepped back, stumbling, flailing, and finally collapsed in a heap by the edge of the creek, his hands sinking into a thick patch of mushrooms.

rest

The alien presence had returned. Or perhaps it had never really left. Nathan wasn't sure. It felt like a whisper, a tickle in the back of his brain. He had thought it a hallucination. Some part of this schism of his soul, between Nathaniel and Nathan, the child he had been, the man he became, and the madman who had tried to kill everyone.

"What are you?"

There was no answer, not really. Just a sense of puzzlement over the question. Or perhaps it didn't know how to answer his question.

"Do you have a name?" He realized then that he was thirsty. No great surprise, he had been walking for hours and covered a long distance. His throat felt parched, and his voice was a brittle rasp. Nathan shifted and leaned over, stretching to reach the creek, to scoop some water into his mouth. Were there parasites in it? Something that could hurt him? He had no way of knowing. The water was so cold it hurt for a moment, took his breath away, before it soothed the dryness. He leaned closer, scooped with both hands, and continued, handful after handful, until it sloshed in his stomach. His fingers trailed through a patch of

fungus, red and frilled at the edges in a deep reddish purple.

no name

not finite

He frowned. What did the alien presence mean, not finite?

"I don't understand."

no name

not finite

It repeated. And Nathan tried again. *"My name is Nathan."*

finite creature nathan

"Yes, I guess you could say that." He shifted and stood up. When he did, the presence faded instantly. *"Wait? Where did you go?"*

Wherever the alien presence had come from, it was gone again, back whence it came, and Nathan was alone again.

Am I hallucinating?

A sudden fear rose in him. It gripped him, hard, in his chest. What if whatever had broken inside him on Calypso was rising again? What if he was still a danger? To the settlement, to Jennifer, and the others? He realized he didn't particularly care about himself. What he had done to the others, to Deeks and Evers, to his wife, that had drawn a hard line in the metaphorical sand. He couldn't go back to life among them. He didn't deserve to. And what was there out here in this alien world? Was he hallucinating some presence, some... creature... Simply to cope mentally with his actions? Would he somehow transfer all guilt to this imaginary creature in his mind next? Was this some complicated matter of transference or self-protection? What would come next? *A demon made me do it?*

"We all have darkness inside of us." His voice was quiet, rough from disuse. The presence in his mind was gone, yet traces of it lingered, feather soft, as if a ghost had taken up roost in the back of his mind.

Nathan looked around at the forest that surrounded him. Like Earth, the forest floor remained littered in vegetation, but unlike Earth, there was far less of it, and sharp rocks hid just beneath, as his tattered slippers could attest to. It seemed endless, this forest, and he struggled to remember the topography of the area. They had all seen the hours of footage from the D.O.V.E. probes. Several landing sites were debated for their proximity to natural resources. Not just water, but open land that was relatively level. The colony needed access to a saltwater sea and mountains that could provide them with natural ores necessary to their future. And, while not as seismically active as Earth, Zarmina's World held areas similar to Earth's Ring of Fire, including several large volcanoes at the edge of the habitable zone. After much back and forth, considering projected weather patterns and trade winds, as well as the topography of the terminator zone in which they were confined, the Landing Committee narrowed their choices to a handful of locations. They had named the sites by order of choice - Site A, Site B, and so on. Nathan had to assume it was Site A that was untold kilometers behind him now. This made sense, as Site A was near the edge of a giant forest, hundreds of clicks across, that eventually led into steep mountain ranges that were rich in iron ore.

The plan had been to establish the colony on Site A, with access to both fresh water via a large river that cut north to south. To the south was a saltwater sea, with ample land to farm between the sea and river. The colonists planned additional settlements, but the first one needed easily workable topography and plentiful nearby natural resources. After all, Earth may well have collapsed completely by now. The virus had been cruelly effective, and the news reports an endless stream of death.

How ironic was it? Jennifer had pushed so hard for them to leave because of the birth rate limits and the infinitesimally small chance that any child they ever had would ever get a chance at something bigger than a shoebox to grow up in. And now, the world they had left had become a wasteland of the dead and dying. A house of death, really. The latest figures Nathan remembered hearing was a 99.6% death rate. How does one get past that? Were there even enough people left to bury the dead?

There's plenty of room on Earth now. There haven't been this few people left on it since 3000 B.C.E.

He remembered the chatter on board Calypso as they discussed the possibility of turning around and returning home. The arguments had been fierce. In the end, without a clear vaccine to reverse the deadly effects of the ESH virus, however, the debates had all ended the same. Stay the course, follow the directive sent from Earth - do not return. It had felt like another blow, if he were to be honest. Another step towards the end of their species. If they left Earth, what were they? Were they nomads? Would they become Zarminians instead of Earthlings? He had wanted nothing more than to return to Earth in those days.

Later, he had wished he had died with the rest. And he would have. Jennifer too. Neither of them carried AB negative blood. It wasn't that much of a leap to give in to the dark dreams, the self-hatred that had been there already.

Mother said there was a darkness in me. Evil. And she was right. Look what I became.

Nathan stumbled. He hadn't even realized that he was walking again. His legs, feet, they just... moved of their own accord. The rest of his body and mind were along for the ride. The stumble had resulted in the last frayed vestiges of the surgical slipper wrenching itself from his left foot. He looked down and could see that the right foot was not far behind. Another hundred feet and he would be barefoot. The sharp rocks would cut him to ribbons in no time, and the soles of his feet ached and bled. He surveyed his surroundings. It wasn't as if he could call up the ordering bot and have a new pair of shoes perfectly sized for his feet delivered to his apartment door. Or even ask NARA for a pair of 3D printed hiking boots.

Native Americans used tanned leather for moccasins. But he'd seen no animals of any mentionable size so far. And even if he did, how would he kill an animal, much less skin it? He had no tools, no weapons, no shoes, no way to make fire. He was on an alien planet, with no allies, no safety net, and no clue how to survive.

Even the survival classes he had taken alongside his fellow colonists were worthless. They had assumed a basic kit of survival gear, not a barely clothed in scrubs, without proper footwear or weapons, dream walk into an alien forest.

For the first time since he had woken up in Medical Bay an untold number of hours ago, Nathan Zradce realized the truth.

I'm going to die out here.

Safe Not Safe

Date: 04.26.2104

The connection between Entity and the organism known as Nathan had abruptly ended when the gangly creature stood up, breaking contact with the fungal mass, spores drifting from his fingers on the breeze.

Entity needed a physical contact in order to communicate. That, or an altered state of consciousness, as the Nathan organism had floated in, so deeply damaged, in the previous weeks. While the Nathan organism could now move on its own, the connection that Entity had with it while it hovered, damaged, in another state of consciousness, appeared to not be its primary plane of existence.

Entity, unlike Outro, had a deep and abiding fascination with these animal organisms. The more advanced, the more fascinating.

It had deeply regretted not intervening all those millennia before when the Visitors had come to the planet. Yes, they had been invasive, much as the beetles that were currently devastating a swath of southern plain, intent on annihilating a new strain of grasses Entity had been cultivating, but the impending eruption of a long-dormant volcano would quickly solve that problem. The new strain of grasses did not have the height and thickness Entity had hoped for, anyway. Losing it was incidental as only the beetles found it attractive, obsessively and devastatingly, so.

Entity followed the Nathan organism's progress across the forest floor. It moved faster than Entity, as most animals did, yet Entity could sense the creature slowing, stumbling more. Whereas before it had stridden upright, legs long, moving apace, now it limped. Was it damaged already? After all the work that Entity had put into it to make it thrive? Entity was ever so briefly irritated, but then recognized that this was an opportunity to continue to study the organism. And despite Entity's attempts to communicate with the other organisms as they sliced, plucked and dug from the soil erecting buildings, planting crops, and causing small waves of localized discomfort, their touch felt different. They differed from the Nathan organism on a deep, unknowable level. And this interested Entity greatly. Captivated it, really.

The Nathan organism differed from the other organisms it had landed with. Despite being of the same shape and size. Its mind was unique. And that generated a deep, abiding curiosity in Entity. An organism independent of other like organisms was alien, yet recognizable. The creatures that roamed the eastern plains in droves were independent of each other. As were the insects and reptiles, even the leviathans in the seas appeared to have divergent consciousness. For these creatures, a consciousness separate from other of its species was expected, and yet, the Nathan organism's mind itself was structured differently. Entity had seen that clearly on the other plane. Entity had tried and tried with the others, but the Nathan organism was different, and because of those differences, a connection had been possible. Was possible again with the right set of circumstances. Had it been damaged so much that it grew different? Entity was unsure.

A rustle of *other* tapped at the edge of its conscious thought.

end it

Outro felt agitated, angry even. Perhaps it remembered the Visitors. It was understandable that it might correlate the Visitors with these new organisms.

Entity responded.

study

learn

Entity could sense Outro's disapproval and anger. It rolled off of the edges of it, where Entity stopped and Outro began, the edges of the fungal line curled up briefly before smoothing once again to connect with Entity.

not safe

Entity tried to reassure Outro.

not same

visitor different

Another surge of anger from Outro and the connection between them cut off abruptly as Outro retreated.

Entity felt concern. It was rare that its kind disagreed with each other. At least, in its own experience, it had never felt the discontent or frustration towards its progenitor that Outro so often expressed towards Entity. Far rarer for a disagreement to turn to anger or the closing of the communication points deep beneath the ground where the threads of fungus wove together, cutting through the earth, even rock. Entity reached out on the higher plane, that space between consciousness and reality, but there was nothing but silence.

For now, Entity and Outro were at an impasse. Entity had complete control over the side of the world that these unknown visitors had landed. Just as Outro had when the first visitors had arrived and began reproducing at a shocking rate.

Entity had spent the small time that the visitors had been on the planet, observing them. No offspring other than the few that were brought with the adult organisms seemed to pop up. For the first time in its long existence, Entity felt concern creep over it. It was a gardener, but also, to some extent, a scientist. All gardeners were. They tested soils, altered plant structure, fed the substrate with more or fewer nutrients. It had spent its existence here on this planet and too many others to count, gently guiding all manner of plant, animal and insect. Its fungal mind was curious, intelligent, and patient. Outro seemed sure that these new lifeforms were the same as those a mere three millennia ago, but Entity remained unconvinced.

After all, the universe was larger by far than even Entity could comprehend, and full of diversity. How could Outro be so closed-minded?

safe not safe

will see

Into the ether it spoke, unsure if Outro even heard. If Entity were human, it likely would have shrugged. Receiving no answer, Entity stopped its attempts to speak with Outro and focused instead on the lone organism that continued to move through the forest erratically. Entity compared it to the memories Outro had given its progenitor of the Visitors. It too was bipedal, but it lacked the thick stump of a tail that the Visitors had possessed. Entity marveled at the organism's ability to stay upright at all without some kind of stabilizing influence like a tail. How did it not fall over? Entity marked the Nathan organism's progress, if you could even call it that, as Nathan lurched through the thick growth, leaving a slick trail of bright red blood spatters now that its foot coverings had finally disintegrated.

Was the organism truly a threat? Was it truly 'not safe' as Outro proclaimed? Entity was unsure. Further observation was necessary.

Re-Making the Man

Date: 04.30.2104

The rains came and went in waves. So did his consciousness.

Nathan had been in the forest for what felt like days. Although in this twilight world, how could one tell? There was no definable change in the light, and this deep in the forest and with the constant fire hose from the sky, he couldn't track the sun at all.

He walked, fell, stood up and walked further. He drank from the small pools of water he found, and stared at the surrounding greenery with an ever-growing hunger. His training on Earth had included foraging for food, but their data from D.O.V.E. remained heavily focused on the open plains, where there were grasses and edible seed pods, not the forest. The densely packed trees had proved too difficult for the D.O.V.E. probes to enter and collect from. The low-hanging branches were home to insects that caught in the tiny, yet powerful engines. This had led to a significant number of probe casualties before the AI-interface had deemed the forest an area better explored once a human contingent had landed.

He could see all manner of plant life, but how much of it was edible and how much of it was straight up lethal for human consumption? Despite everything that had happened, and everything he had done, he wasn't ready to die yet. The ache in his stomach had turned to an ever-present yearning, which had twisted into a constant thrum of need. The bark on the trees, the fat slow-moving insects, even the fire-red lichens and moss were looking tastier by the minute.

How long had it been since he ate? How long had he been out here?

The D.O.V.E. probes had analyzed many of the animals on the planet. A simple dart filled with data gathering devices the size of a red blood cell had allowed them a glimpse into many of the lifeforms and while higher in iron than most Earth beasts, many were confirmed edible. There had been a fiery debate over one particular creature that looked a lot like an Earth horse, although stockier and without hair. Its back spine included a pointed, hard ridge that would accept no saddle, even if one felt inclined to try. The mottled skin had, depending on the angle, been reminiscent of dappled bays. The horn at the crest of the head had earned the beasts, which appeared to run in herds, the term Zarmunicorn, and the arguments about whether Zarmunicorns might actually become the main course at fireside meals had become almost heated. Some felt horror at potentially killing and consuming a beast of unknown intelligence, others seemed inclined to believe it was the human condition and therefore completely acceptable. Nathan had watched the debates with amusement. Meat, real honest-to-God meat from a formerly living animal, was not something he had much experience with. Lab-grown meats had been a staple for decades now, the real thing reserved for those with more money and power than pesky minor annoyances like morals to bother them.

The Zarmunicorns were sighted in large herds that numbered in the hundreds. They seemed particularly at home on the plains, especially those to the south that bordered a freshwater inland sea. Nathan couldn't help wondering if anyone had tried eating them yet. And if so, how they had tasted. His imagination generated the sudden certainty that this world's unicorns would somehow taste like steak and his stomach rumbled at the thought of it.

He was far from any chance at finding out, anyway. Even if the forest had a herd of them wandering about, he had nothing with which to kill or eat one. No knife. No fire. Nothing.

Nathan glanced at his feet. With the thin slippers shredded to nothing, and the sharp forest floor continually inflicting more damage, they now resembled raw meat. Worse, the mud mixed with blood and shredded skin, and they were hot to the touch. Infected, no doubt. Still, he kept on. It was more of a desperate lurch from side to side. Around him the world wavered and flickered, as darkness closed in around the edges of his vision before finally tunneling down to nothing. He'd eaten nothing for days. Or at least, that is how it felt. Without some way of telling time, without a link to

NARA, time was irrelevant. His body was out of fuel, his mind blank.

Nathan fell then, the sound startling a nest of bright metallic blue winged creatures that exploded into the air, buzzing in alarm. His cheek abraded from the sharp rocks on the ground, a rivulet of blood from the wound soaking the edge of one plate-sized fungus that was part of a far larger ring of mushrooms. It would have hurt like hell had he been conscious.

Entity watched him, tracked him, and tried a handful of times over the past few days to speak with the Nathan organism. To no avail. If the Nathan organism had only reached out and touched the patches of fungus that were spread at intervals throughout the forest, the physical connection would have been enough to re-establish a dialogue. But the Nathan organism had not, and Entity chafed as it waited for an opportunity to present itself.

It reached out now, connected through the ether, the higher level of consciousness it had originally contacted Nathan organism through, back when the organism was so damaged as to be nearly brain-dead.

nathan

The creature lay in a crumpled heap. It also seemed to be injured. Of that, Entity was sure. The blood on its face, as well as on the red fluids oozing from the bottom appendages, served as a clear indicator of this. The coppery taste of the blood dotting the delicate sensors of the fungus was odd. This creature was iron rich. Entity could work with that. The iron would sustain and feed an aspect of Entity inside of the Nathan organism. And inside of the Nathan organism, Entity could sustain communication, learn about this unique creature on a molecular level, and be able to make a more informed recommendation to Outro on whether these new arrivals posed a danger.

nathan wake

The Nathan organism did not move, nor stir. And after a few moments, Entity decided. It released spores in a puff of red particles from a nearby ring of fungus. The fungus was tall, nearly half a meter in height, and each was blood-red with black streaks. Broad, perfectly round caps, with blueish purple gills. The wind did the rest, carrying enough particles for the few feet necessary to land on the open wound and the Nathan organism's open mouth. Nathan's saliva instantly dispelled the spores in his mouth; its acids broke down the spores before they could take root in his flesh. One or two spores made it up the frontal cavity, slightly above the mouth, and entered there into the dark moist cavern and rooted quickly. The handful that landed on the open wound, however, were the most successful. Within seconds they were in the Nathan organism's bloodstream, pulsing through, circulating, and a stream of information resulted from this. Including a somewhat concerning fact - this organism was dying.

Entity poked and prodded at the half-conscious mind it now had unfettered access to. The half-formed thoughts included a yearning for food, as well as a powerful fear of dying - either from lack of food, or by eating the *wrong* food.

How... *curious.*

Entity probed the Nathan organism for details, puzzled by the response. Nathan organism ate nutrients from inside of inanimate objects shaped in squares, rectangles. This was perplexing and potentially complicated. What nutrients were inside of these objects and how could they be replicated? Associated images included an intake of repasts that were not from these strange inanimate objects, but that the meals had occurred years ago, in some place very different from here.

Another planet, perhaps the new arrivals home planet?

There was so much Entity didn't know about the Nathan organism or the others. It felt confused as well. Why could it communicate with Nathan and none of the others? The answers, at least some of them, were coming faster as Entity, through its spores, explored the interior of the Nathan organism's body and mind. A circulatory system, alien, yet dizzyingly efficient, allowed Entity access to the organs, the brain. Most curious was the brain, a gray, soft organ that still carried scars from a beating that Entity watched unfold in Technicolor detail, on board a starship that now orbited the planet.

nathan killed

That revelation was the most startling. Only the basest of animals killed within their species. Other species certainly, but their own? This was disconcerting, and Entity briefly wished it could withdraw, pull away from the Nathan organism, and leave it here to die. Entity was a gardener foremost, and gardening meant raising up all species, seeing the worth in the carnivores and the herbivores. It had spent millions of years guiding the evolution of many species, not just the fungal or plant life. Entity could see how each creature was intrinsic to the existence of an ecosystem on a whole. Yes, the carnivores took life, sometimes violently. Yes, the herbivores, if given enough freedom and availability, could lay waste to a field and denude it of grasses, grains, and more. Without the carnivores keeping the herbivores in check, the system became unbalanced.

But a creature who could consciously choose to harm its own? That seemed to defy the unspoken rules of nature. Especially in a highly developed, intelligent organism, this seemed impossible.

why nathan kill

Entity asked. But there was no answer. The Nathan organism was dying. This much was clear. It still lay where it had fallen, unmoving, consciousness far from the present. Entity had a choice to make now. Let this killer of others like it live, or let it die. One or the other. As it was, there seemed to be little time. The organism needed sustenance. Something more than the small amount of water it had cupped in its hands and allowed to trickle down its throat. Entity dug down into the fading consciousness and tried to pull from the organism's memories. A shift occurred, as if opening a path, and the Nathan organism appeared in the ether, haggard, insubstantial, but there.

"It would probably be better to let me die."

need answers

need understanding

Nathan shrugged. "I don't understand it, so how can you?"

what nathan need to survive

Nathan shrugged again. *"Protein, carbohydrates, minerals."* With the words came images, and Entity could see clearly what was necessary. A simple thing, really. Especially since Entity controlled the movements of nearly all creatures on the planet.

Nathan nodded, receiving his own images from Entity. He was reminded of the fungus that invaded and then controlled ants. *"Ophiocordyceps unilateralis."* His mind showed Entity an image of a tiny insect enslaved to a fungus.

ant slave

"Yes, it is." Nathan could feel his death approaching, but he also feared that Entity offered something different, perhaps a fate worse than death.

ask not force

"You ask for permission?"

yes

Entity sensed Nathan's surprise at this. It dug into the organism's thoughts before it spoke again.

free will

"Free will..." Nathan answered. The words stirred memories deep inside. Mother reading from the bible at the kitchen table, or by Emmanuel's grave.

This day I call the heavens and the earth as witnesses against you that I have set before you life and death, blessings and curses. Now choose life so that you and your children may live.

Mother had whispered it, over and over, until her voice cracked and broke. But it hadn't brought Immanuel back from the dead. It had been far too late for that.

Entity waited. Eternal. Patient.

Death was a dark cloud, slipping from the horizon, moving closer, so much closer. Some part of Nathan wanted to live, even if it meant he would be something else. Not entirely himself, but something far different.

"You have my permission."

The thought had barely escaped his mind before he felt Entity move inside of him, the flush of alien energy, otherness, subsuming who/what Nathan was and trading it for another existence.

Nathan died.

Nathan lived.

All at once.

Entity surged through the Nathan organism. Even as the creature's heart slowed, still it pumped blood through the body, slowly carrying pieces of Entity into the smallest of cells. Through organs, the brain. Entity reveled in the experience. The journey stretched, elongated into microseconds, a trip of discovery, learning, around each new bend. Entity could see now how complex the Nathan organism was, how unique. As it delved into each organ, ran down the pathways of blood, of connective tissue, of the multitude of gray folds, it felt the star signature etched deep in the organism's bones. It hailed from light years away. The tiniest, most insignificant of places, a laughably small solar system that held but one point of evolution. Worse, the planet appeared heavily damaged, and tied to a larger planet filled with beings that looked like the Nathan organism, but held no special spark.

Entity marveled at the story that this organism's very existence told. It was alone, different from the rest of the other Visitors. Did it even know it? Did it even know how different it was?

Entity combed through the Nathan organism's memories. At first, Entity found the rush of images jumbled and confused, until Entity sorted, categorized, and realized that the artificial construct of time was the culprit. This linear creature held no understanding of who it really was. Adrift from its beginnings, with only fragments of trauma and pain. It was young. Merely a whisper of a blip compared to Entity, or even Outro, for that matter. Its life would be over agonizingly quickly, even if it could survive its injuries. Entity could clearly see that the Nathan organism's life could be extended with Entity's help. Its death was imminent, its future measured in a few short years, a decade of revolutions around the red dwarf sun this planet currently circled, if even that.

Entity wondered if it was even worth it, saving Nathan organism's life. Such a short, likely ineffectual experiment. Yet here was a chance to study the internal workings of a new species. When considered from a scientific view, however, Entity concluded it was worth trying. It gently lowered Nathan organism's temperature to an acceptable level, one that was more conducive to a fungal variant it had already been working on, and sent the fungus into the dying organism on the forest floor. Nathan organism twitched, convulsed, and then lay still, its life hanging in the ether, its lifeforce a mere whisper.

There was a strong possibility it was far too late for it. But Entity would try. It had all the time in the world and it was a curious being, full of questions for the tiny, impermanent creature it had found. It looked forward to some answers.

Traffic Jam

Date: 11.03.2104

The forest was dense, and the trees' wide canopies made the already dimly lit sky more so. A weak light filtered through, a reminder that this was truly an alien world they were in. Daniel searched the ground for clues, but could see nothing. No sign of disturbed ground, no footprints, nothing. In truth, he was the only one still searching for Zradce, the only one who believed the man might still be alive.

Sam's pregnancy was so advanced, her belly extended and round, that Daniel had considered simply staying home, giving up on the search. She had practically shoved him out of the door instead.

"Go. You're no good to me here. Frankly, you're driving me nuts staring out the window whenever you have a moment free." She growled at him. "It isn't likely he will saunter back into the settlement. Chances are, he's dead." Her face had softened then, one hand reaching up to caress his cheek. "It isn't your burden to bear, Daniel, but if you insist on bearing it, then get out there, follow the search grid, put in the time, and then come home to us."

Us. Her words echoed in his skull. A week, possibly days, remained until he would come home to an "us" rather than simply Sam.

Although there is nothing simple about Sam.

His stomach turned and clenched at the thought of the tiny life he would soon share Sam and their small home, with. Not his child by DNA, mind you. He agreed with Sam and most of the rest of the colonists that the first children would be seed bank babies, for genetic diversity's sake, and he wondered if it would matter down the line.

The question hung there, with thoughts of Toby intertwining, pushing the guilt to the surface. His son, alone on Earth, traumatized by the loss of everyone he loved. Somehow, he was sure that he would love them all.

Children are maddening, wonderful, and an adventure greater than anything else. I only wish I could have seen it that way with Toby. I should have never listened to Janine. No matter how much it would have hurt Luke, I should have stepped up, said something, done *something.*

He hadn't, though. And that was something he would have to live with for the rest of his life.

He had spent months combing through the forest in the search grid the team had established when the news of Zradce's revival and subsequent disappearance had first spread through the colony. Jennifer's panicked face as she struggled to answer the questions of how Nathan had simply appeared, and then disappeared, from her doorstep. They had acted quickly, launching the first search party some two hours after Jennifer Zradce, now Jennifer Lennox, since she had petitioned for a divorce, had raised the alarm. She moved past the terror that her husband might be lying in wait just outside of her door and called for help through NARA. But the heavy rain had washed any sign of him away. No footprints, nothing. They had searched in all directions for weeks until an errant scrap of fabric found attached to a prickly bush deep in the forest by one of the botany team clearly showed Zradce had been there. No one else was walking along the forest floor dressed in scrubs. It had to be him. It had caused a brief surge in interest, and three more joined Daniel for a few weeks before other priorities took over and no other evidence of Nathan's continued existence was found.

Daniel had insisted on continuing working the grid, section by section, long after interest had died down. He did it on his off days, even an hour or two, or a half day here or there, before turning in at the end of a long day of work. Use of a flitter helped, even if the rumblings over misuse of resources had run in waves through the settlement. In the end, Martin Phoenix, who controlled the flitters and other major travel resources, had given him a pass to continue. He'd told the rest of the Council to stuff it, that Daniel's excursions were only a small resource drain, and after what he had done on board the Calypso, it was the least they could do to help him.

Martin hadn't minced words when he visited Daniel and Sam at the door of their cabin. "It's likely a waste of time. The man disappeared into the wilderness of an alien planet with nothing but surgical scrubs and paper slippers on his feet. But if it hadn't been for you Medry, well, there are those among us who will never forget what you did, and the rest, they shouldn't forget it either. Too many of us owe our lives or a friend's or family member's lives to you. Besides, the vote was unanimous. The flitter is yours to conduct your search until you say otherwise."

The grid, monitored by NARA and the Advanced Global Positioning System, still contained miles of terrain to cover. The positive side effect of the search had been nearly 200 more unique botanical samples diligently collected and brought back to Sam and the rest of the botanists.

At least some good is coming from all of this. We're learning even more than ever about this planet's forest structures and ecology.

He stepped out of the flitter, pinned the location for an easy return to the machine, then checked the AGPS on his tablet, and set out into the green canopy. Within seconds, the dense greenery swallowed him whole.

The world was beautiful. So far, it had been mercifully absent of anything truly dangerous. Man was the apex predator on land. In the water, well, most of the denizens of the deep stayed hundreds of meters underwater. An unmanned submarine had vanished rather abruptly on its maiden voyage.

The last images before the connection went black had shown teeth and a maw the size of a small house. Some parts of this world were simply not a place they could safely explore and Zarmina's deep oceans definitely qualified in that category.

Jack would have loved it, even if his dreams for an underwater spiral city would have gone unrealized. Daniel gritted his teeth at the memories and loss he still felt over Jack Dunn's death in Cryo. He hadn't known him well. A few team-building exercises and rounds of drinks and darts in the training before departure. His husband Kevin was a Comm Tech Daniel had worked with on board Calypso. Kevin had talked about Jack endlessly, especially after they had learned of Earth's fate. Jack had been Simon's biological dad, with an egg that a surrogate had carried for the two men back on Earth. Each of the members of Calypso had dealt with their grief and horror over Earth differently, and Kevin's had been to dream of the life they would have upon landing on their new world. He had described Jack's boat; the plans waiting for the 3D printers to produce an exact copy of the catamaran he had sailed on Earth, racing around the world three times and setting speed records with each consecutive trip.

And then the Cryo sabotage had happened and Kevin had stopped talking about Jack, or the catamaran, or sailing. He'd just held their son and grieved, stoic, and silent. Nearly twenty years older than Jack, the lines on his face had deepened, and he had aged significantly. The friendship Daniel and Kevin had begun onboard had widened to include Sam. Nowadays, Kevin and young Simon were regular visitors, especially since they lived just a few doors away in the temporary housing.

Daniel hated Zradce for what he had done. No words of explanation or understanding of childhood trauma from Jacob Carter, their resident psychologist, had been enough. Worse, he hated himself. He could have avoided a handful of deaths if he had just kept going.

"You were bleeding out, Daniel, and you did everything you could. You saved so many lives!"

How many times had he heard those words, or variations, like that? Too often to count. It didn't change the fact that they were dead. That Jack, Kevin's husband and Simon's father, was lost to them forever.

Daniel shook his head. "Get your head out of yesterday, Medry, and focus on the now." He muttered to himself. Silence met his words, and he peered into the gloom ahead. The trees were dense, extremely so, but according to the AGPS, there was a low mountain close by, drowned in the thick canopy of vegetation, but a mountain, nonetheless. In fact, as he squinted ahead and to the left, it looked like the coal-black stones that comprised much of the mountain. Massive chunks, taller than a man, of obsidian. The volcanic activity was long finished, millions of years in the past. The mountains remained, however, undisturbed through the eons. Something caught his eye, a change in the darkness and gloom. More of an irregular shape and a different shade of darkness. Could it be a cave? He would have to get closer to find out. The region provided them with a few caves to explore, and the colony biologists always welcomed any species collection he made. Caves had been of specific interest recently.

The reports of possible Terran life here had been unconfirmed, subject to a margin of error from the drones that they had programmed to run in ever-expanding search patterns. It was possible Nathan Zradce had come through here, but it was also possible a small creature like a mouse or bird had as well. The drones weren't that sophisticated. And the sample was degraded, scant. The data had already sent Daniel on several wild goose chases in the past month. But there was something about the area, with its arching canopy of foliage, that caused him to wonder if it wasn't the perfect place for someone to hide out, to live off of the land. It could be done. The plant and animal life were carbon-based and everyone was raving about unicorn meat, which was barely a step above the lab-grown meat back on Earth, tasteless and unfulfilling.

But if I were on the run from, well, everyone, *I'd hide in a cave. So I'd better check it out.*

But just as he stepped forward to investigate the potential cave, NARA spoke through his communicator.

"Incoming urgent message from Sydan, Sam."

"Accept."

"Daniel, I need you back here. Stat." Sam's voice sounded strained. Was she in pain? Was she in labor?

Daniel spun on his heel, legs moving over the uneven terrain at a half-run. "On my way. Is it the baby?"

A guttural groan of pain sounded. "Ooh! Yes. Hurry!"

He could hear others in the background. Sam was already at the hospital by the sound of it, and she wasn't alone. That was good.

What wasn't good was the cacophony of voices, namely women, who sounded as if they were *all* in labor at the same time. And he could think of at least four who were all in the last month of their pregnancies because he'd seen them all coming and going at the same time as Sam's prenatal appointments. There had been plenty of jokes bantered about that Sam, along with Jennifer Lennox, Kit Tanner, and their doctor Carrie Schrader, could all pop at once. From the sounds he had overheard, that lighthearted speculation might have been dead on.

"Hang on, Sam. I'm on my way!"

The connection went dead and Daniel broke into a run. The baby was coming and nothing else mattered. He had to be there for the birth of their son.

The flitter got him there quickly, although it felt far longer. The plains zipped by, the horse-sized unicorn-like ruminants that grazed there were mere blurs of color. And the hospital, such as it was, a flurry of activity, inside and out. The first births were drawing a crowd of well-wishers. It was historic. After all, the first human children would soon draw their first breaths on an alien world.

He ran inside and found a chaotic scene filling the medical center's largest room, a room typically used for meetings before the community center opened. Expectant fathers, or at least partners, clustered around two of the women. Wes Perdue looked green around the gills, but was holding Kit Tanner's hand, and Martin Phoenix was at Carrie Schrader's side. Another two, Sam and Jennifer Lennox, Nathan Zradce's former wife, were alone, watched over by two med techs and clearly advanced in labor as they groaned their way through contractions.

Someone drew the room's shades and assembled the four beds, each now occupied by a laboring woman. That Carrie Schrader, the colony's doctor, had gone into labor at the same time as Kit, Sam, and Jennifer, was an added complication to their already strained medical staff. Small wonder they had brought all the women into one central space.

Daniel had eyes only for Sam. She, however, had other plans. "Go check on Jennifer. She's all alone."

"But..."

"Just go, I'm only dilated to a five. She's having a baby, and she is all alone." She groaned and shooed him away.

Trust Sam to have made friends with the loneliest woman in the colony. Daniel stood there for a moment until Sam flapped her hand at him and ground her teeth through another contraction.

"Go!"

A lone nurse, who Daniel thought looked familiar, but could not remember the name of, was busy hanging a curtain in the space. She looked at Daniel, then off at Sam, before nodding and giving Daniel a small smile.

"We are understaffed. We didn't expect Dr. Schrader to go into labor so early and Mrs. Zradce here is..."

"Lennox, my maiden name is Lennox." Jennifer's face shone with sweat. "Mayor Phoenix approved the divorce months ago."

Of course he had. Jennifer was as much a victim as the other Cryo survivors.

"How can I help?"

His gentle question brought tears to her eyes and her lip trembled as another contraction moved through her. Her stomach rippled, and she gasped at the pain.

"I..." she groaned, sweat trickling from her brow.

The nurse had already left and Daniel looked around in panic. "You need something for the pain. An... an..."

"I don't want an epidural. Just..." she swallowed and looked away, "Would you mind holding my hand?"

"Of course." He reached out, took her hand in his and winced as she clamped down with surprising strength as another contraction hit. It wouldn't be long now. Daniel estimated the contractions were now less than two minutes apart.

Daniel knew she had chosen an embryo from ARC, rather than using one of Nathan's. And her lack of a partner, or even a friend by her side, betrayed how hard it was for the rest of the colony to separate her from her husband's terrible actions. It wasn't fair. She had done nothing wrong.

"I... ooh... I need to push."

Daniel made eye contact with an unfamiliar nurse and beckoned her over. "Jennifer Lennox needs a private room, stat."

Moments later, after a wild race down a hall, and Daniel was sure this woman was going to break every bone in his hand. Less than twenty minutes later, Jennifer cradled a tiny boy in her arms. His skin was a mahogany brown, and his eyes were dark instead of the trademark blue.

"He's beautiful."

Jennifer smiled, her eyes focused only on the baby. "He is. Thank you, Daniel."

Outside in the hall, Daniel heard Eric Stryder's voice. "I'm looking for Jennifer Lennox. Which room is she in?"

Seconds later, the red-haired chief of police stood by Jennifer's side, his hand on her arm. "I'm so sorry, Jenn. I was down south, dealing with an accident near the lake."

Daniel felt relief flood through him. Jennifer wasn't alone. She had Eric. Which meant he could go find Sam and be with her. He slipped from the room, catching Eric's eye and nodding as the younger man thanked him, then returned his full attention to Jennifer and their baby.

Hours later, he stood holding a tiny, squished creature of his own with dark brown hair, and milk-pale skin with a small sprinkling of freckles. The last baby born of four that day, Lucas Anthony Sydan, appeared at a few minutes past eleven that evening. As soon as the chaos from the last birth of the night had subsided, and they were finally alone, Daniel stared into the newborn's tiny face.

Sam smiled, raised an eyebrow. "Well?"

"He's... perfect."

The fears that he wouldn't love this child, or that he would fail him like he had Toby, they all fell away as he stood holding his son. It didn't matter, not a whit, that he didn't share any DNA with this child. Daniel was smitten.

Two hundred clicks away, in the forest's gloom that Daniel had stood in, Entity's focus turned to the cave opening. Willing change at what was, even for Entity, extreme speed. What had been the entrance to a cave shifted and blurred as a dark fungus grew, obscuring what had been emptiness and now was quickly a wall of fungal growth that was attractive to other vegetation, a thick ivylike substance that grew on vines that were thick and rope-like. By the time Daniel Medry reached the colony two hours later, the entrance had disappeared beneath feet of overgrowth that rendered it invisible and impenetrable.

Later, weeks later, when Daniel finally had the time to resume his search, he chalked it up to a trick of light. There was no cave. There couldn't be. A weird optical illusion, nothing more. What else could it have been other than that?

Extinction Level Event

Date: 11.29.2104

The stream of data from Earth was endless. Worse, the organizational protocols seemed to be thrown out the window. One transmission would have vital data, another, death statistics and reports of uncontrolled wildfires that were apparently burning California down to the ground. Daniel groaned. He had hoped the relays would be functional by now, and with it, Earth would have received Calypso and the colony's communiques in return. That they had survived the trip, barely, no thanks to Nathan Zradce. That they had landed and that the world was optimal for settlement and things were progressing apace.

A little good news for a change.

"When the hell are the relays going to actually, you know, *work*?" Daniel growled. If he had to read another damned transmission that included death and despair in it, he'd...

The door to the claustrophobic communications room flew open and Alex Smart slid inside, his eyes snapping with excitement. "I figured it out!"

Daniel leaned back in the chair and stared at the younger man. He'd heard that before. The solution to one problem revealed yet another problem, and then another, and then another. At this rate, they would never move the delay down to eighteen months, as they had hoped.

"Yeah? What was it this time, the finortener rod?" Daniel asked, nonplussed.

Alex blinked. "The what?"

"Never mind. So, is it fixed?"

"Uh, yeah, I think so. You should see a huge load of messages come in now."

Daniel rubbed his eyes, wishing for the hundredth time he hadn't volunteered to handle the incoming messages and had instead pawned it off on someone else. It felt like a penance, but one that just dragged him further and further down. He turned back to his workstation and jabbed a finger at the refresh button for the queued messages. A few had wandered in since his last refresh, but there was no massive increase. He sorted them by date, then shook his head.

"Nope. The latest transmission is from October 31st, 2100. Happy Halloween." He leaned back. "This is such bullshit. We can't communicate this way. They have our initial messages at least, but we won't have their responses, not for years."

He itched to find out more about Toby, needed to know his son was alright, but all the answers had to wait.

Alex groaned, his shoulders slumping. "Damn it! We dropped relays along the way. They should pair with the relays that D.O.V.E. dropped as well. Everything should work. Jack would've known what to do. The man was a genius. Damn that Nathan Zradce!"

Daniel shook his head. Jack Dunn had been a code reading genius. He had also been one of the five to die in the Cryo sabotage. Grief still clouded Kevin Edmonds and his young son Simon. Jack had a doctorate in history, with a minor in computer languages. Even the most archaic of languages, FORTRAN, FLOW-MATIC, LISP AND COBOL, had been part of his wheelhouse. Daniel had talked with him during an early wake shift on Calypso, where Jack had been working on finalizing the programming of the last relays. And that was where the problem most assuredly was, in the last relays, released as Calypso's deceleration and approach to Zarmina's World was nearly complete. David Farnsworth was juggling his cartography duties with digging through Jack Dunn's notes, just as Alex was doing. Together they would figure it out, but meanwhile, it was a real pain in the ass.

And it was at that moment that another cluster of transmissions came through. Better organized, which likely meant it was from the operating government, the Terran United Planetary Government, headed by none other than Madeline Chen, the widow of RUSA's President Gary Chen. The word that she had not only succeeded him as president of the Reformed United States but also convinced the world to merge under one power had told Medry and his fellow colonists just how bad off Earth was. Even in the years after the Collapse, there had never been consensus, and likely never would.

Humanity seems incapable of peace.

Daniel's screen blinked and another batch of transmissions hit, then another, and another.

The cluster of transmissions was large, but a handful earmarked urgently with red flags drew Daniel Medry's attention. He clicked on the top message.

Alex was pacing behind him, muttering, mostly to himself. "I need to go back and read his notes. I swear, if he actually used FORTRAN, I..."

Daniel held up a hand, hoping Alex would stop talking. What he was reading was running together like a huge puddle of panicked letters.

"No, just, no. No. No. NO!"

Alex stopped in mid-stride. "What?"

Daniel closed the message. He couldn't deal with this. No matter that it had already happened. It felt like death had followed him, come knocking on his door, and was determined to not stop its incessant pounding until everyone and everything that Daniel had ever loved was gone. He stood up abruptly, the chair falling away, clattering to the floor as he slapped the communicator on his chest, "NARA, connect me with Mayor Sebring, stat."

Seconds later, Jackson Sebring's voice sounded in his ear. "Medry, what can I do you for?" In the distance, he could hear the ratchet of heavy machinery. Sebring, like the rest of the colony, had more than one job. He was the acting mayor, sure, along with a handful of others who served as city council members, but he was also heading a mining operation that would help supply the 3D printers with the raw minerals they needed for specific manufacturing tasks required by the growing colony.

"We need to convene an emergency session with the rest of the council." Daniel said, feeling a wave of misery crash over him. "Right now."

There was a pause, and in the background, the machinery continued to pound. Daniel opened his mouth to say the words again, but Sebring spoke, his tone grim. "It's that bad?"

"Worse than you can imagine."

Another silence as the other man digested this. "Aaronson is close, but Phoenix is heading up a recon to the future Sagan Base. He's hours out. It will have to be you, me, Aaronson, Sydan and Schrader. That'll be enough for quorum. Let

Phoenix know, though, it would probably be best for him to head back, yes?”

“Yeah, that really would be best.”

“Okay, so let them all know. I can catch a flitter back, be there by 1100 hours, 1200 at the latest.”

“Roger that. I’ll call in the rest.” Daniel said and disconnected the call before tapping his Comm again. “NARA…”

“What the hell is going on, Medry?” Alex asked.

Daniel avoided eye contact. “I’m sorry, I can’t talk about it until after I meet with the Council.”

Alex swore under his breath, looked as if he wanted to argue, and then his shoulders sagged. “Right. I’ll go back to learning some goddamn esoteric computer language while the rest of you talk about the end of the world.”

Daniel turned away, wincing. Alex Smart did not know how close to the truth he was. Instead, he pressed the communicator again. “NARA, send a message to Fenton Aaronson, Sam Sydan, Carrie Schrader, and Martin Phoenix. The message is: emergency meeting for all city council members at 1200.”

NARA responded, “Sending the message now.”

By the time Jackson Sebring entered the room a few minutes past eleven, everyone but Martin Phoenix was there and waiting. As a one, they turned to Daniel. He sucked in a breath.

"I received an official notification from Madeline Chen of the Terran United Planetary Government." He immediately felt stupid.

As if they don't all know who Madeline Chen is.

Sam nodded at him to continue, her eyes dark with worry.

"The message reads as follows..." He cleared his throat, desperate to speak over the block of dread forming there. "An asteroid over fourteen kilometers in diameter, one not previously tracked but likely the fracturing of 486958 Arrokoth, better known as Ultima Thule, in the asteroid belt, is on a collision course with Earth. All attempts to deflect it using the planetary defense system have failed. We expect impact will occur on August 9th, 2104 at approximately 8:10 GMT, resulting in an extinction level event on Earth. We are sending as many lifeships as we can to Mars, the Moon, and to Zarmina's World. More to follow in further communiques."

A silence descended over the group. It didn't last long.

"August ninth? That means it has already happened."

"Extinction level event."

"This isn't possible. This *can't* be possible."

Sam stood up and ran for the trash can near the door, retching into it. The rest didn't look so far behind. Everyone's face had paled, and Daniel could see the glimmer of tears forming in Fenton's as well as Carrie's eyes.

"The relays still aren't on-line, so we are stuck at a four-year delay. We don't know for sure it has happened, I guess, I mean..." Daniel's voice petered out. As if the Earth's population being reduced to less than one percent hadn't been bad enough, the impact of the asteroid would ravage their home world. An extinction level event. That's what the transmission had said. Those three words echoed as they repeated over and over and rolled through his head. His head pulsed in time.

Extinction level event. Extinction level event. Extinction level event.

Daniel walked over to where Sam was still crouched and placed a hand on her shoulder. She continued to retch. All he could see when he thought of home was death and destruction. They were likely dead. All of them.

Boiling seas. Fire from the sky. An asteroid that size, it could set off a chain reaction in the Ring of Fire. Earthquakes, eruptions, tsunami. A fucking nuclear winter. And Toby is there. I never should have left him!

"Medry."

Daniel blinked. "What?" They were all staring at him.

Sam's hand gripped his tightly. She was standing now, pale, her mouth tight, a sheen of sweat on her brow. "Fenton asked how much we could reduce the communications delay."

"If we can get the damn relays to come on line? A 520-day delay, maybe less, is the best we can hope for. There are multiple variables - solar radiation, orbits, asteroids, unforeseen damage. Smart is working on it." His lips felt numb. His whole body did.

Why the fuck do I get all the bad news? Why can't it be someone else?

Carrie Schrader cleared her throat. Her face was pale, pinched. "We need to decide on what to tell the others. We don't know what has happened to Earth and we don't have that data yet."

Martin Phoenix frowned over at his partner. "Are you suggesting we withhold information?"

A wave of discontent washed over the group, and Carrie held up both her hands, as if she could push it back. "I'm saying that we have all been through a lot. There is not a single person here who hasn't lost someone. Either on Earth or on the Calypso. What I'm saying is that, despite appearances, many of our people here are *fragile*. We're seen firsthand what happens when someone breaks. Do we really want to see it again?"

"We need Carter in on this," Sam said, quietly, sinking into her seat slowly as if she had aged a dozen years. She reached for a napkin and pressed it against her mouth.

"Agreed." Martin Phoenix said and glanced around the room. "Any objections to bringing him into the meeting at this time?"

The rest of them shook their heads.

"Does anyone know where he is?"

"NARA, please give us a location on Jacob Carter." Martin said.

"Dr. Carter is in the cantina." NARA responded.

"NARA, patch me through to Dr. Carter, please."

A few moments later, a knock came at the door and Carter took his place at the table. His lips flattened into a line at the grim news.

"And with the communications array still not aligned, we do not know what has happened to Earth," Martin explained.

Daniel's headache was rapidly expanding in size and strength. He stood, swaying. "I need to go."

Sam stood with him. "I left Luke at the care center, but he will need feeding soon."

"But we haven't come to a consensus!" Carrie said, looking scandalized.

"Does it matter?" Daniel said, a bitter note in his voice. "They wouldn't have sent a transmission like that if it wasn't a damned sure thing. It's happened. There truly is no going back. And maybe we get a fresh wave of colonists, or maybe they bring the ESH virus 22 light years away and infect us and we all get it and die. Or worse, some of us get really damn lucky and get to watch anyone we have left die as well."

Sam caught his sleeve. "Daniel!"

Carrie winced and glanced over at Jacob Carter. "This is exactly why we need to figure out what to say to everyone else. Because of responses like this.

And worse." She covered her face with her hands. "We were healing, if one can, after a virus wipes out everyone you knew and loved. And now this. It's..."

"Inconceivable." Fenton said, his eyes haunted.

Daniel wanted nothing more than to flee the room, to scrub his mind clear of the past hour. But he was part of the council. He had a front-row seat to the end of the world. "So, what do we say? Or, not say?" All he wanted was to hold their baby close and pretend he hadn't seen that transmission. Perhaps Earth had deflected it, stopped it, reduced the damage. It was possible, wasn't it? The planetary defense system put up over thirty years earlier had helped destroy several sizable chunks of rock before they could affect Earth. Testing the theory proved successful; the system had prevented more than one asteroid impact in the past three decades.

"Go to your son, Medry. Sam." Jacob Carter said gently before he turned to the others. "I think that this needs to be discussed further. A day or two won't hurt. Anything longer might cause significant trust issues with the rest of the colonists. I would strongly suggest the city council call a town hall meeting to discuss this before something leaks."

Martin nodded. "Daniel, Sam, can we trust you to wait for the council to decide on this before sharing the knowledge with the others?"

"Of course." Sam answered for both of them. Daniel gave a tight nod, not trusting his voice. The emotions welling up, the helpless and hopeless feelings felt overwhelming.

They headed for the door, let it close behind them and Daniel strode down the corridor, eager to escape to the outside. Suddenly, everything felt too small, too enclosed and claustrophobic. He pushed on until they were outside in the fresh air.

God, I've had enough canned air to last a lifetime. A lifetime. Something Luke and Janine never had. Their lives cut short and Toby left alone in the ashes of the dying world.

"Daniel, please slow down." Her hand slid into his. Sam knew his heart, knew his agonies, his guilt. "We will find him, Daniel. We will."

"You can't know that, Sam."

She reached up, placed her hands on his cheeks, and stared into his eyes. "They will have given him a priority seat on a lifeship, Daniel. Because of you, or even because of who adopted him. The scientist, Dr. Aaronson. You've read her work, her papers on the ESH virus. Think about it. You *know* this. We *will* find him. I promise you."

It was a hopeful dream, an empty promise, really. But in that moment, he believed her. After all, what choice did he have?

Incoming

Date: 07.18.2105

NARA's voice cut through Luke's wails with quiet efficiency. "Communications requests your presence, Daniel Medry."

Even the baby stopped bawling, although perhaps he sensed Daniel's shift in mood. Luke wiggled in Daniel's arms, stuck a thumb in his mouth, and stared up at his father. There were still tracks of tears running through the dust on his tiny cheeks.

Daniel sighed, "I have to go, little man." The baby's face shifted, morphing from sadness into a wide smile.

"Go." His son babbled in return. "Go, guh, go!"

Sam swooped in, picking up their son. "That's right, Luke. Daddy needs to go. But he will be back in time for your bath, don't you worry." She shot Daniel an irritated look. "After all, it was Daddy who let you play in the dirt, wasn't it?" Her irritation melted away as she noticed his expression. "Do you need me to come with?"

Daniel shook his head. "No, no, you stay here with Luke. Besides, he's ready for a nap, and you look like you could use one yourself."

She was over five months pregnant with their daughter and with the extra gravity, and everything else that was going on, including an active little boy who was crawling everywhere. Sam looked exhausted. There were shadows under her eyes and she moved slower with each day that passed.

"Someone else could do it." Sam said, biting her lip. "It doesn't always have to be you, Daniel."

She knew how much he dreaded reading the transmissions, and with every tweak and improvement to the array, more news came in from Earth, and the time between sending and receiving was narrowing. This meant more and more news. Much of it was bad.

The continuing restrictions on reproductive rights were chilling enough. Here on Zarmina's World, most of the colonists felt the need to bring children into the world if they could, but they also hadn't watched most of the world die around them. Taking away the right to bodily autonomy, to choose where and when a woman would have children, was a fundamental right that all RUSA citizens expected. But with a mere 15 million people left on Earth, and a small fraction of that expected to survive the Ultima Thule asteroid, the Terran United Planetary Government handled things differently. And the reports of increasingly draconian measures in the name of protecting the children showed children were being removed from their parents in record numbers.

The colony had politely refused to consider several of the newer ordinances the TUPG had passed and there was talk of declaring Zarmina's World a sovereign world, and government, in their own right. After all, it wasn't as if Earth could pass sanctions on them 22 light years away.

Alex Smart and two others had been working on the project nonstop for months. They had whittled down the delay to just over three years. Today might be the final push to whittle it down to the 505-day delay mark, which was the minimum they could expect from Earth.

"I know. But bad news just seems to find me." And it did. The news before the extinction level event had broken had been of wildfires burning out of control along the west coast of the Reformed United States, stretching from south of Los Angeles, all the way north of Seattle. Then there were the troubling reports of reproductive freedoms being restricted, and how abortion was now completely illegal worldwide. There were transmissions detailing increasingly draconian liberties being taken by Children's Protective Services, removing children from their natural parents. It was unnerving. The overcrowded Earth that they had left replaced with a planet in crisis - not just because of the impending asteroid, but from the remnants of humanity that were left. The enormity of their changed reality remained a staggering concept to them. How was it possible to go from eleven billion people, to a mere 15 million, and that terrifyingly small number, with a 14-kilometer asteroid headed toward them, now suddenly *too many*?

Daniel closed his eyes, thinking again of Toby. Was his son even alive? He dreaded knowing the truth, but he dreaded *not* knowing even more. That's why he hadn't asked to be released from Comm duty. Perhaps it was his penance. He remembered the last night he had spent with his son on Earth, staring at the stars, showing the boy that distant cluster of stars where he was going, so sure Toby was better off with Luke and Janine. Better off never knowing the truth.

Sam's hand, softly cupping his face, brought him back to the present.

"There are others who can take this burden, Daniel."

He shook his head and looked away. "I'm fine. Really, I am."

"Are you?"

He met her eyes. "I have to do this, Sam. For Luke and Janine. For Toby."

She kissed him softly, sighing as she did. "Okay."

Luke wailed behind him as Daniel set down the path towards the settlement and the distant Comm building. The ground was dry now, a sharp departure from the seemingly endless rains of the month before. He waved at Fenton Aaronson, who was operating a small leveler, preparing his new homesite for a foundation. His wife was due any day. Twins no less. Fenton said that they ran on both sides of the family. A few feet away, Fenton's dog woofed in concern and ran over to Daniel. The dog kept looking over his shoulder, obviously concerned about his human and the enormous machine.

"Hey Dunkin', don't you worry, I think Fenton knows what he's doing." Dunkin's tongue lolled from the side of his mouth. A fawn color over most of his body, Dunkin' sported a white chest and dark, kohl-like outlined eyes. A good-looking, happy boy, and one of the first dogs produced by the artificial wombs. The pup was already a solid 20 kilograms, and from the look of his leg muscles, the pittie would top out at over 30. Fenton had asked for a dog that could handle the extra gravity, and NARA had produced a list of dogs with strong hearts and compact, muscled frames. Pitbulls had topped the list. Loyal, family-oriented, and protective.

"What more could I ask for?" Fenton had said the other day, stroking the dog's head as it chewed on a large stick.

Daniel hoped his own request would come up soon in the lottery. There were limited spaces available, but now that the goats, sheep and pigs were now well into their second and sometimes third generations, the artificial wombs were opening up to less "necessary" requirements, like dogs and cats.

Growing up, he had walked the neighbor's dog, a rough collie with a narrow nose and tri-color markings, every week for a neighbor. He'd had other motivations at the time. She was several years older than him and far more interested in her Honors and AP classes than she was in walking a dog or talking to a kid whose voice cracked with regularity. Daniel had walked the dog for nearly two years until the family sold the house and moved away. By the time they did, he had bonded with the collie and liked him more than he ever liked the girl. There had never seemed to be the right time to get a dog. At least, not until now.

And Luke will need a dog. A boy needs a dog.

He stared at the building that held the artificial wombs on the east side of the settlement. It wouldn't hurt to check in real quick, would it? Sure, they'd notify him, but why the hell not ask, just in case the tech was busy with other things? His steps slowed as he considered taking a quick detour, only to hear Alex's voice calling.

"Medry!"

No rest for the wicked.

Alex looked stressed. Hell, he looked as if he hadn't slept. "Thanks for coming in."

"What's up?" Daniel asked.

"Another red-label communique," Alex answered and pointed to the terminal.

"Shit." These were never good news. The last one had been about the asteroid, something that had already hit Earth, even though they wouldn't see that for another few months at least, depending on if the relays finally stopped giving them trouble.

If they could just fucking work, that would be really nice.

He sat down at his console and clicked on the communique, then entered his Level II password. Alex's pass capped out at Level III. Daniel's clearance allowed him to view nearly every single communique, except for those reserved specifically for governmental-level decision-making. This seemed whimsical at best. He still didn't understand why they coded a 14-kilometer wide extinction-level-event asteroid as Level II, yet considered any legislation affecting bodily autonomy at Level I. But there they were.

TRANSMISSION PACKET
TPC TO ZWC
/BEGIN TRANSMISSION
CONFIRM ARRIVAL OF TWO LIFESHIPS EN ROUTE FROM EARTH. NOSTRADAMAS LIFESHIP CONTAINS 189,542 UNINFECTED SURVIVORS IN CRYO AND SKELETON CREW OF 15. THE MAYFLOWER LIFESHIP IS COMPRISED OF 95,527 ESH-POSITIVE SURVIVORS. PLEASE CONFIRM SAFE PASSAGE FOR ESH POSITIVE INDIVIDUALS.
/END TRANSMISSION

"Holy shit." Daniel breathed. "Holy shit!" The uninfected survivors. Sure, he could understand that. Sending ESH positive survivors to the only place unexposed to the virus, and thus risking everyone, seemed beyond foolish.

Alex's reaction, having read over Daniel's shoulder, was even more extreme. "What the actual fuck are they thinking, sending ESH positive survivors here? What the actual fuck?"

Daniel stood up. "You shouldn't have read that, kid. But since you have, I'm asking that you keep your mouth shut about this until the emergency council can meet and figure out what to do. We had three suicides after the news of the asteroid broke and we can't afford any more losses. You get me?"

Alex stared at him for a moment, then had the decency to look chagrined. "Sorry Medry, I wasn't thinking."

"It's okay, man, we just..." He stopped and closed his eyes. Would the hits ever stop coming? When the fuck was he going to get some good news for once? His thoughts swirled, a building maelstrom of conflicting emotions. They would have to put them on the far side of the planet. But would that be enough? Were they still at risk? ESH had gone airborne. How many parts per million would it take for an infected on the far side of this massive new world to infect one of his people? This colony had to survive. "We just need time to figure this all out." He hated how weak that sounded. Figure it out, yeah, like exactly *how* did they go about figuring it out?

Hours later, in yet another emergency council meeting, Fenton Aaronson had all eyes focused on him as he scribbled equations on his pad with a stylus, his face grim. "This will take more than my rough estimates, but I think we will be okay if the ESH positive group lands on the far side of the planet. If they target the southern plains, the trade winds would move south before rising and then move past us to the northern edge of the mountains. And that's assuming the ESH virus could survive the cold side of the planet, much less be at any level of concentration." He waved his hand dismissively. "Disbursement, and all that. Besides, they are working on a cure, and who knows, by the time they land, we might all have a solid way forward. We won't have to isolate from them forever."

"The southern plains?" Jackson Sebring frowned. "What is the water situation like there?"

"It's good. A nice, solid aquifer underground, with a network of springs throughout and plenty of valleys that provide shelter from the trade winds." Fenton shrugged. "It was high on our list for potential landing sites, but the volcano was looking active, so we passed and took this spot. The volcano likes to talk a lot, but more in-depth drone studies show it will be a long time before it does more than blow smoke and growl at us."

Carrie spoke then, "The Uninfected's on the Nostradamus are all in Cryo, except for the skeleton crew." She shrugged. "Since *they* aren't a threat to our health and safety, I propose we encourage the Nostradamus to establish orbit, and bring them down in batches, take them out of Cryo slowly. Daniel, once you have the rolls, and we can suss out family units and more, we can prioritize a list and figure out who can wait and who should be revived from Cryo. That way, we don't overload our reserves and food stores with too many mouths to feed, clothe, and house."

Martin Phoenix frowned. "Do we even know if that is what they want? What is Earth saying about the viability of the planet after impact?"

"Ten years." Daniel replied. "They estimate at least ten years until the nuclear winter induced by the sediment and projectiles thrown into the air completely clears."

"Jesus. And they think they can stick people underground for that long?" Martin whistled. "Do they really think any of them will survive?"

Daniel shrugged. "Nature will out, I guess. They must leave a majority on the surface. Whether they will survive, and what the others currently underground will eventually be able to return to, it's all up in the air. After all, it's been a hot minute since the dinosaurs were wiped out. We don't exactly have a road map here."

Fenton spoke then, "We have seventeen months to get our shit together, people. Before we have a massive influx of new residents. Mayflower will have to figure things out on their own, but we can help those on board the Nostradamus, and take our time decanting them from Cryo." His voice rang with the same authority as it had on board the Calypso. "By the time Nostradamus and Mayflower arrive, we will have a plan in place, food and shelter ready."

The others nodded. It still didn't feel real. Especially the thought that Earth, or at least the world they had known, was in ruins even now. That it had been for nearly a year. Still, it didn't feel real. Not without visual confirmation. That was coming. And each of them needed to see it for themselves even if they dreaded doing so. The dying of their world was already eleven months in the past.

Cataclysm

Date: 12.27.2105

As the day of the incoming broadcast approached, Daniel felt his dread growing. It might have already happened on Earth, but for the colonists, each doom-filled message they received was yet another terrible blow from the world they had left behind. The estimated day of impact, August 9th, 2104, had occurred over a year earlier, but because of the transmission delay, one they had finally whittled down to just over sixteen and a half months, today they would finally see the true devastation.

As if the ESH virus hadn't done enough. How much more could their home planet bear? Or humanity itself?

As the date had drawn nearer, the alcohol consumption ticked up, as did tempers and frayed nerves across the settlement despite the festive season. Someone had put in a request for tinsel, garland and some kind of festive sparkly giant bells with the 3D printers that made the colony look like Yule had puked on everything. Daniel wasn't sure if they were overcompensating for the last few years when 3D printers were still reserved for the more important things, or if this was a direct response to the impending destruction of humanity's birthplace. Whichever it was, it was over the top and visually overwhelming.

They had celebrated Yule two days earlier with Kevin and his son, Simon. Exchanged gifts with each other, tried a new vodka distillation from an overrun of potatoes, and tried to not think about the impending doom of Earth. It wasn't easy. A pall had fallen over the colony and no one said much about it. In fact, they seemed to avoid discussing Earth. But now that Yule was out of the way, and any potential food coma or alcohol-induced stupor well recovered from, well, it was time.

Daniel wondered if anyone felt like him. Did they share this desperate fantasy that somehow, at the last minute, Ultima Thule would simply slice past and miss Earth? Maybe just give the old girl a memorable meteor shower and be on its way?

All the models and projections had unequivocally dashed that hope. Yet the dream of it remained. Just as death is a distant and alien possibility until it knocks on your door, Daniel held hard to his hope of a reprieve. He knew Tobias had secured a place in the Cheyenne Mountain Complex, one of the safest places on Earth. Deep within the earth, his son would live for up to a decade or more before emerging to a changed world. At least, that was the plan. Anything could go wrong with that plan, really it could. And every day that passed, Daniel found himself in knots, just imagining the terrible possibilities.

"Are you ready?" Sam interrupted his thoughts. She had the baby swaddled against her, gently snoozing. "Lucas just finished nursing. I think we have a good two hours before he wakes back up."

"Yeah, let's get down there."

She gave his hand a squeeze, and they set off down the hill to the colony below. They could see others milling about, walking out of their homes, heading toward the central meeting space. A week prior, after much deliberation, the screens were put into place. There were those who felt that they should view the destruction first, before releasing it to the public. The vote was close, with almost as many wanting to delay the release of images until it was reviewed. But the cat was out of the bag, and delaying it would only cause additional tension. That was the overall consensus, and Daniel and Sam had both thought it best. Today would not be easy, but hiding it, or delaying it as if their fellow colonists were infantile and in need of protection, well, that was far worse.

Daniel had dreaded this day. He had struggled to smile or enjoy Yule, their first Yule as a family here in their new home. The pall of what today would bring had hung over them like a black cloud.

Jennifer Lennox, with Eric Stryder holding Jennifer's daughter, Jane, in his arms, joined them, nodding silently. No one spoke any common pleasantries, not then, and not when they joined dozens of others in the open square. Everyone was silent, only the occasional bark of a dog, trudge of footsteps, or wail of a baby to cut through the thick silence. They were all dealing with their own demons. Guilt over leaving loved ones behind, worries about who remained and would those who sheltered on the planet survive. The impending destruction of their home planet weighed heavily on their minds and robbed them of the wish to make small talk.

Daniel didn't need to be in the Comm building for this. He was grateful for that. He wanted to be with Sam and Lucas, and have something to hold on to in the moments to come. The transmission packet would include multiple satellite viewpoints and he had already worked out with NARA how to go about broadcasting the satellite imagery to the screens. All it would take was a single voice command. He looked around at the crowd, and realized he and Sam were standing in the middle, ringed by the other colonists. To one side, slightly elevated by a shipping crate, their mayor, Jackson Sebring, was standing. He tapped his comm and murmured into it. Seconds later, the speakers squealed slightly and his voice was amplified through it.

"Fellow colonists and citizens of Zarmina's World. In a few moments, NARA will show us feeds from the satellites that surround, well, surrounded Earth on August 9th of last year. The viewscreens will soon show us the devastating impact of one of the largest asteroids our world has ever seen. I know you know this, and that with your presence here today, you believe you are ready to see these images. But know this." He paused, took a breath. "There is no shame in looking away or taking your time to absorb the moments that come next. No matter how far we have come, no matter if we never return, the birthplace of humanity, of almost all of us here today, holds a special place in our hearts, our souls. All the feelings you have today are valid and understandable. We have asked Dr. Carter and his associates to extend their hours of availability for the next few weeks, as we all take the time to process what we see next. Remember, we are stronger together than apart. The people of Earth will survive. Here on Zarmina's World, in orbits around the Moon and Mars, and deep within our very planet. We will survive. We will rebuild what has been lost and humanity will not lose its light."

A murmur ran through the crowd. Jackson turned, picked out Daniel in the crowd, and nodded to him.

"NARA, stream the latest transmission packets from the satellites surrounding Earth, please."

"Streaming in five, four, three, two, one…" NARA's dulcet tones responded.

The screens flickered to life. Six separate images appeared on the screens before them. Each a vantage point of a specific satellite. Before them was Earth. Beautiful blue, wreathed in white clouds over the oceans, green and brown continents. The images cycled to the dark side, then back to the light side. In one image, viewers could see a massive lifeship dwindling into the distance, safe from the asteroid's path, but within optimal viewing distance.

They must have had front row seats, Daniel mused. *Front row seats to the end of the world.*

The crowd murmured again as a large ball of light turned one satellite image to white and then black.

"Satellite 8H539 ceased transmission." NARA intoned.

Other satellites also turned yellow, then white, then returned to showing a tremendous glare as the asteroid arced past them, traveling at over 14,000 kilometers per second. NARA, who Daniel had prepared beforehand, stopped, rewound, and then played the next pieces of footage slowly, so that it was clearly visible to the human eye. The asteroid, once past the satellites, streaked toward Earth. The pieces separating, encapsulated in fiery light as they punched through the atmosphere, tails of fire following them as they made the final descent.

Then nothing. For two, three, four, even five seconds. There was nothing past the afterglow of the asteroid's descent. Hope bloomed in Daniel's heart. Other asteroids were blasting past satellites, destroying them. Several more images went black. And then, a dark pimple on the surface of the planet appeared. It grew like a boil, darkening, expanding. Around its edges, red and orange, but the blackness kept expanding faster and further. The dark, roiling clouds came next, spreading darkness across their home world, an insidious infection of the grotesque.

One by one, the satellites grew dark, until only two remained. They showed a hellscape forming on the surface and in the atmosphere. It was destruction on a massive scale. It took Daniel's breath away. His chest constricted, his heart felt crushed.

Some were silent, others sobbing, and a few keened their distress. Wailing as one would at the funeral of a loved one. And wasn't it so? Mother Earth, ravaged by decades of abuse, poisoned and used. The deaths of billions in the past decade, and now this. Their mother, the cradle of humanity, disfigured and in flames. The atmosphere quickly becoming unbreathable. On the surface, some fourteen million unfortunate souls remained. They had survived the ESH plague, the years of struggle after, and the heartbreaking fight to repopulate the Earth. And now this, this surely unsurvivable event. Would any of those burrowed deep underground actually make it? And those millions on the surface? It seemed impossible and even as he had believed himself to be prepared for this moment, Daniel found himself unmoored. Tears he didn't remember shedding flowed down his cheeks and dripped into the alien soil at his feet. He clutched Sam tightly and sobbed with the others. It felt as if his soul was being ripped from his body.

Later, hours later, back in their house, muzzy-headed from the distilled moonshine passed around long after they turned the screens off, Daniel felt fog-filled and unfocused. It wasn't the alcohol. At least, not only the alcohol. It was grief. Sharp, deep, as if a knife remained buried in him. Only this time it wasn't in his shoulder, but his heart, and his stomach. Perhaps his very soul.

"He's alive, Daniel." Sam's body was warm in his. He curled around her, needing the skin-on-skin contact. As if he were her child as well. He could feel Lucas' warm little body, already in a deep sleep after a long feed. He would sleep most of the night.

"We don't know that."

"Perhaps not. But until proven differently, that's what I choose to believe." Sam was steadfast, her voice calm. "Tobias is in one of the safest places on Earth. And humankind has survived against incredible odds. In another six months, maybe a year, they will broadcast a signal. Have faith."

Faith.

What an odd choice of words for her to use. And yet, faith was just what he needed. Not in a divine being that would save them all, but in something far more tangible. The force of a human will to survive often by simply believing they could. Against all odds, against all forces.

Tobias was strong. He'd survived the deaths of Luke and Janine, of a refugee encampment. He'd found his way into Julie Lynn Aaronson's life, studied the ESH virus, and attended one of the most elite scientific colleges in the country. If anyone could survive, it would be his son.

There had been no answer to his message sent. Had Tobias received it? In the chaos of those last days, it might have been lost or delayed. Perhaps his son was already deep underground. He'd wanted him to know the truth, just in case he hadn't already figured it out, but there had been no response to the vid Daniel had spent days crafting.

His brain spun, tangled in alcohol-thick webs of chaos. Images of the bombardment of Earth now burned into his brain. Daniel sunk into sleep, his body finally succumbing to exhaustion and grief. His dreams filled with rock walls, cave ins, and the Earth in flames.

Who Are We?

Date: 01.05.2106

Eric Stryder stared at the graffiti for a moment. The paint was dry, and he would try to pull up footage, but there were few cameras here. They weren't necessary. At least, not until now.

Back on Earth, every street was under surveillance, both public and private. It had been that way for nearly a century. It had reduced crime. Especially since the cameras became better quality, and facial recognition software had become standard.

This, however, was the first graffiti Eric had seen since leaving Earth behind. And it signified that, despite few voiced objections to the incoming lifeships from Earth, there was at least someone who felt strongly.

LIFESHIPS FROM EARTH BRING VIRUS & DEATH

He had to get this down... now.

Eric tapped his Comm unit, "Stryder to Council. We have a situation at the cantina you may want to see."

He tapped the Comm twice to enable camera mode. "NARA, please send the following image to all members of the Council."

It was early, just past 0500. He could remove the graffiti before anyone else saw it. A quick command to a cleaning bot did the trick.

It didn't, however, remove the problem. Seeing the graffiti, it pointed to unrest, fear, and both were problems for their struggling colony.

A squeak of gears and a robotic chirp of greeting came seconds after his request. The cleaning bot got to work, no need for chitchat or questions, and moments later, the words were gone as if they had never existed.

But Eric knew they had been there. And so did the Council and whoever had painted them there. He made a note to investigate who would have requested any paint supplies in the past few weeks. The Council would probably want to know.

By early afternoon, Eric was standing in front of the Council. No one looked happy. Fenton Aaronson yawned, rubbing his eyes and looking haggard. At five months, his twins still weren't sleeping through the night.

"So, do you know who did this?" Sam asked, staring at the image on her tablet.

"I narrowed it down to two men who recently requested paint from the 3D print units. Marshall Briggs is down on a fishing and cartography expedition and has been for the past ten days. Richard Knox has a playhouse for his daughter in the exact green."

Carrie Schrader scrolled through her own tablet. "Knox, Richard. Mechanical engineer, minor in geology. I think I met his wife, but I don't know him."

"I've worked with him on some of the bigger infrastructure rollouts. He helped install the power grid and plan the sewer lines. He's a good guy, but he's scared, and likely had plenty of liquid courage in him." Martin frowned and paused before continuing. "The problem is that we've already heard grumbles and fears over the lifeships that are coming. And considering that, despite precautions, the ESH virus escaped Earth and infected the moon colony, space stations, and even Mars. It's not like he's not the only one who is worried." He turned to Carrie. "You've received the reports from survivors of the Mars Colony. Is there a cure for the ESH virus? And how effective is it?"

Carrie shrugged. "Honestly? I'm unsure. The two Mars survivors, or at least the ones who had remained unexposed to the ESH virus, were from the Chinese contingent on the far side of the planet. From what I understand, they kept them isolated from the ESH-positive survivors at Huygens until an experimental cure was ready. It seemed to work for them, but who knows as to its efficacy on a large scale?"

"And Earth had its hands full creating the lifeships and getting as many off-planet or underground as possible. So, all they are saying is that it *appears* to work." Sam added.

The room settled into silence.

"We need to ensure strict isolation protocols. No one, and I mean *no one*, leaves isolation until 50 days after revival from Cryo." Jackson said, his fingers templed in front of him. "What about keeping them in orbit?"

"That could work. And it would go far to assuage others' fears." Carrie answered.

"That's an exponential amount of supplies needed. Because we can't just uncork them from Cryo all at once, we'd overload resources on the lifeship and on the ground." Jackson Sebring chimed in. "How many people would come out of Cryo at a time? Five? Ten? Twenty? We're going to need to set aside food and create a plan for processing them or plan on leaving most of them in Cryo for *years*."

Daniel's fingers flew as he accessed the records for the Nostradamus lifeship. "It looks like we could leave over 80% in Cryo for a while, possibly years. Hell, that was probably the plan, anyway. There are over 100,000 souls on ice right now. It could take us a decade to prepare a city for them here on the surface."

"We need to get ahead of this. Address it head-on rather than ignoring people's fears." Fenton added, "We need to show them we are taking their safety seriously."

"What do you suggest, Captain?" Daniel asked.

"We come up with a coherent plan of action. Call a town meeting. Talk to them." Fenton answered. "They deserve the truth, and they deserve a say in what happens next."

Two days after the Council meeting, an all-hands meeting was called for Sagan Base. There had been two more incidents of graffiti, and the atmosphere felt charged with fear and anger. Jackson Sebring stood at the podium, waiting for the cacophony of voices to quiet down.

"Thank you all for coming tonight." His voice rang out across the crowded room. The roar fell to a murmur, and then to silence. "Let's get straight to the main issue. The two lifeships headed for Zarmina's World. On board these two ships are over 200,000 souls. Half are ESH-positive, the other are UPs, uninfected persons."

"Yeah right! Tell that to the Moon and Mars colonies!" A man's voice rang out from the crowd. Murmurs rose in response, the vast room's occupants restless, afraid.

Jackson nodded. "Yes, that absolutely is a concern. From what we understand of this ESH virus, it is the most dangerous killer humanity has ever encountered, and we must take every precaution we can to ensure it does not spread past the far side of the planet. That is where Mayflower will disembark and where they will stay, far from us, until we have determined that the cure is 100% effective and the virus has not mutated."

He paused, as the murmurs grew, "We have Dr. Schrader and a team of researchers examining the cure, and when they have clear data one way or the other, they will share it with us. I'm urging you to give them the time they need to learn everything there is about the virus and then complete the tweaks on a vaccine. We will keep everyone updated."

A woman's voice, from the back of the room, shouted, "What about the Nostradamus? Are we really going to allow those people access to this continent? Why can't we tell the lifeships to turn back?"

Jackson shook his head. "All but a skeleton crew are in Cryo and there they will stay until we have a cure for the virus, are absolutely sure none of those in Cryo have it, and can prepare for that many people landing here on the planet. We estimate it will be at least one decade, and the plan at this time is for them to stay in Cryo. Only those who have isolated for 50 days and show no signs of the virus will be allowed on Zarmina's World."

The murmurs, angry voices, and rumbles of discontent continued, rising in volume.

Fenton stood up then.

"Who are we?" Fenton's voice rang strong across the meeting room. He paused and surveyed the room, letting the question sink in. "That is what each of us needs to ask themselves. Your fears are our fears, all of us. We have children, loved ones, and we have sacrificed so much to be here, in this place, so far from Earth." He paused again. "And most of us have lost everyone we ever knew, ever loved, back on Earth." He spread his hands, turned and eyeballed several of the louder dissenters. "Earth is currently uninhabitable. Humanity, all of it, is in peril. Our very survival as a species is at risk. In our fear, our love for those we have here, we mustn't forget that there are over 200,000 people, survivors, who need our assistance. We must help them in whatever way we can. We can do this safely. If we follow all biohazard containment protocols until the virus is eradicated, and the sixth mass extinction has passed. Help us make that a reality."

After two more hours of questions, the colonists dispersed. The consensus was that the Mayflower be allowed to land on the far side of the planet. Meanwhile, the Nostradamus would remain in orbit. Fear was still rampant, but Eric Stryder hoped there would be no more graffiti.

Filled With Darkness

Date: 06.02.2106

"What the hell are these plants, anyway?" Anton Webster asked as he ripped even more of the serrated leaves out of the ground. The plot of land had seen an infestation of the plants in the past week, and they were crowding out the lines of lettuce and herbs.

Fenton swore and stuck a finger to his mouth. "Razor-sharp, they are as well!"

Anton dug into his rucksack and tossed the former starship captain a pair of gloves. "Try these."

"Sure will, as soon as I can get the blood to stop. Got any bandages in there?"

"Of course. First aid kit for all my friends." Anton answered, digging down deeper into the rucksack.

"Thanks." Fenton dug into the kit for gauze, his other hand dripping blood. "Damn, we should gather this for Sam to identify. This has got to have anti-coagulant properties. One minor scratch and I'm pouring blood!"

A small puddle of it had gathered on the soil at his feet.

Anton raised his eyebrows at the sight. "Damn, Cap, you sure you're cut out for farming?"

Fenton grinned. "It's in my blood. My grandparents on both sides, heck, even my great-great-grandfather, my namesake, Fenton Perdue, was a farmer."

"So, the whole starship captain thing was just a side gig?" Anton asked, winking.

"You caught me," Fenton snorted. "Just a farm boy pretending to drive a tractor to the stars."

He stopped the blood flow and wrapped the bandage tight before slipping on the gloves. They were thick, but pliable. He wouldn't be impaling himself on any more of the local flora with these on. He straightened and looked at the field.

"This growth, it seems... aggressive. Almost as if it is speeding up. But what's changed? The weather's holding steady, so why is it suddenly showing such increased growth?" Fenton frowned. It felt like a puzzle that he didn't have all the pieces to. What was he missing here?

Anton stood up from where he had crouched, squinting at the far edge of the field. He'd had the bots plow it six days ago, and already the native plant life was making a comeback.

"Newly turned soil? Perhaps it is easier on the local plants?"

Fenton walked over to the outer boundary a mere ten feet away. The soil was light, easily dug, not compact, not full of clay like the thick Missouri soil he remembered as a child. "Got me. This seems easy enough and the natives aren't as close together here as they are in the areas we are seeing incursions. But unless we get a handle on it, the

181

native plants will choke the life out of the Terran variants."

"Damn it. We need these crops." Anton bent down and pulled out more of the invaders. "Sam's tests detected a nasty side effect to this native."

"Oh yeah? What?"

"Yet another variant of emesis colonicus."

"The shiteberry?" Fenton asked, his eyes widening. The shiteberry had quite the reputation after one colonist had picked it, at the edge of a line of Terran crops, not realizing it wasn't some thornless blackberry, but a native plant instead. A couple of "blackberry" pies served up at the cantina that night had caused a wave of diarrhea that downed anyone foolish enough to ingest a slice. Three had ended up hospitalized after consuming more than one slice. The symptoms had lasted for days.

"Yup."

"Jesus Christ, everything on this planet is determined to make us shit ourselves to death." Fenton grumbled.

Anton snorted. "It sure seems like that, doesn't it? So, what do we do about this native taking over?"

"Fire?"

Anton looked pensive. "That's better than glyphosate."

"That it is. That shit caused all manner of merry hell back on Terra."

"I'll program the bots and get the perimeter plus another fifty meters out flamed. Clean the rest of this up by hand." Anton tossed a bunch of the leaves as far as he could from the cultivated crops. "Give me a hand with the western edge?"

"Yup."

An hour later, Fenton straightened, groaning. A hot shower, preferably a nice, long soak, was just what his body needed. He didn't know if he would get it. The twins were crawling and close to walking. Home had become chaotic, with two small boys determined to get up to plenty of trouble. A leisurely soak in a tub was a distant memory, as was a full night's sleep. Even now. The boys often woke up screaming with nightmares, which, according to Joanna, was unusual. Hell, he had nightmares, too. Perhaps the end of their world, and the trauma they had all been through in the past two years, contributed to it all. Could children inherit trauma and nightmares? He didn't know. Still, if he hustled, he might have time to soak his aching back before they woke from their afternoon nap.

The reek of the burning plants was giving him a headache. Fenton was feeling every one of his fifty-six years as he climbed into the passenger side of the flitter and let Anton handle the rest.

Entity noted the destruction of its experiment first as an accident, then recognized it for what it was. A deliberate destruction of the flora it had cultivated for millennia. The plant's structure and use were complicated, and Entity considered it a keystone species. The quadrupeds, which Nathan organism called Zarmunicorns, used it to combat a variety of ailments, including consuming it in order to end the reproduction of a bloodthirsty parasitic worm that was rampant in the tall prairie grasses. It also served as an integral part of the diet of several prairie ruminants That the Visitors had chosen destruction instead of cultivating another area free of the experimental plant disturbed Entity more and more. First, they had clawed up wide swaths of soil, which destroyed several variants, before they attempted, rather poorly, to replace Entity's experiment with one of their own. Entity had nudged the remaining variants, adding more growth hormone to the soil, neatly delivered via the fungal substrate, and attempted to mitigate the damage.

And it had worked. Until today, when the bipedal visitors had unleashed fire, destroying over 90% of Entity's long-lived experiment in mere moments. And while Entity did not indulge in such odd reactions such as anger, it felt more than just disturbed. Perhaps Outro was right. These creatures might actually be a pestilence on the world. Perhaps.

The drops of blood from one of the bipedal visitors had fallen, with almost a cunning accuracy, onto a fungal sensor node. Entity had seeded the area with the nodes in order to keep close tabs on the plants' growth and health. The nodes damaged during the clawing of soil had mostly regrown, and lay thickest at the perimeter of the Visitor-infested planted field.

Long after the creatures had left, and the fire consumed most of Entity's hard work and dedication, Entity analyzed the wealth of information held in those drops of blood. One of the most startling discoveries was that the blood from the bipedal organism known as Fenton differed in several key ways from the Nathan organism. Entity found this fascinating. From the Nathan organism, it knew key points about human reproduction, genetic variance, and more. But that didn't explain these markers, not at all. Entity was knowledgeable in billions of species, carbon-based and otherwise, and it knew, beyond any doubt, that Nathan organism and Fenton organism were different, markedly so. There were enough differences in the genetic markers to make the organisms completely different species. What that meant when compared to the rest of the visitors remained a mystery. A mystery that Entity wanted to solve.

end them

destructive

Outro's presence skimmed past Entity's, viewing the destruction to the crops through Entity's own nodes. Entity could feel Outro's hostility. If it had been a color, it would have been red and black, the color of blood and rot.

visitors destructive yes

Entity answered in return.

cannot study visitors if dead

Entity pointed out that fact gently. Discontent roiled through the connection between parent and child. Outro was different, so different, and this still surprised Entity. It remembered its parent, but there was not such a divisiveness in thought and action between Entity and its parent. How was it that Outro was so very different? Was the difference because of the visitors? Was Outro reacting to the visitors in a way that made sense, that Entity was placing sanctity of life above common sense? Entity did not know. This had never happened before.

visitors destroy

visitors pestilence

infection

must die

Entity possessed no arms, no face to roll its eyes. It had no way to show through body language, like the bipedal lifeforms it was currently studying, how much it disagreed with Outro. But disagree, it most certainly did.

study

learn

adjust

Entity responded as gently as it could. Why did its child not see that these creatures were worthy of study? Outro's presence at the edges of Entity's boundaries vanished then. Outro clearly did not agree. Likely, it could not see any reason for continuing a fruitless discussion with its clueless parent. Outro's silence felt both petulant and foreboding to Entity.

Entity let the keystone species go. The quadrupeds would suffer, most assuredly, and the other flora and fauna that depended on this plant in the vast plain would also adjust, for better, for worse. Entity turned the disagreement with Outro over and over in its thoughts.

Yes, the bipedal visitors were destructive, and that in itself was an annoyance. A significant distance from this experimental field was another visitor-introduced plant. The nodes had detected the unusual growth of a non-native species. A million of the plants, possibly more. The species grew fast and was already disrupting a ground cover that Entity was cultivating. Yet another keystone species of flora whose beneficial qualities were necessary to both surrounding flora and fauna. Entity contemplated destroying the vast plantings the bipedal visitors had done, but ultimately waited. Perhaps the non-native species the visitors had planted would stop their rapid growth before they affected the cultivated groundcover. Perhaps. And if not, well, Entity knew of a particular form of fungus this alien plant would easily succumb to. Entity had, of course, already identified the genetic components, as well as its weaknesses.

Were the visitors dangerous? Invasive? Destructive? Were they a pestilence, as Outro insisted? Only time would tell. And Entity had time, plenty of it.

Arrival

Date: 12.21.2106

"They're here." Alex Smart panted as he slid to a stop in the mud outside Daniel and Sam's cabin. It had been raining for seven days straight and today was the first day in a long time that there was even a hint of light on the horizon.

"Er, well, in orbit. And Phoenix is asking if you'll go up with him and meet the crew of the Nostradamus."

Sam held their newborn Lila close, her mouth set in a grim line. "Full suits."

"Of course." Daniel wasn't about to argue with her.

There were still fears, plenty of them, and with Lila, born just over a month ago, the family of four had plenty to lose. There was no one in the colony willing to become infected with ESH just to see if the cure worked. Instead, it was time to administer the vaccine to the crew of the Nostradamus, and set in place the production of an additional vaccine for every man, woman and child that emerged from Cryo.

The town hall meeting nearly a year ago had resulted in a flurry of research and protective protocols that ensured the colonists of Sagan Base would continue to be safe and virus-free. Ellie Satler, Carrie Schrader, and Ellen Lowry had parsed through the data sent from Huygens Outpost on Mars. There a sibling duo had created the vaccine in order to help two UPs from the Chinese outpost be able to integrate in with a handful of other survivors. After several months of examining the reports, as well as corresponding information from limited trials on Earth, they verified the data and produced a test batch of the vaccine. They then began production for everyone currently in Sagan Base, as well as for the incoming lifeships.

The distribution of the vaccine was complete, and only the youngest children experienced minor side effects, such as irritation and low fever. Luke overcame it with just two days of fever and a bit of grumpiness, possibly because of his new molars. Lila was due to receive the vaccine in just two more days, at her next checkup.

The grumbles and fears of infection from the incoming refugees had eased significantly and finally disappeared entirely. They were far too busy now, anyway. Somehow, they had to help assimilate nearly 100,000 new colonists on Zarmina's World. With less than three hundred original colonists, the task would not be simple and already Martin Phoenix had been in discussions with the Nostradamus crew about exactly how this would get accomplished.

Comms were out because of flooding in one of the smaller power stations. The colony was building a new power station, raised on a low hill instead of at the bottom of one. Thankfully, none of the other power stations were affected.

"The comms being down is a colossal pain in the neck," Alex groused after Daniel kissed Sam and headed out the door and down the hill. They passed by Fenton's property and the twins screeched and waved at their older half-brother as the two men passed. "They've had me running all over hell and back like I'm a messenger boy. I've got houses to build!"

Alex was one of the team responsible for creating housing on the planet, a job he was quite happy doing when the rain wasn't trying to drown them all. All work had stopped during the onslaught nearly a week ago as a storm system had crawled over them, then stalled, dumping more rain than they had ever seen before. Of all the challenges colonizing an alien planet provided, a lack of water was not one of them. The cisterns were full, the roads partially washed away, and the power station that helped provide their communications array was under a meter of water.

"Eh, another week, maybe two, and the rains will move on." Daniel replied, as he stumbled over a large rock dislodged by the rain, then slid down the thick mud. "Damn, it's slick as hell out here!" The path would need to be re-laid once the ground dried out. They were coming to the end of the wet season, thankfully.

"Tell me about it," the younger man pointed to thick mud caking his knees and down his legs. "I stopped counting how many times I fell hours ago. The mud is like glue!"

As they walked, shuffled through the thick mud and tried to not fall on their asses, Alex asked, "Is everyone committing to the ten-year plan I heard mentioned? Ten thousand Cryo revivals per year?"

Daniel shrugged. "That's the plan. How well it will go remains to be seen. That's a shitload of new colonists. My head hurts from all the Council meetings and numbers and goals."

"Hell, at least you're on the inside, helping decide, getting all the deets." Alex neatly avoided a slippery pit of mud and water where the plasticrete had collapsed in the heavy rainfall.

"I guess. It isn't as fun as it sounds, though, believe me." He stopped, steadied himself for the last leg of the hill. It wouldn't do to show up at the base, needing to be hosed off before he geared up for the flight into orbit. "I've thought of resigning. I need to focus on mapping and plotting with Farnsworth and help prepare Uruk for the new settlement. But then Sam suggested she resign and I stay on." He glanced over at the younger man. "Why don't you throw your name in the hat as her replacement?"

"Me?"

"Why not? You've got what it takes. I think you'd be an excellent addition to the Council." He winked. "Besides, the group needs young blood. The average age is what, sixty?"

Alex snorted, "You and Sam aren't all that old, not by a long shot." They were nearly at the bottom of the hill. "But yeah, I'd be interested."

"Good deal. I'll put in a good word for you with Phoenix. He was asking for recommendations."

The shuttle stood waiting outside of the hangar and Martin was stacking the first round of vaccines into the cargo hold.

"Morning, Medry. How's Sam doing?"

"Sleep-deprived." Daniel grimaced. "You know how it is. And I think Luke's teething. He had me up half the night."

Martin clapped him on the shoulder. "Well, I'll pilot the shuttle then. You relax, take a nap."

Daniel laughed. As if napping through 4.2g's of acceleration was going to happen. "Yeah, I'll be sure and do that."

"Let's suit up and get to it. I've got a dinner date planned with the missus." Martin and Carrie Schrader had begun dating soon after planetfall.

Their daughter Martina was the same age as Luke and two other children.

Oddly, births synched up on the planet. No one could explain it, but there had been at least four more instances of multiple birth days, even women who were due weeks apart. When one woman labored, at least two more would as well, and the babies were born on the same day. It made it challenging and frantic at the med center, and Carrie and the other doctors could not explain it. But at least they now planned for it.

Daniel wondered if some unknowable primal switch in the colonists' genome had activated, sensing humanity's dire future and compensating for it. Especially with the sudden spike in twin and triplet pregnancies in the past year. The other option, and one that seemed rather popular if impossible, was that the planet itself was affecting the births and the multiple pregnancies. How often had he heard others joke that there was "something in the water"? It fascinated Daniel. Was it simply coincidence? Or something more?

He mulled over it as he suited up, climbed into the seat, and belted himself in. Moments later, he regretted eating the small plate of eggs that Sam hadn't wanted to finish. The g forces made the light meal feel like a boulder sitting in his stomach, compressing his organs. Daniel tried to think of anything else past the discomfort and difficulty breathing, and failed miserably.

Moments later, they achieved orbit, and he regretted his meal once again. How it burbled about, weightless and directionless, as if it had forgotten to follow the path to his guts.

"You okay there, Medry?" Martin asked. Daniel could detect a note of amusement.

"Yeah, I'll uh, be okay. Just a stupid landlubber mistake."

"Ate something?"

"You know I did."

Martin Phoenix laughed. "Sorry. Hope you feel better, because we're docking in five minutes. You toss your cookies and you'll end up staying up here on-board Nostradamus for the next 45 days."

"Shit. Right. Got it." He felt his face redden. It was a rookie mistake. One he knew better than to do. Sam would not be pleased if he screwed this up. "I'll be fine. Let's dock, unload, and get back home."

His nausea subsided to an acceptable level and twenty minutes later, they stood, still suited, on board the massive lifeship. Not that it *looked* massive from inside. The mass of the ship remained filled with Cryo units. The skeleton crew on board was half the numbers that Calypso had on its journey out. There was no one available for experiments. It hadn't even been a certainty that the massive ship would stay. It was more of a gamble that Zarmina's World would take them in. If not, well, they could have easily returned, and with a few years' wait, Earth would likely have recovered enough for them to return to the surface. The TUPG's plan had a double benefit: it saved people from the planet and gave them a new home, free from the ESH virus, where they could live alongside the Calypso's crew and colonists, with the option of coming home.

There were three women and one man there to greet them. The captain stepped forward. She was tall, with coal-black skin and white flowing hair. Daniel was sure he had seen the man before. He looked so familiar, but he struggled to place him.

"Welcome on board, Nostradamus. I'm Zara Desdemona, and this is my first officer, Pele Gauthier. Also, Anthony Vogt, and Jenn Rivers Vogt."

The astronomer, the grandson of the man who had discovered Gliese 581g. Daniel felt a wave of fanboy excitement roll over him.

Martin nodded to each. "Thank you. Welcome to Zarmina's World. I'm Martin Phoenix, the mayor of Sagan Base, and this is Daniel Medry, a member of our Governing Council." Jackson Sebring had stepped down in March and nominated Martin for the position. There had been two other contenders, but Martin had won the election by a large margin.

Daniel stepped forward. "Mr. Vogt, it's an honor to meet you. I was there in '92 when you gave the speech announcing the mission to Zarmina's World."

Anthony Vogt smiled, "I have heard good things about you as well, Medry. As I understand it, most of the colonists owe you their lives."

Daniel's face flushed, and he hoped it wasn't noticeable through the helmet. He had done what anyone else would have done.

"And I understand you have brought us a vaccine." Captain Desdemona asked.

"Yes, ma'am. We spent the last eleven months double-checking all the information on the vaccine, reproducing it in enough quantities to inoculate our people, and 1,000 doses for you and other priority personnel, with more on the way," Martin answered. "You should have received all research notes from the Mars and Earth teams, as well as the medical team on the planet. And we've brought the doses on board for you."

"Thank you for this," Jenn said. "I'm heading up the inoculation program on board. We've already been reviewing the notes and the four of us, as well as all crew currently out of Cryo, will get inoculated today."

"Perfect," Daniel said. "That starts the clock. We look forward to welcoming you on the surface in 45 days."

Initial testing showed ESH antibodies within three days of inoculation. The 45-day wait was overkill, but necessary for the peace of mind of their fellow colonists. It had been something they could all agree on as it mirrored the incubation time, and then some.

Minutes later, the cases of vaccine delivered, and a few more pleasantries exchanged, Daniel and Martin returned to the shuttle. They would go through full decontamination protocols after landfall, and the shuttle too.

Zarmina's World would soon see its human population expand exponentially. It was both exciting and overwhelming. It was the beginning of their ten-year plan. By the beginning of the next

year, their numbers would rise from 297 to over
10,000.

An Argument Against Man

Date: 12.28.2106

Nathan felt... different. Better in some ways, and decidedly not better in others. Here in the cave, time was irrelevant. A strange state of being for a human used to clocks and timelines. Still, the importance of it had diminished in the time he had spent here.

Whatever Entity had done to him, whatever it had put inside him, it was still changing him in subtle and not-so-subtle ways. He no longer needed food. Nor did he particularly want it. Still, the memory of it, of meals he loved, his favorites, the richness of ice cream, for example. He missed those experiences.

In whatever ways Entity had changed him, one thing was clear: there no longer was any hindrance in communication. He was one with Entity. Or at least, a vestigial limb. While he could not sense all of Entity's thoughts, he was certain that Entity could sense all of his. He could feel the alien presence sift through memories, knowledge, as if through the files of a computer. And while he could sense curiosity, touches of emotion, alien as it was, he knew nothing about the creature other than what knowledge it willingly shared with him.

Day in, day out, it combed through his memories, asking questions, clarifying, deep discussions on everything from human sexuality and reproduction, to the history of humanity, even philosophical discussions. Entity appeared particularly interested in science and ecology.

In return, it informed Nathan of its own history, such as it was. He was in awe of it. The enormity of Entity, a planet-wide intelligence, and a fungus at that, contradicted anything that Nathan understood about such organisms. Sure, physarum polycephalum could solve mazes, learn new things, even predict events. It could mimic transportation networks and choose the best food. But it couldn't think or communicate like Entity could. Fungi, or at least Terran fungi, could communicate across their mycelial networks. They could grow in strategic ways that preserved resources. Hell, they could even remember where they found food and return to that location.

But Entity was so much more than that. Entity had saved his life as well.

Nathan's existence was no longer what it had been, though. His body felt different, changed at almost a cellular level. When he asked Entity about it, the being gave only simple answers that said little. Eventually, though, Nathan pieced together enough to understand that in saving his life, Entity hadn't actually healed him, but changed him irrevocably. These changes likely meant Nathan's end, sooner rather than later. For now, however, he was alive, in a sense.

The darkness of the cave was absolute, his bodily needs nonexistent because of Entity's changes, and Nathan's consciousness ebbed and flowed according to his interactions with Entity. Between these moments, there was nothing. No feeling, no light, no dreams, nothing.

nathan kill

Entity had said nothing in response to his memories of killing Deeks and Evers, and of his attempt to kill so many more in Cryo. And the thought of it now was jarring.

"Yes, I killed people. Good people."

wrong mind

"I wasn't in my right mind. I thought..." he struggled to convey the confusion he had felt to this alien lifeform. *"Occasionally, humans have mental failings, depression, confusion, paranoia. And I've... seen... things. Visions. Of, the future? I don't understand it. But my mother..."*

progenitor

"Yes. My progenitor. One of them. I didn't know my father. My mother, my progenitor, saw visions, suffered from... delusions."

delusions

not real

imagined

"Yes."

Entity withdrew, the silence and blackness of the cave wrapping around Nathan. He was used to it.

Time was irrelevant, but if it had been relevant, or if he had cared, he might be surprised to learn that over two and a half Earth years had passed while he was in the cave.

The oneness with Entity dictated an acceptance of sorts. He was no longer who he had been. Not Nathaniel and not even Nathan. Allowing Entity to enter his body, which saved his life, had changed everything.

When Entity returned, it said something that rocked Ethan's world.

human dangerous

"Me?"

no

man

"I'm a man."

not human

"Do you mean I'm not human now? Now that you changed me?"

no

not human

nathan other

man dangerous
outro sure

Nathan struggled to comprehend. First, Entity was clearly telling him he was not human, which made little or no sense. But also, the way Entity said the word Outro, it felt different, as if...

"Outro?"

outro

child

"Outro is your child?"

yes

"Help me understand what you mean by Outro is your child."

Entity paused for a moment, then sent a flood of images into Nathan's mind. He reeled, absorbing the new knowledge like a sponge, understanding that Entity had done something unique and unusual. From the brief collage of images, Nathan came to understand that this did not happen often. Entity's child was merely a teenager in the larger scope of things. And that teenager was millions of years old. In mere minutes, Nathan absorbed the history of millions, no, billions of years that Entity had lived. He felt, in the dizzying display, the conflicting emotions Entity had toward Outro, who was full of teenage angst and harbored a deep resentment of bipedal life forms. He had seen the brief, violent end of the first bipeds to land here on the planet, and Nathan could not help but fear for the colonists at Sagan Base.

"And Outro thinks man is dangerous?"

yes

Nathan pondered this for a moment. *"Did the colonists do something?"*

destroy

When Nathan did not respond, Entity elaborated.

destroy experiment

burn plants

destroy work

"But the colonists aren't aware. They didn't know." He knew by now that Entity was essentially a planet-sized gardener. It had shown him visual cues in the cave's darkness that clearly illustrated that. And more than just a gardener. Entity dabbled with the genetics of plants and animals alike, although it seemed far more focused on plant life and far less

certain about how to deal with the intricacies of an animal such as himself.

He was certain that the colonists did not know that Entity even existed. How could they? Entity was outside of their scope of understanding. Man had studied Armillaria solidipes and determined the mushroom was over 2,500 years old and over ten square kilometers in size. But Armillaria didn't *think*. And it certainly didn't conduct experiments, genetically tinker with plants and entire ecosystems, or even, to some small extent, animal lifeforms. Explaining, hell, making them believe in a reality that was straight out of a science fiction vid was problematic at best. Nathan was sure that Sagan Base did not understand that what they had done, burning Entity's experiment, was tantamount to assault.

He tried to explain it, visualizing the moral equivalency to a dog pissing on a fire hydrant, to help Entity see that humanity was not Entity's nor Outro's enemies. They couldn't be. Perhaps at the beginning of the last century, when humankind's Industrial Revolution was in full swing, polluting the land and water and killing off entire species indiscriminately. But certainly not now. At the edges, the far edges of Entity's attention, he could feel another presence. Hovering in the ether.

Listening but saying nothing. It felt different from Entity. Sharper. As if he were skirting around someone holding a wickedly deadly blade. Was this Outro? He tried to focus his words, his thoughts, toward that distant presence. But it wasn't having it. Nathan didn't feel it withdraw so much as he felt its *absence*.

ignore or destroy

only options

now more are here

With the message came images of an alien race landing on the planet, on a vast plain that bordered a large inland freshwater sea. He racked his brain for memories of anything like it, and could think of nothing that big on Zarmina's World now. Which likely meant that whenever this had happened, it had been a very long time ago. Mountains and valleys had risen and fallen in the time since.

One could never confuse these creatures with humans, yet they shared some basic characteristics. They walked upright, like a man, although balanced on a thick, ridged tail that trailed behind them as they loped. A creature that seemed at home in the sea as much, if not more, than on land.

Nathan watched as the images showed the alien species land in enormous spaceships that cracked the ground, then unfolded slowly, converting from a spacefaring vessel into one meant to serve as a home. And while Nathan could not tell from the images Entity sent how much time had passed, the alien species seemed to multiply overnight from a few into hordes. Their offspring living only in the sea from birth to young adulthood and then emerging onto land. He could see that some of them had been culled by the denizens of the deep. However, this was corrected. Entity showed memories of the creatures concocting a paste that somehow protected them from harm. Whether it made them invisible or repellent to the monsters of the deep, he was not sure. This, however, was apparently the least of their problems.

As Nathan experienced the deluge of images, seeing the creatures multiply exponentially, he could feel the anger that rolled through these images. Indignation over them, changing the landscape, rage even. And he realized it wasn't coming from Entity, but from what had to be Outro. Knife-sharp, black around the edges, rage. And finally, as the last of the images presented themselves, his guts twisted as he watched the eradication of a species happen. It might have happened hundreds of years ago, or a millennium, or even longer. Perhaps these creatures evolved, learned space travel, and came here while the dinosaurs still ruled Earth. Every one of them, however, down to the tiniest of squirming, fleshy swimming babies, had been eradicated from the planet. The adults reduced to oily black streaks while the deep sea monsters snatched the babies up, consumed them.

Finally, the last image was of massive lifeships. They orbited Zarmina's World and Nathan knew they were from now. He recognized the markings on the sides of the ships. How Entity could see them when they were still in orbit, he did not know, but he could clearly read the names of them. The Nostradamus and The Mayflower were multitudes larger than Calypso. How many people were on these ships? Twenty thousand, one hundred? Maybe more?

What would Outro do if they landed? What would Entity do? Of the two, he only really knew Entity, but after seeing what he had seen in the image dump, he knew that Entity had not stood in the way, nor tried to stop Outro. Why?

"You did not stop Outro from killing that alien species."

outro side

entity side
different

"You each have a side of the planet? One side is Outro's, and the other is yours?"

yes

Nathan, suspended in the web of fungal growth, shuddered. There were thousands and thousands of colonists in orbit. They wouldn't all go to one side, would they? And if they went to the side Outro controlled, and tried to colonize it, how quickly would this go badly? How would Outro react to this many?

"If you told Outro not to kill them, would it listen to you?"

no

This could happen to the colonists unless he convinced Entity there was another way. How long, after all, would Entity be willing to ignore the destruction of its work? Perhaps Entity would be more resistant to culling than Outro, but now that one invading species' extinction has been witnessed, how easy would it be to shift to a preventative approach that more easily accepts culling after a previous one?

entity leave

"What?"

outro ready

entity leave

"Outro is all grown up and you will leave soon?"

yes

"You will leave this planet? And Outro will stay?"

yes

Nathan felt an icy wave of fear wash over him. Entity would leave the planet to Outro. And Outro had already shown exactly what it thought of invasive species.

"There has to be another way."

Entity did not respond. Instead, it withdrew. Nathan's audience with it was over. It was busy, after all, with running half of a planet's worth of experiments. Nathan was only a small part of Entity's focus.

How long until Entity leaves? A few months? Maybe a year? A millennium?

Nathan remembered a joke he had once heard. Something about millennia being but a moment to

God and being asked by a man for a million dollars. "Of course, son, in just a moment." Entity was a lot like God. Nathan doubted he would get a straight answer on *when* Entity planned to leave, but when Entity did, humanity's time on Zarmina's World would begin counting down.

In the absolute darkness, Nathan pondered on the situation. The irony of it did not escape him. Once, he had been so certain that man's fate was to end - back on Earth and in space. He'd certainly done his best to help God out, to bring the other colonists to God and usher in the dawn of an existence without humankind, so sure that everyone was dead back on Earth.

Now he had to figure out how to save their lives. All of them. The colonists on the surface and the untold thousands in orbit around Zarmina's World.

An Unexpected Proposal

Date: 02.03.2107

Below the deck, the group of children played, hyped up with sugar, zipping between the maypole and birthday decorations.

Jack linked his long fingers around Kevin's and sighed at the scene before them. A breeze ruffled his blond hair.

"I can't believe he's eight. It seems like yesterday we were bringing him home from the hospital."

Kevin sucked in a breath, painful in the cool air, and tightened his fingers, feeling his partner's warmth. How he wanted it to last, to pull him close and never let him go.

Instead, he smiled and said, "Linda used to say, 'Don't close your eyes for too long, kids grow up far too quickly.'"

Jack leaned his head on Kevin's shoulder. "You are doing so well. Simon looks happy. I can't believe how tall he has gotten!"

"He misses you, you know." Kevin could smell Jack's clean scent, the hint of his favorite aftershave. "We aren't the same without you."

"Would that I could stay here forever with you."

"Then stay." Kevin could hear the tremor in his voice. He missed him. Oh God, he missed him so.

"It's too late for that. Far too late."

"Late, Dad. Dad?" Jack faded away, his body disappearing, then his voice, and Kevin blinked in the dim light, aware of Simon's voice in his ear. "Dad?"

The dream faded, his love slipping away as Simon tugged at his arm. "Dad?"

Kevin snapped awake, "Hmm, what? What is it, son?"

"You were dreaming, Dad. And talking in your sleep. It woke me up." His blond hair was tousled and he rubbed the grit of sleep from his eyes.

"I'm sorry, Son. Was I loud?" Even in the gloom, he could see his son's shoulders hitch up a bit.

"Sort of. I was dreaming too. Of Daddy. Were you?"

"Yeah, I was."

"A good one? Or a bad one?"

Kevin wasn't sure how to answer that. Whether he was reliving the Cryo sabotage or discovering Jack in his everyday dreams, it hurt. It hurt that he was gone; it hurt that Simon had only a quickly fading set of memories of him. Kevin struggled each day with the hurt that he could not share this planet and these memories with Jack. They had dreamed about it so much, watched the vids taken by the D.O.V.E. probes over and over, even picked out their perfect spot for building a house on the edge of the Northern Forest, with a large inlet where Jack could have sailed to his heart's content.

He realized Simon was waiting for a reply. "A good one, yeah, it was your eighth birthday party."

The bed dipped slightly, and he answered the unasked question next. "Sure, climb on in."

Simon clambered in, followed by Antoinette, the collie pup who had graduated from puddles and yips to a long-legged, bed-hogging cuddler. She didn't seem to understand that she wasn't lap-size anymore. She wedged herself into the space between Simon and Kevin.

Even the dog had been Jack's idea. He had campaigned for one in the months leading up to their departure and insisted that Kevin submit an application that put them in the queue for an artificial womb reserved specifically for colonists' pets. A year had followed, as they set up camp, built the house, and settled into some kind of routine. One that seemed empty without Jack.

Jack had paged through image after image of dogs with Simon before departure and they had both fallen in love with collies, especially after seeing an old black and white vid series of a collie named "Lassie." Kevin had dutifully submitted the application and detailed the specs for a collie.

He hadn't really thought about it after landing. He was still blindly going through the motions, pretending to be alive and interested, trying his best to cover up his broken heart, his anguish. But the call, nearly nine months ago, had woken him from his funk.

"Your pup will be ready to come out of the tank in a week," Sarra Drenowski, the head veterinarian at the livestock production center had informed him.

He had met Jack soon after his divorce from Linda. He hadn't even really understood it. One moment he had been out enjoying the live concert, and the next minute he was drowning in a pair of gorgeous blue eyes, blond hair, and a five o'clock shadow that, try as he might, Jack could never seem to escape from. Kevin had fallen in love, hard. So much for being a straight man with an ex-wife and nearly grown daughter. So much for meeting someone his age. Jack had been all of two years older than Kevin's daughter, Anna.

It was more than Anna, still reeling from her parents' divorce, could take. She had backpedaled, avoiding her dad's phone calls, refusing to attend their wedding, and not even responding when he had told her she had a younger brother and that they were leaving Earth.

And as much as it hurt, as much as he missed the easy comaraderie they had shared when she was younger, Kevin had understood her shock. It was second only to his own. Falling in love with Jack had blindsided him, took him to a place where his heart and mind were one and he could see it mirrored in Jack as well. He hadn't planned it, hell; he hadn't even fantasized about being with a man until Jack's fingers had laced into his and they had moved together to the beat of the music. All he knew was it had made him feel complete. As if destiny had written this chapter of his life onto his soul before his birth. A secret joy to be unwrapped and discovered.

Kevin could hear Simon's steady breathing. The boy was already fast asleep. How he wished it could be so easy for him. But even now, the edges of the dream still curled around him, and he could smell Jack's aftershave wafting on the breeze. It wasn't fair, not at all. Jack had so many dreams, so many plans. They both had. And it all seemed hollow without Jack here to accomplish them.

Antoinette's ears twitched at Kevin's deep sigh. She shifted position and groaned slightly.

Kevin lay there for another hour before giving up and rolling out of bed. By then, Simon had turned sideways, his head resting on Kevin's chest, snoring slightly thanks to the remnants of a cold he had caught at school the week before. The boy didn't even stir as Kevin slipped the pillow under

Simon's head and walked out to the kitchen to make some coffee.

There were few clues to the time of day in this world. Unless you watched the sun's progress closely, it was simply a matter of the sun rotating along the edge of the line of sight. Never fully sunny, never fully dark.

The colony was progressing well, and births had been steadily climbing. Nearly sixty children had been born since their arrival nearly three years before, thirty-two in the past twelve months. Kevin had been cross-training as an EMT and attended three births in the past month. They had all been bittersweet - joy at new life, and a reminder that he and Simon were alone. Jack had been the fun one, the life of the party, and the one who handled all of their social engagements. Without him, well, Kevin couldn't seem to connect well with the other parents.

The exception to that had been Daniel Medry and Sam Sydan. Although they didn't have any children Simon's age, their friendship was one of the main pillars that kept Kevin tethered to the other colonists. He was looking forward to visiting them. Simon had asked if they would be at the birthday party, but Sam had just had her third child and it was easier for Kevin and Simon to visit than the other way around. The promise to take Simon to see Daniel and Sam had satisfied the boy, and they had scheduled the next two days to head up to their friends' homestead, some two hundred clicks away.

The clicking of nails on the floor announced the dog's presence even before Antoinette's cold nose bumped his hand. She walked past him and whined at the door.

"Okay girl, out you go." The dog wagged her tail and ran outside. So far, they had encountered little in the way of large indigenous animal life on Zarmina's World. At least, not on land. The oceans and even the freshwater seas and lakes were another matter entirely. On land, there were insectoid creatures, more varieties of fungus than you could shake a stick at, and the scales tipped up abruptly and showed an elusive, yet unique land mammal. The size of a small pony, the Zarmunicorns, were shy creatures. They seemed to congregate in small herds, comprising five to seven individuals. Their bodies rippled with muscles and their horns were small, singular affairs, only eight centimeters long.

Thankfully, nothing on the planet seemed to want to kill them. Well, other than the leviathans in the sea. Land was safe, the water, not so much.

Kevin stood in the doorway and watched as the dog galloped in a wide arc, stopping to bark at a Zarmunicorn that had wandered away from the herd before Antoinette circled back, a stick in her mouth. She bumped his hand with it, asking to play.

"Sure, girl, sure." Kevin threw the stick as far as he could. His mind was still in the dream. Jack had wanted a whole passel of kids, three, even four more. Kevin already had a grown child, so it had seemed less important to him, and they had held off. The opportunity of a lifetime, to travel to a new world, had captivated them both, and they had thrown all of their energy into the preparation and departure. He had promised Jack they would have more children, knowing how important it was to him. And Kevin had been more than willing, especially at the sharp rejection from his firstborn. Finding a surrogate wouldn't be as easy, but he had struck up a friendship with Elizabeth Cook, the world-renowned journalist. She had been very interested in helping them become parents again after Landfall.

"I'm not maternal. Not at all." She had shrugged her shoulders. "God knows I tried with my sister's kids, but no, I wouldn't be looking for a co-parenting kind of thing. I would just like the idea of helping someone out."

She was perfect for their needs, and Jack had already insisted that this time, Kevin should contribute the sperm since Jack had with Simon. "Imagine it, we will have two mini-me's running around."

Occasionally, Kevin's thoughts strayed from his grief over Jack, to the loss of Elizabeth as well. It hurt. Not as much. They had barely known each other, but still. Her death and Jack's in Cryo had taken away any hopes Kevin had of ever having more children. It was a hard pill to swallow.

Worse, Simon kept bringing it up. He had remembered their talks back before departure and often asked Kevin if there would ever be any little brother or sister for him to play with. Kevin usually joked, "You don't even like to play with Lila when we visit Daniel and Sam. You realize a baby would be even younger than that, don't you?"

It didn't seem to deter the boy. Thankfully, today was not a day he was interested in talking about it. Instead, he'd dressed himself without being reminded, which was quite unusual. All Simon wanted to talk about was his birthday party, which Daniel and Sam had kindly offered to host.

"Everyone from school will be there. Even Miss Maria, because she's Miguel's mom and I told

Miguel he had to come because he's my best friend."

Kevin tousled his son's hair. He had met Maria Gonzalez when Simon entered her class last year. The widow of another Cryo victim, Esteban Gonzalez, they had connected over shared grief and their boys. Although a year younger than Simon, Miguel and Simon were inseparable.

Hours later, after a round of gifts, cake and ice cream, Kevin stood watching Simon play with Miguel, the Medry-Sydan clan, and a handful of others on the meadow below Daniel and Sam's house. It had been hours, but none of the kids showed any signs of tiring, and he wasn't ready to end things and return to the large, empty house. A warm hand on his arm, and he turned to find Maria. She smiled up at him.

"You have been quiet today. Is everything all right?"

"Yes, well, no. I mean..." He took a deep breath and shared with her his dream. "It's as if Jack is reminding me, I need to do more than just exist."

Maria sighed. "I've had those dreams, too. It's... hard. Even now. It's been so long that Miguel hardly remembers him. He asks me, over and over, when I will find someone else to be his dad. He sees all the babies at the center and wants me to have 'just one more.'" She smiled sadly. "And heaven knows, I would love another child. I would. But not alone. Not on this big planet, with only a little boy by my side. I suppose I sound old-fashioned."

"I fear I have the same discussions and the same conclusions." Kevin answered. "The only difference is I certainly cannot create a child without significant help."

Maria laughed, and it reminded him of his wife Linda's laugh. Musical. Warm. They had been best friends, then almost reluctant lovers. He had never felt the fireworks for her. Perhaps, if he had thought about it long enough, he would have figured out why. Instead, he had let her lead the way. In their relationship. In bed. And followed her obediently into marriage. It hadn't been intentional or well thought out. His work and research absorbed him, and things simply fell into place.

Despite this, it had been no great surprise twenty years later when Linda told him she had been seeing someone else and wanted a divorce. Their only child, Anna, had just graduated and struck out on her own and he hadn't shared a bed with Linda for years.

"Do you want more children, Kevin?" Maria leaned in, her brown eyes boring into his. It took him by surprise, the directness of her manner. And despite knowing her only as a fellow colonist, as Simon's teacher, he found the truth spilling out.

"As crazy as it might sound at my age... yes... I do. We, I mean, Jack and I had wanted a few more, but..." He didn't finish the sentence. That future was gone now, along with his handsome, blue-eyed husband. He expected her gaze to shift away, as most others did. It was hard to see a loss in another.

Maria, however, did not look away. Her eyes were full of compassion, loss, and shared pain. He sensed she wanted to say more. Instead, she simply nodded, slipping a warm hand around his arm and turning to smile at the children playing in the meadow below, a single tear tracking down her cheek.

A month later, she asked to speak with him after school. Miguel and Simon, sensing an opportunity for a few minutes more of play, streaked away out into the fresh air, heading for the small playground that had just been installed.

"I need to ask you a question." Maria said. Kevin watched as Maria chewed her lip, closed the classroom door to give them more privacy, and took a deep breath, before she blurted, "I was wondering if you would consider a possibly different living situation than the one you currently have."

At his look of confusion, she explained further. "We both lost the loves of our lives on board the Calypso. I think you know exactly what I mean when I say I don't believe I will ever have that again, but... we have a lot in common, you and I. Not just both having lost the love we thought we'd have until we were old. We both want more children. You and Jack had planned for more. And our boys, they're close. My husband would have said they are like brothers from another mother."

Kevin blinked at her. Understanding came in a rush of clarity. "You want to have a child with me?"

"Well, yes, maybe even..." she bit her lip. "Perhaps we could live together? We don't need to marry. Honestly, I always thought Esteban was a tad old-fashioned, insisting on it. He was Catholic, bless him. But yes. I think, I mean, I know we don't know each other well and perhaps we could do a trial run, but my Miguel needs a father figure in his life. And perhaps Simon could benefit from my presence? He's a sweet boy and honestly one of my favorite students."

The last brick slipped into place. "Live together?"

Maria shifted uncomfortably. "I've bungled this, haven't I? Ugh, I'm sorry. I thought perhaps since you'd been married before, to a woman, I... Look, forget I said anything." She stepped back and Kevin reached out a hand, capturing hers with his.

"Wait. Just... Please. I'm not saying no, it's just a lot to take in." He paused, his mind awhirl with the idea of it. The house Jack designed had been built to spec a few months after landfall. It included five bedrooms, three of them with full ensuite layouts, the other two bedrooms shared a Jack and Jill bath between them. Jack had dreamed of filling the rooms with children, but wanted the en suite rooms for a potential surrogate live-in situation should it come up. With just Kevin and Simon in the house, they knocked about in the place and Kevin had toyed with giving it to another colonist should a larger family have need of it.

They had more than enough room for Maria and Miguel there. The boys would love it, and he couldn't help thinking it would be nice to cook with another adult and said as much.

"I hate cooking." Maria said, looking apprehensive.

"I rather love it." Kevin smiled in return. "I'd like to try."

A few months later, after a quiet dinner, just the two of them, the boys asleep in a tent in the yard, Maria told him she was pregnant with a girl. He kissed her, hugged her and remembered another baby girl, long ago, and billions of miles away. He sat alone, long after she had gone to bed, and wondered what Jack would have thought of all of this. Kevin wasn't in love with Maria, but he felt love for her. And for Miguel as well. Theirs was a relationship built on mutual respect and kindness, as well as practicality.

Kevin hoped Jack would have appreciated the good news, maybe even been a little excited. It wasn't the future they had both dreamed about, this life. But it was a good one. And for that, Kevin was grateful. And for a moment, on a gentle breeze from the open window, he swore he smelled Jack's cologne.

Jacqueline Estelle Edmonds was born on February 3rd of the following year. Her two older brothers adored her.

Far Side

Date: 02.11.2107

Mayflower had been built in sections on Earth, then assembled in orbit. The intention to land the massive craft on the planet was a modern engineering miracle, a first of its kind. With nearly 100,000 souls on board, and nearly all of them in Cryo, the plan for the lifeship was two-fold.

It could return those on board, all ESH-positive, to Earth, should the need arise. But the architects of the enormous craft had hoped it would instead serve as a home base, a temporary home, for the thousands in Cryo as they slowly decanted and forged a future on the surface of their new world.

If the ESH virus had taught humanity anything, it was that to confine their species to just one world was a recipe for disaster. Mayflower's original destination was far more distant. An impossibly ambitious trip to the Kepler system, over 1,400 light years away from Earth. The modifications to the Alcubierre-Mesner drive promised to cut the journey from 350 years down to 224 years, give or take a decade. Most of that time would, of course, be spent in Cryo. They selected the crew, and they were building the ship when the ESH virus began to spread.

Work on it had stopped in its tracks. That is until Ultima Thule threatened to end the human species forever. Just as Chicxulub did to the dinosaurs. Then it became a race to finish Mayflower and a half dozen other lifeships. They were lucky. The ship had been 90% complete and its efficient engines shortened the journey to Zarmina's World by nearly two full Earth years.

Minerva Runchin sat in a small jump seat on the command deck and stared out of the viewscreen at an alien world. All the images, from D.O.V.E., the unmanned exploratory vessels that arrived mid-

21st century, to those from the colonists who made landfall on the opposite side of the planet nearly three years ago - nothing could prepare Minerva for the reality of it. She marveled at the twist of fate, some random sequence that pulled up her name as one of those lucky enough to escape Earth's terrible fate and journey to this distant planet.

"It's beautiful, yes?" Ona Hallila asked from a few feet away. She spoke English well, with only a tiny burr at the end of her words to betray her Finnish origins.

"Yes, I suppose it is." Minerva's chest was tight. It had been that way since she woke from Cryo four days ago. Staring at this world from space, and now, the descent into the twilight of the terminator, it all felt like a dream she would wake up from. The images from Earth flashed through her mind. This world wasn't home. The mission leaders dangled the possibility of a return after ten Earth years like a carrot in front of every person on board the Mayflower.

"Safety in the stars. A chance at a new life on a new planet. And if, after Earth has recovered, you wish to return, there will be space and opportunity to do so."

That had been the carrot. The promise. But really, could any of them be sure? An asteroid that size had destroyed the dinosaurs. And Mars had once had an atmosphere. It had once had a thick atmosphere that kept enough heat for liquid water to flow on the surface. What had happened to it to make it lose all of that? And could that happen to Earth?

And Minerva couldn't help wondering how sure they were that there would be a home to return to after all.

"We are entering the atmosphere in five, four, three, two, one..."

The massive ship shook and Minerva felt her stomach drop. She was thankful she had not eaten this morning. None of them had. It had been the last thing on their minds as the crew prepared for the last leg of this trip, landing on Zarmina's World.

The view changed from the dark of space lit with stars and a planet with a thin, hazy blue layer around it to that of a bright wall of fire and flame. *A glowing plasma layer*, Minerva thought, the wording for the article forming in her head as she stared at the bright glow outside of the viewscreens.

This was her job, why she had been revived, while so many others slept. To serve as witness. To report to those on board Mayflower and to anyone who still survived back on Earth.

It's what you do, M. Report the news. Tell people what you see.

Sitting on the command deck, she felt useless as she watched and listened to the crew using their training to land this massive spacecraft on the surface of the planet below.

They would be thousands of klicks away from Sagan Base, here on the far side of the planet, both in the terminator, connected by the north and south poles, but on their own, to live or die, separated from the first human settlement until they were absolutely certain the ESH virus was no longer transmittable.

"Status on landing thrusters?" Renata O'Day, Captain of Mayflower, asked, her voice calm.

"Deploying landing thrusters in three, two, one... deployed." Gabriel Sulkava answered. Despite his steady voice, Minerva could detect a tiny tremor of excitement in her lover's voice. She'd spent enough time with him, in bed and out, to recognize the nearly imperceptible tell. For Gabriel, this was the opportunity of a lifetime, and one he could soon share with his wife and son. Crew members were allowed the chance at priority revivals, and he had told her last night as they lay spooned in his crew coffin.

"You understand, don't you?" He'd asked, his voice uncertain, and slightly nervous. "I put in the request and they will be one of the first wave pulled from Cryo."

"Of course." Minerva had said in return, deliberately hiding the myriad of feelings and hurt his words had brought to the surface. Of course it would not last. How could it? That he and his wife and son had all survived the ESH virus and the chaos after had been a rare thing. And that they had made it into a lifeship, their family intact, was damn near a miracle in the desperate last days before Earth's destruction. Shipboard romances didn't last. How could a mere affair survive all of that?

Still, it hurt. Every time they had decanted her from Cryo to serve as witness, to report on their voyage, Minerva and Gabriel had fallen into bed like two lovesick teenagers and fucked like rabbits. They had never discussed his family, but she had known he had one. And perhaps because he never spoke of them, she had hoped, tried not to but failed, and dreamed that the affair would survive. She had thought of what it would be like, on this alien planet, with Gabriel at her side. And those dreams had made living on an alien planet palatable, even possibly enjoyable.

Minerva had imagined him sitting his wife down and telling her gently that, despite all that they had been through, he'd fallen in love with someone else, that he would still be a father to their son, but that he had met his soul mate, the one, and no one could keep them apart.

But of course, that wasn't what had happened.

The lifeship passed through the outer atmosphere, and the fiery chaos outside evaporated. She could see a vast planet rushing up to greet them as the thrusters engaged, screaming as the ship hurtled towards its doom, the vast piece of machinery shaking and quaking.

Minerva felt sure they would all die. How many times had she thought she would die in the past eight years? The ESH virus had killed her family, every member. As an adopted, half Korean, half German baby, she hadn't looked like them and often felt like she didn't belong, but they had been her family. After they were gone, there'd been riots, chaos, food shortages, and government collapse as every underpinning of social framework came crashing down around the survivors. What is a social framework without someone to provide the frame, or the work? She'd been a journalist without a country, a child without a parent, a sister with no siblings. And that had all been before Ultima Thule, or Azrael, as the TUPG and Chairwoman Chen referred to it. Planet killer, angel of death, had come to kill off the terrified and traumatized remnants of humanity.

The roaring scream of the thrusters, fed by the engines, reached a crescendo and Minerva's pulse matched, the artery in her neck bulging, her heart pounding, and then...

They landed with a jerk. One she felt emanate through her feet, her legs, her tailbone, which ached in surprise, and even her spine. They were on the planet. Alive! And seemingly unscathed.

Minerva unbuckled her restraints and stood slowly. Her knees creaked in protest and she could feel every bit of the extra gravity pulling at her, punishing her.

Cheers and claps sounded through the room. The professional calm dissolving into a sense of relief, even joy. Their long journey was over and they were safe on the surface of an alien planet. A planet that would become home for now, and for some, likely forever. Minerva had conducted the onboarding surveys. Over half of the surveys returned by the adults on board, a mere 31,000 of the total aboard, had showed a strong interest in making a go of it on Zarmina's World. Only time would tell if they still felt that way after they had experienced the strong gravity and primitive conditions that came with settling an alien planet. The rest of those in Cryo were children, most of them orphans. The last gasp of hope for humanity remained safely unaware, still in Cryo, deep in the bowels of Mayflower. Most of them would stay there. Children weren't what they needed right now. Hard labor awaited those revived, or the soon to be revived. They had the enormous task of creating the new colony. They would break ground, build homes, mine needed minerals, and create an infrastructure for those waiting in Cryo. And slowly, agonizingly slowly, they would bring out those children into a new world of possibility. Minerva stood amongst the revelry, lost, alone, and tried to imagine what kind of world those children would wake up to in a few years. The trauma of losing everyone they ever loved, their homes, everything, and finding their way on this alien world, was almost too much. It felt as fair to her as being dumped by Gabriel did. Perhaps she would adopt one or two. Better than waiting for a man to truly commit to her, to love her as she deserved to be loved. She left the control room and silently slipped into her assigned crew coffin to indulge in a well-deserved pity party.

Some fifty feet below the scorched and damaged surface of the planet, Outro seethed. Once again, its domain invaded. A vital, multi-millennia experimental ecosystem destroyed, burnt beyond recognition. The bipedal creatures were a blight, worse than any mindless ruminant that trampled over a few fields or stripped vegetation. Entity was weak. Entity espoused *patience* and *time* and *examination*. These things were antithetical to Outro. What was needed now was decisiveness, action, and retaliation. Still, its parent had one piece of advice that Outro would take. Study. Outro would study these bipedal invaders. It wouldn't take long. And once it had enough information, it would plan a proper end to a creature that would so casually destroy several millennia of work. And then it would rid the rest of this planet of the pestilence, once and for all.

No Virgin Soil

Date: 04.05.2107

The overgrowth of the forest was thick, impossible to move through quickly. The canopy above blotted out what little light there was, and the ground, spongy from the last rain, sucked at their shoes.

"Vitun metsä" Onerva swore a few feet behind Gabriel.

He glanced back at her. Her hair had come loose from the neat ponytail, victim to the vines and plant life that surrounded them. Her face was red, shiny with sweat.

"Let's stop, yeah?" Gabriel asked. He felt a trickle of sweat run down his back, the material already sodden, stuck to his shoulders, and he could swear he felt something crawling on him. "I could use a break."

Onerva sighed with such deep relief he couldn't help but laugh. A large log was conveniently nearby, and the two fought their way over to it and both sat down with groans of pain and relief.

The canteen from his pack still sloshed with water, but they would need to turn back soon. They'd been out here for hours trying to find the anomaly that the scans from orbit had insisted were here. So far, nothing.

"What was that you said back there? Vito metsa?"

Onerva frowned, then grinned, "Oh, vitun metsä. Um... fucking forest."

Gabriel snorted. "Yeah, fucking forest is right. I'm thinking NARA sent us on a wild goose chase. There's nothing here but," he turned to her, "how do you say fucking trees?"

"Vitun puut."

"Veeton boot?"

"Vitun puut."

"Yeah, that. Vitun puut."

Their laughter disrupted the hum of the forest. All went silent for thirty seconds, a minute, before resuming their clicks and warbles. Life carrying on, despite the existence of alien invaders.

Onerva groaned. "This gravity. My bones ache every night. It makes it hard to sleep."

"Yeah, same. And then if I'm not waking up sore, I'm waking up from some damn nightmare." Gabriel reached down, slipped off one shoe and sock and rubbed his foot, feeling the tendons and muscles flex in relief as he did. They needed more arch support in higher gravity, something that felt lacking in the currently assigned footwear. He'd have to ask Tanya if she could design arch supports and get them printed via the 3D printers.

As if she could read his mind, Onerva asked, "How's Tanya?" It was a loaded question, and they both knew it. Their son was still in Cryo, but Tanya had mad design skills and had worked with the 3D printers back on Earth, helping design the new cities after they abandoned the old ones filled with the dead. They had decanted her from Cryo in the first wave of revivals. They needed her skills on this alien world. His wife did not know about his affair with Minerva. Sure, Gabriel had wrestled with just telling her, but the time never seemed right. Tanya was wrestling with a lot, not knowing if her sister and brother-in-law were alive back on Earth. They'd made it into one of the underground sanctuaries, but that meant nothing, not with a killer asteroid slamming into your home. And any transmissions from Earth were few. Chitchat between family members, even if it was a "Dear God, tell me you are alive" was simply not a priority. Besides, chances were high that they, too, were in Cryo. Tanya was struggling with the high gravity. She had inherited a rare disease on her matrilineal side that manifested as early-onset osteoporosis. In a normal set of tests for a colonist to Zarmina's World, she would never have passed. But these were not normal times.

And if all those things weren't enough, Tanya missed their son and kept waking up screaming from nightmares. Once awake, and once she had woken him and half of the corridor with her screams, she couldn't remember what the nightmare was about.

And of course, Onerva knew about the affair he'd had with Minerva. They were close friends.

"She's doing okay." He paused, pulled the shoe off his other foot, along with the sock, and shifted to focus on the aches emanating from that foot. "She uh... I mean I haven't..."

"Ei minun asiani." Onerva said, shrugging, then repeated it in English. "Not my business."

Gabriel nodded. He'd figured as much. Onerva didn't do drama. She was down to earth, matter of fact in her view of the world and their current situation.

"But truth is best."

"Yeah, I know. Just trying to find the right time for it." His feet ached slightly less thanks to the impromptu massage and just for a moment he stretched them out over the moist ground and wondered if he should ask after Minerva. He'd thought their trysts were fun, exciting. He hadn't felt as if they were getting emotional. It had been just sex for him, after all. He'd found Minerva gorgeous, sexy as hell, and fun to be around. But now he had to wonder, how had she felt about it all? He'd never hid the fact he was married. That his wife and son were in Cryo and that he loved them both very much. Hell, he'd talked about them with her. Hadn't he?

In his mind, it had been clear. A dalliance, a diversion, one that, while enjoyable, was merely transient. Had Minerva thought it would be more?

"How is Minerva doing?"

Onerva didn't answer. She stared into the distance, her head cocked to one side, eyes squinting through the overgrowth.

"Is that...?" She stood up abruptly and strode toward a patch of dense overgrowth.

"What?"

"I think I see something. Something... *manufactured*, not organic." She began walking towards it, her entire focus on something he could not see, but she obviously did.

"Onerva, wait, let me get my shoes back on." Gabriel shifted, dropping a sock, his bare foot sliding across the mossy ground and into a prickle of sharp pain. He looked down to see a shallow slice on the side of his foot, blood already welling up and dripping from the wound. What the hell had cut him? And if it wasn't deep, why the hell was it bleeding so much?

"Ow! Fuck! Onerva, wait!"

Gabriel slid the sock back on, smearing blood on his hand. He watched as the sock turned red. "Christ, I barely scratched it!" He shoved his foot back into the boot, hoping the compression would help stop the blood flow. Gabriel stared briefly at the ground, wondering what had cut him so badly. A nondescript plant in the center of a patch of mushrooms, really more like slime mold, held serrated leaves. He reached for his pack. Judging from the amount the slight wound had bled, he'd bet the plant's leaves had anti-coagulant properties. He slid on a glove, plucked it from the ground, and added it to a collection bag before shoving his other foot into its sock and boot, and scrambling to follow Onerva as she called out.

"Gabriel! You must see this!"

He hobbled after her, swearing, his foot stinging as he stumbled through the thick overgrowth toward Onerva's voice. The vegetation was so dense that a few dozen steps had taken her out of sight. He could hear her, though.

"Aivan mahtavaa! Gabriel, it is amazing!"

Seconds later, he joined her, gaping in wonder at the structures she had spied. The scans had been accurate. There was something beneath the canopy. Something manufactured, not grown, something made by another creature. Humankind was not the first visitor to this world.

In front of him were the ruins of a round-topped structure. Vines and plants twisted and turned around it. Branches from the trees lay draped across it, and a tree grew through another structure on the left. On top, a white-bleached set of bones of some creature lay covered in moss and broken branches. And he could see more beyond it. At least a dozen of the round-topped structures in various stages of decay. One was a mere suggestion of what it had been. The dome collapsed in the middle, and only jagged bits of the building structure reaching desperately for the sky. Another nearby had several trees rooted into the top of it, and moss or lichen hung in tendrils above the dark circular holes. It gave them the appearance of open, hungry maws hoping for a human-sized snack.

"Holy shit," Gabriel breathed. Onerva was already peering into the dark shadows of the ruins, her hand on a vine-covered pillar.

"Definitely not plant. I can't identify the substance used for the structure, but it has almost a glassy sheen to it beneath all the plant growth." She dug into her pocket for a knife. "I'll try to get a sample, but we might need a hammer and chisel." She worked at it for a moment, muttering under her breath, before shaking her head. "Definitely not going to give up its secrets that easily."

They both stood in silence, staring at the structures. Now that he was here next to it, he could see the vague remnants of a path. The path curved toward one of the other structures, but a large tree intersected it, almost as if the forest had grown up afterwards.

The buildings themselves were probably three meters tall, which made them a tad short in human standards. The circular openings varied in size, and clearly appeared to be doorways or windows. For what, a species that were slightly shorter than humans? Possibly a meter, or one and a half meters in height?

Onerva carefully stepped inside of one structure, having to duck as she did so. Gabriel, who was 198 centimeters, had to fold himself almost in half to step inside. His injured foot squelched as he did so. Would the damn thing ever stop bleeding?

"Do you think they are still here?" Gabriel asked, and Onerva shook her head.

"Definitely not. The D.O.V.E. probes would have detected that. The world has some ruminants, but no intelligent life other than us and Sagan Base."

Her fingers trailed down the exposed pillar. Up close, he could see what she meant about the glassy sheen. "This has been here a long, long time. How long, I couldn't tell you, but this is huge. Something was here, either native or an alien species that was bipedal and slightly shorter than us, and they either left or died out a long time ago."

"And if they died out..." Gabriel didn't finish the sentence. He didn't have to. They both were thinking it. If something had killed out another race that settled here, perhaps, just perhaps, it could kill them too.

Onerva shrugged, "Sagan Base has been on-planet for years, and nothing untoward has happened to them."

"Yeah, well, that's on the other side of the planet." He tapped the glassy surface. It was hard as a rock, and he couldn't even see scratches where Onerva had tried to use her knife.

"We need to inform the captain about this and get a team out to inspect it. Run tests."

Gabriel nodded, staring up at the ruined, plant covered roof which grazed the hairs on the top of his head, even as he bent low. Another step, another squish from his injured foot. He looked down, gaping at the red splotch that had now wicked through the tan canvas.

Onerva followed his gaze. "You're injured."

"Yeah, the littlest damn scratch and the fucker won't stop bleeding."

She tugged at his sleeve and pointed to a nearby clump of rocks. "Come on, I'll doctor you up and then we'll contact Base. Get an AGPS flag on this place and head back, yeah?"

"Yeah."

He sat on a large, smooth boulder and slid off his boot. As soon as he removed his sock, the wound dripped onto the plants below. Fat drops of blood. "Jupiter's balls. What the hell is with this wound?"

Onerva snorted at his epithet, slid the first aid kit out and sprayed the open wound. Gabriel hissed in response. It stung.

"Hush, men are such babies."

"It stings!"

"Antiseptic spray, and it has a coagulant as well."

Seconds later, the blood slowed, and the small puddle of blood accumulating on the forest floor grew no more.

"There. That did the trick." She winked at him and bandaged his foot. "You get a look at the plant that did that?"

"Yeah. I collected it. It's in my pack."

"Excellent. Harinder will want to examine it." Harinder Logan had been living an ethnobotanist's dream since being revived from Cryo in the first wave.

Gabriel frowned. "He's welcome to the damn thing. I hope it's the only one of its species."

Onerva's laughter echoed through the forest as they headed back to the edge where a flitter was waiting to take them back to Heinlein Base. Behind them, the forest floor absorbed the drops of Gabriel's blood. The forest floor was thick with fungal growth, and the fungal nodes transmitted the genetic information in each drop of blood to Outro.

Entity had refused to share the human DNA with Outro, using only the same tired advice to be patient, to give the colonists time, to examine the situation. The same thoughts, over and over, as the creatures had once again made incursions on Outro's fields of study, fouling the plants and their results with their very presence.

Outro seethed at the intrusions. This side of the world *belonged* to Outro, just as the other half belonged to Entity, if only for a limited time. If Entity was unwilling to deal with the invaders, Outro was more than willing to step up. After all, in another millennium, perhaps far less, Entity would leave. It was the way. Once it had reproduced, created a caretaker for a world, it was time to move on. And while time in itself was a construct that Entity and Outro rarely bothered with, they were both in agreement with this. In time, this planet would be Outro's and Entity would find another, just as it had so many times before. This was the way of their kind.

The initial results of the blood raced into Outro's knowledge nodes and it began breaking it down, piece by piece, molecule by molecule. By the time it was done, it would understand how these bipedal invaders lived, and how they died. It wouldn't be long until this world would return to the pristine place it had been, and Outro would spend the next million, perhaps even a billion, years guiding the flora and fauna through its experiments. All it would take was a few tweaks - to the plants and animals - to make this world fully inhospitable to these bipedal interlopers that Entity seemed so partial to. Outro felt something akin to smug satisfaction then, as it dreamed of making every one of the invaders die horribly.

Darkness Spreads

Date: 05.01.2107

On the surface of the far side of Zarmina's World, deep in Outro's territory, Mayflower's crew and refugees continued to spread across the planet's surface. They had made their landing close to a freshwater lake with multiple tributaries spread out like fingers through the land. The spot had been especially attractive since the D.O.V.E. probes had taken soil samples some three decades before. It had been high on the list of choices for the Calypso, but eventually they had decided on the far side of the planet because of the potential for volcanic activity to the west. The massive Mount Dumas smoked and sputtered, but the potential for an eruption was less important than a ship full of ESH-positive refugees infecting the last ESH-free humans in the universe.

Outro ignored them mostly, although the invasive bipeds appeared far from done with their mindless destruction. As if it hadn't been enough to scorch an enormous meadow with their massive ship and smother anything that could have survived, now they were digging and planting invasive, non-native seeds and setting in place structures. These smothered the native life and consisted of some lifeless material that resisted all of Outro's efforts to break it down using insects or plants. Whatever it was, the flora and fauna Outro sent to destroy it failed to so much as dent or chip it. Yet another indignity upon all the others.

Instead, Outro focused its studies on the genetic components of the Gabriel organism. It also encouraged the growth of more of the serrated-edge plants with anticoagulant properties. For a solution to the invaders to be the most effective, it needed more blood samples. Outro set the plants to pop up in and among the structures, which appeared to be where the bipeds rested immobile for up to one-third of each day. Sometimes more, sometimes less. They were restless creatures and as they entered a rest state, Outro reached out to their simple, base minds. It wanted them to know how repellent and unwanted they were. Outro was unsure what the bipedal creatures retained after returning to an active state, as it wasn't sure they were even intelligent enough to be communicated with in any other way than their odd vocalizations. They were, most assuredly, even more primitive than the first bipedal invaders, who had communicated through movement, color and vocalizations. The first invaders, however, had not had the same rest state. When they entered rest state, their bodies, their respiration, presented as a hibernation state, and it was a rare occurrence. Outro hadn't studied them long, though. They were invasive species, after all, and not welcome.

In order to be effective, and not waste time waiting for one approach to kill them off, Outro focused its intent on creating a multi-prong line of attack. It would not stop at just introducing a fungal variant that would kill the bipeds. It would also employ the local fauna to help with this. A few tweaks to a large quadruped and an infestation of a particular fungus that could move into the creature's brain and take control, and the usually peaceful creature became enraged. These quadrupeds, with a single large horn emerging from their foreheads, dubbed Zarmunicorns by Sagan Base, lived in large herds of fifty or more. A group of violent ruminants running through the settlement would certainly cause chaos, which could help with the collection of random samples of DNA. A week after Outro had collected the Gabriel organism blood sample, it sent a large herd of the Zarmunicorns through the bipeds settlement in the middle of a workday. The large hooves and horns of the Zarmunicorns trampled and gored twenty people. Medics placed two severely injured people in Cryo until a full medical facility was installed.

The blood that soaked into the ground, some fifteen samples, gave Outro just what it needed to finish its work. With these multiple samples, it now understood clearly the potential weaknesses the bipedal organisms had for certain fungal and viral components.

Over the next week, as more of the invaders' buildings rose, some bipeds returned to investigate the ruins of the first invaders' domains, crumbling and ruined as they were. Outro created the first of three fungal delivery systems. One was similar to the Terran Lycoperdon echinatum, that when disturbed, released a large, but mostly invisible cloud of spores. Those spores, when inhaled, were lethal within one to three days, depending on the size of the individual. Outro pushed those to grow along the edges of the ruins as an experiment.

Two bipeds were excavating the largest, most intact ruin of the first bipedal invaders. Discovered days after the first smaller structures, it had been part of the original spacecraft. Outro watched as the bipeds pulled vines away, burrowed into the open edge of the ancient craft, and continued vocalizing. It was a shame, really, that they were so invasive, such a pestilence. If they had simply stayed in orbit, perhaps done something less aggressive, attempted to communicate, Outro could forgive their disruption of its work, its millennia of research. They appeared to be curious creatures and interested in other bipedal creatures, if their focus on the ruins was any sign. But they seemed singular in their approach. As if nothing else mattered but bipedal life. Outro had seen the creatures hunt and consume quadruped ruminants and creatures of the air. It sensed the bipeds digging into the soil, removing plants, and from the excretions deposited in a waste lagoon, they were omnivores.

This expanded Outro's choices in plans of attack, should the spores fail to be fully effective.

Above all, Outro wanted one thing - the entire removal of the invaders from its land. Soon, Entity would share Outro's understanding of what these creatures were. Entity was soft, slow, but Outro saw them for what they were better, having learned so well from the first invaders. These creatures had no right to be here, and they were not welcome, not at all.

Unaware they were being scrutinized, Gabriel stood sweating, despite the dimness of the canopy and lack of direct sun. He wished he was at Heinlein Base instead of back out here, struggling through the thick overgrowth with Rajinder Fet. His legs, back and head ached, and he'd had only brief stints of sleep the night before. Tanya's nightmares were constant and loud. There was no sleeping through them, and she wasn't the only one. He'd slip into sleep only to wake with a shout moments later, already unaware of what had caused the nightmare. And now that they had arrived on site, Rajinder was deep in concentration as he examined the ruins.

The images they had taken of the discovery had motivated Captain O'Day to request a look through the refugee roster for someone who could tell them what they were looking at and how old it possibly was. Rajinder's name had popped up, along with two others, all in Cryo. The other two would have taken some resources to get to. In the back half of the ship, the Cryo units were stacked fifty deep and twenty wide, like some nightmarish rendition of the vintage game Tetris 3D.

They'd decanted Rajinder from his Cryo unit, given him a day to recover, and then sent him out with Gabriel to learn as much as he could from the ruins. The number of people Gabriel knew, compared to the untold tens of thousands he didn't, and likely never would, was small and did not include Rajinder. Native to India, his English was impeccable, with the British accent. He was of average height and build, with salt and pepper hair, as well as a neatly trimmed beard and mustache. When he wasn't muttering to himself as he took vids, dug at the ruined buildings, or typed notes - his lips stretched wide in a gleeful grin. Gabriel had lost count of how often the man had described the ruins as an opportunity of a lifetime. The guy was as happy as a pig in mud.

Gabriel just wished he could take a nap. Along the outer edge of the forest opening, he could see several fallen trees, as well as what looked like a large mossy area. There were few insects in this world. At least, when compared to Earth. And little really in the way of thorny vegetation, that odd serrated-edge plant being the exception. Nothing with thorns, at least not yet. In the ship were thousands of native plants, thorny varieties included, which were waiting to be transplanted into their new home. All identified as having high potential for success based on the D.O.V.E. probe soil reports.

He could take a nap. He doubted Rajinder would even notice. The man had disappeared inside one of the larger ruins, already having identified the smaller ones as possible family homes and the larger as communal in nature, indicating an organized society. He'd added a lot of other words in, and pointed to the possibility of the long-gone denizens possibly having a large, thick tail that provided additional stability to a bipedal frame.

The moss looked cushion soft.

A hammock would feel like a five-star hotel right about now, Gabriel thought, a rueful smile on his lips. He walked over to the mass of moss. It was roughly the size of a double bed in width and length. It called to him seductively, promising he could rest his aching bones and red eyes for just a moment.

He stepped closer, and a tiny, almost imperceptible puff of air or particulate flew into the air from a clump of fungus on the ground. Barely noticeable, but it set him to sneezing.

Once, twice, thrice. God, his nose itched now!

"Salud! You alright out there?" Rajinder called out. And Gabriel said he was before another sneezing fit overtook him. By the time it finished, his nose ached and a small soreness was developing from the harsh coughing fit that had followed the sneezing.

"I'm fine." Gabriel reflected on the history of blessing sneezes. History was full of stories of the superstitious being afraid of demons popping out of the sneezing person's body and infecting anyone nearby. And in terms of infectious disease being spread, the superstitious weren't so far off. They couldn't have known at the time that a sneeze, traveling at speeds of up to 160 kilometers an hour, could produce up to 40,000 droplets or travel as far as one and a half meters and remain in the air for ten minutes. Still, they had suspected there was danger in a sneeze, and they hadn't been wrong there.

Had it been the tiny puffball mushrooms? Could that have set him off?

Gabriel had never been that susceptible to allergies, not like some of his agemates who, like him, grew up in overcrowded cities with claustrophobic housing. The perfect scenario for the spread of disease.

He stepped onto one of them on purpose, and found himself in the throes of a sneezing and coughing fit, before he stepped away, his headache intensifying from a level five to a level nine.

Suddenly, the mossy bed didn't look half as appealing. His right eye watered uncontrollably and the fiery feeling in his throat was spreading into his lungs. He coughed, mucus suddenly filling the back of his throat. He spit, a glob of yellow streaked with red landed on the mossy carpet, right next to a series of tiny mushroom rings mere centimeters in diameter.

I feel like shit. Here I am, in the middle of nowhere, getting sick with the flu on an alien planet. How's that for bad luck?

Rajinder found himself entranced inside the alien structure. The excitement at this ancient find, which he estimated to be between 3,000 and 5,000 years old, had him happier than he had been in a very long time. Happier than he ever thought he could be again after losing Aditi. His soul mate, his love, and his partner in all things. Aditi had stood by his side as he traveled the world. The Incan ruins in Peru, a collapsed necropolis near the Valley of the Kings, and even deep into the Amazon jungle to discover pre-Columbian civilizations hidden deep beneath vines and rotting vegetation. They had never wanted children. A rare, unpopular position to take and one that both their families seemed deeply disappointed by. But as Aditi had said repeatedly, the skeletons, the ruins, were their pride and joy, not teething and potty training and being trapped by a child's many needs. And they'd been happy, so happy.

The ESH virus had robbed him of her. He'd considered ending it all. All he wanted was to find her again in the next life. To commit suicide, though, it could have harmful consequences in the next incarnation. And as much as he missed Aditi and wanted to join her, he also didn't want to harm his chances to be with her again in the next life.

He traced a set of whorls and lines carved into the glassy interior pillar and wished he knew what the creatures, now long dead, looked like. There was an incomplete skeleton on the floor of the building. A contorted set of bones that were clearly nothing close to human. "Aditi, you would have loved this."

"Raj?" Rajinder heard Gabriel croak from outside. "I'm uh, I'm sorry, but we need to head back now."

Rajinder blinked. Surely, they hadn't been here that long. What time was it?

"Now?"

"Yeah. I'm sorry, but I'm uh, I'm not feeling well." Gabriel's voice sounded raspy and raw.

He climbed out of the entrance hole, bending slightly to do so. A hanging vine brushed against his face as he stood upright outside of the greatest discovery he could ever have hoped to be a part of. Evidence of an alien species on an alien planet over 22 light years from Earth.

Gabriel stood nearby, leaning on a tree for support, his skin both red-blotched and pale. He looked quite unwell, alarmingly so.

"It uh, it just came on so quick. I slept poorly last night and, well, I guess I didn't realize I was so under the weather until now."

"Okay, well, yeah, we should get you back to Base, right away." Rajinder tried to calculate if there was any way he could help Gabriel hike out, fly him in the flitter back to Base, and then return on his own.

Probably not. They don't seem to want anyone out on their own until we know more about this planet.

It seemed a little foolish, these precautions. After all, on the opposite side of the planet, the colonists had been coming and going for years. It seemed an overabundance of caution. And Rajinder was looking at the discovery of a lifetime. The last thing he wanted was to leave, but Gabriel was looking terrible.

"Let's get you back to Base." He said and, turned around, headed the wrong direction, stepping directly into the same patch of puffball mushrooms. Rajinder's sneezes and coughing fit drowned out Gabriel's croaked comment about his going in the wrong direction as he activated the puffball mushroom cloud at his feet.

Four long hours later, they emerged, stumbling, pale, and shaking from the thick underbrush. It had taken them less than two hours of hiking to get to the ruins, and now twice as long to get back. Both men were hacking, coughing, and spitting globs of yellow and blood-tinged sputum up, steadily worsening with each hour that passed.

Outro analyzed the sputum that landed intermittently on the fungal sensor nodes. Yes, the two bipedal invaders were both infected and responding as expected.

it begins

If Outro had been human, a triumphant crow would have accompanied the words. Entity said nothing in response. That side of the world was Outro's to do with as it wished. And in truth, in another millennium, possibly less if the solar winds shifted, the entire world would be Outro's anyway. Such was the way.

A flitter, on autopilot, arrived at Heinlein Base shortly before dinner. Inside it, were Rajinder Fet, his eyes glassy, unfocused, his normally dusky skin mottled in red and white patches, his breathing raspy. Beside him lay Gabriel Sulkava, who had sunk into a coma shortly after collapsing into the passenger seat of the flitter.

By the time most of the settlement would be in bed for the night, Gabriel's heart stopped twice and all brain activity ceased. By morning, Rajinder Fet was dead as well.

"Whatever is out there, we don't need anyone else exposed to it. That forest, and those ruins, are off limits," Captain O'Day announced, her green eyes snapping.

"Agreed." Mireille Marcelin, the only member of the TUPG council currently out of Cryo, rubbed her forehead, sleep-deprived and fighting off the beginnings of a debilitating migraine.

"Message Sagan Base. Ask them if they know what could cause this." Mayflower's Captain continued, "We need to be sure this doesn't happen again."

TRANSMISSION PACKET
HEZW TO SBZW
/BEGIN TRANSMISSION
TWO DEAD FROM FAST-MOVING ILLNESS. HEALTHY IN MORNING, DEATH IN LESS THAN 14 HOURS. ANY HISTORY OF SUDDEN ONSET OF SYMPTOMS INCLUDING FEVER, BLOOD IN MUCUS, AND LABORED BREATHING? PLEASE ADVISE.
/END TRANSMISSION

But it was far too late. Outro had already spread the seeds of the spores in and around the settlement. By the next morning, the infection had killed or was killing most of the fifty-eight souls— mostly crew members and a few specialists. Their lifeless bodies lay where they fell. Above them, the enormous lifeship, powered by its own nuclear generator, continued to preserve those in Cryo. Ninety-five thousand two hundred and eighteen ESH-positive refugees from Earth remained in

Cryo, blissfully unaware of the deadly spores that lay just outside.

Dust to Dust

Date: 05.02.2107

Outro had much work ahead. The invaders' ship was monstrous, an affront to Outro's sense of order. It sat there, an ugly scar upon the land and clearly still operating, despite having no one left to need it. It hummed and Outro found this both fascinating and repulsive.

Outro did not know that there were more on board, so many more. Had it been able to access the computer logs, it would have known that. Their bodies were all in Cryo. For all of Outro and Entity's many talents, a fungal entity has no use for a computer. A computer had no organic qualities, and therefore could not possibly be a form of communication.

For Outro, the deed was done. The threat vanquished. It would be easy enough to replicate the puffball pestilence in the future when it assumed control of the other half of the planet. It wondered if it could figure out a way to convince Entity to let it try. Perhaps Entity had seen enough of their atrocities on its side of the world and was ready to be reasonable.

Outro reached out...

it is done

Outro felt Entity shift and move to the edges of Outro's domain.

all of them

Entity asked in response.

yes

Outro answered.

a pity

Outro felt a surge of resentment. A pity? Really? These things were vermin!

a pity

Outro responded. The question hung in the air.

unknown potential

That was all of Entity's response. *Unknown potential.* As if these bipedal, carbon-based lifeforms had potential for anything except destruction. They crawled over the skin of the land, burning, poisoning, and disrupting. What potential was there?

Some arguments are unwinnable. Outro knew it was right. Surely, somehow, eventually, Entity would come to see the truth of it. These bipeds were invasive vermin. After a few more years and more of its territory's defilement, Entity would understand.

For now, however, Outro had a task before it. It wanted every part of these invasive vermin removed from the face of this half of the planet, and that was proving to be difficult.

The massive ship, constructed of non-organic materials, seemed inaccessible. One of the crew members, in some pathetic attempt at self-preservation, had fled inside and sealed the door.

Outro sent vines to access the inner reaches, through whatever means necessary, with little success.

Mayflower's hull proved resistant. The walls were smooth expanses, interrupted only by occasional seams, round plugs, antennae that jutted out. And Outro's genomic study of the invaders and assessment of their decaying bodies confirmed a basic incompatibility with the frozen, oxygen-deprived vacuum of space. Similar to how Entity had described its own journeys between the stars, Outro understood that these bipeds also required a kind of impenetrable protection during their own trip from one planet to another. But whereas Outro or Entity only needed a part of their larger selves, a few microns of life buried deep within an asteroid, these bipeds needed a monstrous ship to hide away from the vacuum of space inside. Highly inefficient, and now a stain upon Outro's territory.

Already, Outro had sent the fast-growing vines to take root, cover the structure, and find its weaknesses. Everything had a weakness, and nothing an insignificant bipedal species would create could be the exception to that. Each day, the vines grew higher, thicker - covering the skin of the ship with gray-green life. On the ground, fungal ground covers similar in appearance to Terran lichen grew. It riddled the corpses, accelerating decomposition, but the bipedal invaders' outer coverings stopped it. Again, Outro found a substance that was not organic and resisted its attempts to break down the coverings into the more basic building blocks of life.

It was as if, even in death, these creatures were determined to be a thorn in Outro's side.

Radio Silence

Date: 05.07.2107

The silence from Heinlein Base filled Jason Axler's dreams and kept him tossing and turning all night. By 0400, he'd given up trying to sleep and instead paced back and forth in his small house, forcing himself to wait until a decent hour. It wouldn't do to wake someone up at the ass crack of dawn, after all. Not Mayflower, and certainly not anyone here at Sagan Base.

The work was hard. They might not have to terraform the planet like the Mars colony, but it wasn't as simple as sticking plants in the ground. And the construction, mining, laying of sewers, and so much more infrastructure went into creating a home than any of them had realized. The denizens of Sagan Base worked hard, and slept hard, and the last thing he wanted to do was wake anyone up early. Finally, at 0700, he allowed himself to go back to Communications, and try once again to reach someone, anyone, at Heinlein Base.

"Heinlein Base, Heinlein Base, come in." he listened to the static for a moment, hearing nothing. "Heinlein Base, Heinlein Base, this is Sagan Base, over."

Nothing but static.

Nothing via the transmission packets since that concerning message about two men dead from a mysterious, fast-moving illness.

He sat back in his chair, frowning at the communication array before him. It was time to get someone else involved.

"NARA, please connect me with Daniel Medry."

"Connecting now." NARA replied. There was a short beep.

"Medry here." He sounded tired. No actual surprise there. Most of those who had kids sounded chronically sleep-deprived. And Daniel Medry and Sam Sydan had three now, with a fourth on the way.

"Hey Medry, it's Jason. I'm uh, I'm a little concerned over here and I'd like your opinion."

He could hear the other man yawn. "Sorry, yeah, whatcha need?"

"I'm not getting through to Heinlein Base. I've checked all the equipment, twice, and... nothing. It's been six days since the last contact."

"Six days?" Medry's tone sharpened, the sleepy tone vanished. "Which method did you try?"

"Both. I've sent the transmission packets and tried them via the comm relay system."

"And no answer in six days?"

"No, not since that transmission about those two guys, Sulkava and Fet, dying of some fast-moving illness." He pulled up the message, "It reads 'Two dead from fast-moving illness. Healthy in the morning, death in less than 14 hours.' They wanted to know if we've had anything like this and I asked Dr. Schrader before replying, but we hadn't."

"Yeah, no, we certainly haven't. And this was all six days ago?"

"Yup. I didn't have any messages for a couple of days to pass on. And it was maybe a day or two past that when I thought to reach out. I've been trying for two days, well, three counting today, and no answer."

"Shit." There was a pause. "I'll be in soon. Contact Mayor Phoenix and apprise him of the situation. I'll go through all the steps and figure out things from there."

"Got it. See you soon, Medry." Jason replied. Seconds later, he was speaking with Martin Phoenix, who sounded as concerned as Medry had. A few minutes later, Daniel walked into the Comm Unit, a look of concern on his face. A half hour later, after checking, rechecking, and quizzing Jason, Daniel looked even more concerned. He smacked the Comm unit on his shirt.

"NARA, please connect me with Martin Phoenix." A moment later and the mayor's voice, accompanied by a loud hammering in the background, came through.

"Phoenix here. Medry? What do you know?"

"I think we have a problem here. We've got zero communications from Heinlein Base for the past six days..."

"Jason filled me in on that, yes. And it's not a failure on our end?"

"No, sir. And nothing I can see on their end. When we ping the receiver, it replies, there's just no one answering on their end."

"I see." The hammering sounds continued. "Call a Council meeting. We need to sort this out."

Daniel nodded, rubbing his eyes. He hadn't been sleeping well. And it wasn't just the kiddos waking him up. Both he and Sam kept waking up from nightmares, the kids too. By the time he realized he was awake, and usually on his feet, the details of the nightmare had completely vanished from his mind.

"Will do, Mayor. See you at 1300?" The Council was scattered across the continent. Things had been quiet since both lifeships arrival a month prior. It would take a few hours to assemble everyone.

"Yep, Phoenix out." The sounds of hammering cut off and Daniel looked up at Jason.

"Check everything again. Send a transmission packet. I'll see if I can get connected to the NARA on Mayflower, but I'm not sure the permissions will allow for that."

Jason nodded. "Should I reach out to Jacey Wyatt, or maybe Zach Jenkins? Those two have mad skills. They might get us a workaround with the Mayflower NARA."

Daniel grinned, "Yes, do that." His grin faded. "Call up to Nostradamus, and see if they've had any contact, either."

"Will do."

Nostradamus had taken things slow. The first group, inoculated against the ESH virus, had made the trip down to the planet nearly four months ago. The group of fifteen had eventually grown to nearly one hundred, and after a few mediocre harvests threatened to limit their resources, Captain Desdemona had limited the revivals until things stabilized on the surface. They didn't need to overwhelm resources, after all, they had time. The captain and much of her crew had visited, then returned to the Nostradamus. Now that they had a vaccine for the ESH virus, she had already announced her intention to return to Earth. Zara Desdemona was due to take a turn in Cryo while others cared for the orbiting ship and its precious contents. They had to at least wait for Earth to recover. It would be another seven years before Earth would be ready for their return, possibly longer.

Jason went through all the steps again. Comm messaging, transmission packets, and finally he called Zach Jenkins. His friend answered and Jason could hear giggles in the background.

"Zach here. What can I do you for, Jason?"

"How are your hacking skills, my man?"

A door closed and with it the giggles. "Fair to middling. Whatcha got?"

"I need a hack into Mayflower's NARA."

"Oof, Jacey would kick ass on that, but she's on maternity leave, as in, went into the hospital today. Twins. I could give it a go, though. I'll bring Laney. She's been polishing her skills."

"Right. I need it ASAP. I'm here in Communications. When can you be here?"

"Well, lucky you. We're both off today. See you in twenty," Jason heard a door open again, and more giggling, "Yeah, make that thirty minutes, maybe forty." The comm went silent.

Jason grinned. They made a cute couple. And forty minutes still gave them four hours until the Council convened.

Forty minutes on the dot, Laney and Zach walked in, hand in hand.

"I know you asked for Zach, but I figured I could help." Laney grinned up at him.

"She's a natural." Zach added, then reached out to tickle her side. She pushed him away, giggling.

Jason rolled his eyes. They were in the throes of puppy love. Great for them, not so much for someone single like him, although the latest group from Nostradamus held promise. The beautiful and exotic Pele Gauthier had caught his eye. Former First Officer, she now worked for Communications, installing cell tower relays afield right now. Eventually, they would stretch north and south, past the poles, allowing them standard comm access to the far side of the planet. That wouldn't be for a year, possibly two. Pele moved between overseeing the tower installation and returning infrequently to her position on board the Nostradamus whenever a new set of Cryo revivals was required. Like most others on board and on the surface, she used her skills in multiple positions.

She'd be gone for another week, but Jason was gearing up to ask her out on a date. He figured he'd better make his move soon if he didn't want to lose his chance.

Zach and Laney settled at a large table, pulling out their tablets, fingers flying over the keyboards. "So why are we hacking the Mayflower NARA, anyway?" Zach asked, eyebrows raised.

Jason shifted uncomfortably, "I'll need you to both agree to not say anything until Council says it's okay, but..."

They both stared at him. Laney spoke first. "We promise. Now dish."

"They've gone silent. I'm getting no responses. Not to the radio, not to transmission packets. And it's not on our end. I'm double, triple-checked."

"Shit." Laney said, her ebullient tone gone. "That doesn't sound good at all."

"No, it doesn't. I'm working on getting eyes in the sky. There's a satellite I can redirect, but it will cause issues for those up north if we move them for too long."

Zach's fingers danced on the keyboard. "The D.O.V.E. mother ship, yeah? On it. If we uplink to that, I can probably bounce it off the Nostradamus and see if I can connect to NARA that way. We should be able to at least ask NARA for updates."

Laney scooted closer to the table. "I'll access the mainframe to redirect for video."

It was almost noon before, simultaneously, both Zach and Laney whooped in victory. "We're in!"

"Hang tight," Laney said, "Let me see if I can't get these images enlarged, and... Oh... oh no..." Her voice died away as the image transformed from grainy pixels to a grim image of bodies scattered across Heinlein Base.

The image, taken from space but enlarged to where it appeared they were merely a few meters above the base, showed bodies crumpled, decaying, limbs splayed.

Jason stared at the vines and plants that covered the ground. He could see them wrapped around the ship, easily covering the bottom two meters and inching higher. "What's with all the plant life?"

"Who cares? What killed them? And are they all dead?" Laney snapped back. "I think those are more important questions."

Zach's voice was subdued. "I'm patching in the Mayflower NARA now."

"NARA, are you receiving?" Jason asked.

"Yes, this is NARA." The computer program's voice sounded exactly like their own here at Sagan Base.

"NARA, can you please connect us to Captain O'Day or any other member of the Mayflower crew?"

"I'm sorry, I cannot do that."

"Why not?" Jason asked, frowning.

"All crew member bio-functions have ceased."

"All of them, NARA?"

"Yes."

Laney spoke up. "NARA, what is the status of those in Cryo?"

"All Cryo units are stable." NARA responded smoothly.

"NARA, how many are inside the Mayflower at this time?" Zach asked.

"There are ninety-five thousand two hundred and nineteen individuals on board the Mayflower."

"How many are in Cryo?"

"There are ninety-five thousand two hundred and eighteen individuals in Cryo."

"There is one crew member on board that isn't in Cryo?" Jason asked, his hopes rising that there was someone on board who could tell them what happened.

"Yes. There is one crew member aboard, a Minerva Runchin, but that crew member's bio-functions ceased at 2345 hours on 05.02.2107." NARA responded.

Jason's heart dropped.

"NARA, how many are dead?" Jason asked as he watched Laney pointing at and counting the dead in the image.

"Fifty-eight individuals' bio-functions have ceased."

The three looked at each other with dread.

Jason spoke again, "NARA, there seems to be an above average amount of plant life in the immediate vicinity of the Mayflower. Can you detect this with Mayflower's external sensors?"

"One moment." Seconds later, NARA spoke, "Yes, there is an abnormal amount of plant life. In reviewing external scans over the past few days, it seems there was an expansion of growth beginning seven days ago."

"Seven days, that's how long it's been since the last transmission packet or any radio message of any kind," Jason whispered, his tan face pale, drawn.

"They're all dead. But from what?" Laney asked, her eyes full of tears. "What could have gone wrong?"

"I don't know," Zach said, pulling her close to him. "But we need to find out."

The Emergency Council echoed Zach's sentiments an hour later and reviewed the few pieces of information Jason and the others could provide. The next morning, Daniel piloted a flitter with Sam, Laney, and Martin Phoenix, up over the North Pole and down into the far side of the world where Heinlein Base was located. By the time they arrived at midday, they could already see a stark contrast from the day before. Where there had been bodies, now there were just masses of plants, with an occasional bone sticking out. A ribcage here, a skull there. The ship itself, enshrined in vines and creeping plant life, was now one-third, and in some places one-half, covered.

The decay of the bodies seemed unnaturally advanced. What should have taken months had taken days.

They conversed again with the Mayflower NARA, ensuring that yes, the ship was sealed.

"Someone did that. And it's keeping those in Cryo safe," Martin mused.

"I'd like to get samples of some of those plants," Sam said.

"No way. Something down there killed fifty-eight people. The hell any of us are getting out, getting near that, or even risking picking it up on the outer skin of the flitter." Daniel replied forcefully and Sam glared at him, opening her mouth as if to object.

"I agree," Martin replied, lending his support. "There's no way to know what killed them, and I'm not risking any of you to find out."

Sam's shoulders slumped. "I know you are both right, but damn it, how will we know if we don't take samples?"

"Fifty-eight people died here. Our lives, our settlement, it depends on every one of us staying safe." Martin answered, "I'll see if we can't repurpose some D.O.V.E. probes and have them collect and analyze samples without human involvement."

This seemed to satisfy Sam.

They hovered there, taking image after image of the plant life, the bodies, and making observations before finally leaving.

"All those people," Laney whispered. "We have to get them out of there."

"And we will." Martin said, and patted her shoulder, his mouth grim.

Within three weeks, the scans from space showed Mayflower completely covered in vines. Close examination of the plants would reveal five new species never seen before. One in particular, a fungus, caught Sam's eye. It reminded her of a Terran mushroom, Lycoperdon echinatum. A puffball mushroom known for spreading spores, millions of them, when disturbed. The recommissioned D.O.V.E. probes collected multiple samples in the area. And after a month, one thing was certain - the puffball look-alike was absolutely deadly to humans.

What stumped Sam, and the rest of the colonists, is that they could find no evidence of the mushroom anywhere else on the planet but there at Heinlein base.

With regular reports from the NARA on Mayflower, the Council waited until they identified an antifungal compound that would counteract the puffball's deadly effects. Until that time, there was nothing they could do to help those in Cryo. No one was happy with this answer. No one at all.

Total Loss

Date: 05.10.2108

"Lucas Anthony Sydan! You get over right now, young man!" Sam's strident, exasperated voice could be heard all the way outside.

Daniel looked over at Lila and raised his eyebrows. Her tiny mouth was frowning. "Mama's mad."

"I can tell Pumpkin. Any idea why?"

"Luke said he was gonna study his pee." The little girl answered, her focus on the pile of stones in front of her. She was stacking them with a quiet intensity, slipping in smaller rocks in between larger rocks, wedging them into a solid low wall.

"Wait, what?" Daniel asked, setting down the curved wood piece he had been carving for the banister railing. Sam was worried that the baby would fall without the railing to hold on to. "Say that again, Lila?"

"I tole you, Daddy. Luke said he was gonna study his pee. And I tole him it was stinky, and that Firelli was gonna get into it and he didn't listen. And then Firelli got into it and it spilled all over the bed and now Mama's mad."

Sam's voice was rising. Daniel debated going inside to help. "Um, *which* bed, Lila?"

"Yours."

"Shh-oot." Daniel changed the wording at the last second.

"You said a bad word, Daddy. But it's okay, I'd say that too if I had pee on my bed." Lila commented, not bothering to look up.

Luke was yelling back now, not the least bit fazed by his mother's anger.

"It's an *experiment*! Daddy *said* I could!" Daniel heard him say clearly.

"Now you's in trouble too, Daddy." Lila commented, frowning harder at her pile of rocks.

"*Daniel Medry*!" here came Sam, her curls bouncing and her eyes snapping as she stood at the open front door, "Did you tell our son he could save his urine for an experiment?"

"He did, he did!" Luke was at her side, pointing at Daniel, desperate to share the blame.

"Now wait, I don't remember *any* of this."

"Tell the truth, Daddy, you got's to always tell the truth." Lila muttered and carefully adjusted her miniature rock fence, moving a tiny stone chip into place.

Daniel took in the set look on Sam's face and threw up his hands. "I've got nothing. I have no idea what Luke is talking about." He turned back to his daughter. "And thanks for nothing, kid. Talk about throwing me under the bus."

"What's a bus?"

"Daniel, please come in here and help me deal with this." Sam's eyes snapped with anger, her mouth set and teeth clenched. "Firelli is covered in stinking week-old urine, and the rest of it is soaking into our bed. On *your* side."

"Ah, Christ." He set down the wood and the knife he had been using to carve the banister with.

"Thank you so much for sparing us a few seconds of your precious time, Daniel," Sam sniped. There would be no placating her.

"Honey, I was making the banister, like you asked." As soon as the words left his mouth, he knew they were a mistake.

Sam's mouth tightened even further. She spun on her heel and marched away, a wave of old urine in her wake as she carried a still-dripping Firelli to the bathroom.

He called after her, "Would you like me to wash Firelli? Or should I clean the bed up?" There was no reply and he could hear her muttering under her breath as she ran the water for the bathtub.

"Dad, you told me I could study my pee, you *did*." Luke, standing at his elbow, his pants soaked with the urine, was insistent.

"I do *not* remember that conversation, Sport, so why don't you refresh my memory?"

"You said we learn by experimenting."

"Oh-kay."

"So I experimented. I kept it so I could see if it changed colors and I was gonna look at it under the microscope, but then Firelli messed it up."

The boy followed as Daniel walked into the bedroom and took in the messy, stinking scene. The reek was overwhelming, and Daniel's eyes watered as he opened the two windows as wide as they could go.

A gallon container, now mostly empty, lay on its side next to the bed, his and Sam's bed, and there was a large yellow puddle on the floor.

"Just how much urine did you save, son?"

"All of it."

"All of it for how long? A day?"

The boy rolled his eyes. "No, for a week. 'Cause it had to be a proper experiment."

Daniel laughed. It was horrific, all of this urine, the reek of it, and he wondered if their bed was worth saving, but all he could do was laugh. Sam emerged from the bathroom, glaring at Daniel, but his laughter was contagious. Before long, she was laughing too. Luke stared at them, confused.

The house intercom chirped, and NARA's steady voice interrupted their mirth. "Incoming call from Aaronson, Joanna for Sydan, Samantha."

Sam tapped her individual comm, a small button on her shirt, "Morning Jo, how are you?"

A tiny transmitter, audible only to the wearer, was installed in each comm. This allowed for at least partially private conversations. Sam listened for a moment, nodded, and said, "I'll be there in an hour. Right. No, no, I'll take care of it. You have your hands full right now. Sam out."

"What was that all about?"

Sam frowned. "The weirdest thing. You remember the mass plantings we did down south? Of the Paulownia trees? Quick growing, good for furniture, ready for harvest in just five years?"

Daniel nodded, "Yeah, it will be a nice resource, better than the thneed trees." The thneed trees, native to the planet, produced wood that was rough, easily splintered. It had proved difficult to work with. The Paulownia trees, however, would allow the colonists to create wood furniture and structures more easily.

"Well, Wesley Perdue just called it in. We planted over one hundred thousand seedlings. They were doing great, and then overnight, they have all died."

"Yikes, I thought you tested the soil extensively?"

"We *did*. There was nothing out of the ordinary. In fact, the soil composition was perfect for the seedling's needs. It makes no sense. Anyway, I'm going to take the flitter down there and see what I can figure out."

"Now?"

She grinned at him. "No time like the present. Besides, you can help our future urine specialist learn all about clean laboratory techniques."

Daniel groaned, "Are you sure they don't need help with, I dunno, something, down there at the farm?"

"Nope, your place is here," came her quick reply. "Here with the kids, handling the cleanup process, you'll do great." She grinned smugly at him and turned to find her knapsack.

A few minutes later, Daniel watched the flitter disappear from view. "Help me with the cleanup, son, then it's off to the bath with you." He turned back to the house, "C'mon kid, let's talk about the proper storage of specimens while we do it."

Luke trudged after him. At nearly four years of age, the boy was curious and intelligent. So was Lila. Their little girl was showing strong leanings toward building and design. She made walls of pebbles that held, sometimes serving to trip the unwary, and had a corner of the yard devoted to her various engineering projects. Even Firelli showed plenty of signs of high intelligence. She was already a year old and already forming dozens of words with a wispy baby lisp. That high intelligence hadn't stopped her from getting into the bucket of urine, however.

The past four years had shown Daniel just how difficult, overwhelming, and surprisingly joyous raising children could be. And with three of them, he and Sam had their hands full.

Sam took in the scenery as the flitter jetted past the familiar terrain, turned and headed south towards the giant auto-farms established to feed the growing colony. The farms were in a pleasant, broad valley, surrounded by miles of fence to keep out the unicorn population. The colonists had found that the Zarmunicorns, better known as unicorns, had a predilection for Terran vegetation. Unfortunately, they did not have the intestinal fortitude to digest it. Although the Terran vegetation made the Zarmunicorns horribly ill, they were undeterred and would invade a section of crops, devour and then regurgitate them. They continued this behavior until they consumed the crop. The Zarmunicorns would then head for the next crop as if they were hoping for a better outcome.

After losing large swaths of harvests to the marauding native animals, Wesley had insisted on installing the fencing. The panels, printed by the large 3D printers, would last for decades, and the automated diggers had neatly drilled holes through the soil, gravel, and solid stone in several spots along the perimeter to enclose the farm.

The animals had then been driven out, forced away from the food source that they had been so attracted to.

The fence disappeared from view as the flitter landed next to the enormous swath of Paulownia crops. The trees stretched on and on, planted in neat rows, stretching as far as the eye could see. They were three years along now, and quite tall, most of them topping eighteen meters in height. Another two years and they would be ready for harvesting.

Well, at least that had been the plan. Sam stared at the catastrophe before her. The gray fungus had left the trees almost completely defoliated, their brown leaves lying on the ground.

"Sam!" Wes Perdue jumped out of his flitter, strode over, and hugged her. "How are you? How are Daniel and the kids?"

"Hey Wes, good to see you!" She hugged him back. "The kids are great and infuriating all at the same time. How about yours?"

Wes began dating Kit in the weeks after planetfall, both of them moving slow. Kit had still been recovering from losing Mike Deekins in the Cryo sabotage. Pregnant with Deeks' child, she had been reticent at first, and Wes hadn't pushed it. Slowly he had become more of a daily presence in her life and when the scan had showed not one baby, but two, Wes had been there holding her hand. The twins were born the same day as Luke, a boy and a girl. The boy, Michael, who everyone called "Mikie," was the spitting image of Deeks, while Kethryn favored her mother.

Tiny Lizanne, another perfect replica of Kit, joined the twins two years later, and now Kit was pregnant again.

"The kids are great. Kit is feeling huge and useless, her words not mine, and I was doing great until I saw this." He pointed to the trees.

"Wow, we have some serious die off occurring here. How long has this been going on, Wes?" Sam picked up a leaf and rubbed at the gray fuzz.

"That's the thing, Sam. They were fine yesterday. As in, absolutely one hundred percent fine."

Sam stared at Wes, then back at the trees. "No way, Wes, this has to have been going on for days, if not weeks."

"Sam, I'm serious. I was out here *yesterday*, taking soil samples and checking things over. Everything was *fine* and now this." Sam could tell by his tone that Wes was telling the truth, but the truth was impossible.

"Wes, this fungus. I've studied it. It moves *slow*."

"I swear to you, come back to the house and see my samples. I took them yesterday, including the leaves, bark and soil, and have them back at the barn. There isn't even a *trace* of fungus on them, and now it's covering everything!"

"How many trees are we talking about?" Sam asked, now examining the bark of the tree. She could see the gray lines of fungus threading through the bark.

"All of them."

"All of them in this quadrant?" Sam asked, looking up at Wes with concern, "That's a lot of trees. I know folks have put in their orders for most of this wood already."

"No, Sam. Not just this quadrant. *All* the Paulownia trees we planted. All one hundred thousand of them, overnight, dead."

Sam blinked. It wasn't possible. "I think I'm going to need some more samples."

Wes nodded and beckoned to her, "C'mon, I've got the supplies here in the flitter."

"We will need to take samples every one hundred yards. We need to test for contaminants, verify the type of fungus this is, and get a comprehensive soil test."

"Yep." Wes handed her a pair of latex gloves.

"I'll send the flitter back. Daniel might need it. And it looks like I'm going to be here for a while." She keyed in the command for home and the machine rose in the air, pulled slowly away and then sped up, quickly disappearing from view.

Hours of samples later, Sam stared into the microscope, her brow furrowed.

"Have you contacted Anton Webster yet?"

"I've got a call in, but he isn't answering. He might be out of range. The last time I talked to him, he was heading for the Northern Mountains and you know how spotty reception can be there."

"Well, we need to talk to him. Stat. Nagel too. I've never seen anything like this."

Sam's neck ached and her eyes burned. The samples across all the tested areas were the same. Spores of the fungus, a fungus that had shown up often across the planet but never in the amounts it was here in the Paulownia tree grove. This didn't seem possible. They had purposely chosen the region for its lower fungal presence in the soil - a benefit for the Paulownia seedlings since they were quite susceptible in the first few months to fungal infections.

But these weren't seedlings, they were trees that were taller than a three-story building. They shouldn't still be susceptible to fungus after three years, not like the seedlings were. And the massive amounts of fungus. It would have taken decades for it to appear and would have been clear long before they ever planted any of the trees.

Sam was staring at a mystery.

"Here, Kit sent sandwiches out. You must be starving by now." Wes handed Sam a sandwich. The bread was dense and still warm from the oven. Nestled in between the thick slices was bacon, tomato, lettuce and one of the new cheese blends that Kit had been experimenting with making.

Sam took a bite, her eyes closing as her mouth filled with the crunch of bacon and the flavor of the fresh tomato.

"Oh my, this is so good!"

Wes grinned. "We just pulled an heirloom tomato from A.R.C. - it is called a Cherokee Purple. I think it is my favorite - so flavorful!"

Sam was about to ask for some seeds when a large series of crashes shook the ground. "What the hell is that?"

Sandwich in hand, she sprinted outside of the barn, Wes on her heels. The tremendous crashes continued, an enormous cloud of dust and particles filled the air. Sam stood gaping in shock at the gray cloud roiling towards them.

"The Paulownia grove, the trees are falling over!"

Kit and the children had appeared in the doorway of the farmhouse, "Get back inside, the fungus, it's in the air!" He called to them, making shooing motions. "C'mon Sam, we need to get out of this and wait until the air settles."

Once inside, Wes instructed NARA to enact emergency filtering protocols on all ventilation.

They had not had to use them since the eruption of Mount Dumas the second year after land fall.

By evening, such as it is in a twilight world where the sun never truly rises or sets in your portion of the land, the trees had all fallen; the wood fractured and spongy, suffused with fungal spores and useless for any kind of harvest. They had spoken with Nagel Lowry. And Wes was still trying to track down Anton Webster. Nagel and Joanne promised to be at the farm first thing in the morning. Sam had put in a call to Daniel telling him she was spending the night.

As she fell asleep in the guest room, she couldn't help but think of the gray fungus and wonder whether the Paulownia trees were the end of it, or if their problems were just beginning.

The Grand Reveal

Date: 02.23.2110

Nathan Zradce was dying. It had certainly been a long time coming. Entity had both saved his life and been responsible for the state it was in now. Riddled with fungus, his organs were failing, his blood thick and slow.

nathan dying

entity failed

"You aren't a god, Entity. You saved my life, even if in saving it you doomed it. I should have died six years ago."

The creature, once human, croaked.

"I hope you have learned that humans are not your enemies."

Despite what Entity had revealed to him, that on some deep, genetic level, he was not like the other colonists, he still thought of himself as such. What else could he be? He turned his thoughts away from that, focusing instead on the concerning events that had occurred since he had been here in this dark cave. He worried that Entity's interest in humans was giving way to Outro's continued pogrom of distrust. After all, he knew about the Paulownia trees that Entity had destroyed. Had felt Entity's frustration over the destruction of its crops, its experiments. Nathan understood that Entity and Outro were at heart: gardeners and scientists. But that didn't mean they could relate to the scientists that now walked through their world. As much as he had tried to explain human behavior, Entity either did not understand, or did not believe him. Perhaps it was because, as Entity insisted, Nathan was not human. Or at least, not the same species of human as the others.

As time had passed, and Sagan Base had expanded far beyond its borders, Nathan sensed Entity's growing unease, distrust, and unhappiness. More and more, though, he feared what would happen when Entity departed. That, of course, was confusing, hard to truly understand. The most that Entity had said was that when the solar winds came at just the right angle, Entity would know it was time to leave and find another planet, another testing ground, another place for its experiments.

That would leave Zarmina's World to Outro. Total control and authority, to a being that clearly hated humans. He thought of the terrible fate of the colony that had settled in Outro's territory.

"I must warn them. They deserve to know the danger they are in."

nathan hunted

"Yes, I was hunted. But I deserved it. I killed people."

nathan kill

wrong mind

"I wasn't in my right mind. But that doesn't matter. What matters is that they are in danger when

you leave. And I must warn them so that they don't end up like that other colony and ship."

tried warning

"You've tried warning them?"

through other state

"Through another state? Like you did with me when I was in the coma?"

yes

humans don't listen

tried all this time

humans don't listen

Nathan thought about this. Entity had come to him when he was deeply injured. Through the ether, an almost psychic connection of sorts. Was it how Entity had tried to interact with the others?

"Are they conscious or unconscious when you have tried warning them?"

what is conscious unconscious

Nathan thought for a moment. *"Are they standing? Moving about? Or is it during their rest state, when humans sleep?"*

There was a long pause.

rest state

"You come to them in their dreams?"

what is dream

"Humans dream during their rest state. Primarily to process and merge memories from their waking lives. A sort of mental housekeeping." He visualized cleaning a room with a broom, hoping this made sense to Entity. *"We don't always remember our dreams, though."*

not remember

"No. Dreams are... well, they are unreliable. They aren't fact, but a more psychological extension of us, a way to, I don't know, understand the world better while decompressing."

humans not remember dream

"Not always, no. And you've been warning them? All this time?"

yes

"Then I'd say they don't remember it upon waking. So, somehow, I need to warn them. It needs to be me, Entity."

nathan changed

"I'm changed from who I was? Yes."

more not human

show

And suddenly, there was light. Bright. Blinding. Nathan could see nothing but a wash of white from the distant opening of the cave. Despite the world being twilight, more than sunny, the light now felt white-hot, piercing, and overwhelming. He squinted, felt the vines and fungal nodes that covered his body fall away. Nathan collapsed on the ground. His legs could no longer carry him. How long had it been since any of his muscles were used? He moved his arms, his hands, running his fingers down his sides and realizing that his body was stick thin, bony, wasted. He'd not used it, after all. Not for years.

"I can't walk anymore, Entity. My muscles have atrophied."

One attached vine twitched. Nathan could feel it along his back. Entity remained connected to him.

creature help

Nathan wasn't sure what Entity meant, so instead, he focused on trying to get his eyes to adjust to the light. He was weak as a kitten and as the white-hot brightness faded, and his eyes slowly adjusted, he could make out shapes, colors. Much of it was blurry, but he could see that his body was mostly naked. The fibers from the clothing he had put on that night so long ago had degraded and fallen away. His skin was white, gray, and mottled with green fungus. It wasn't just on him; it was a part of him. And likely the reason he was dying. If only he could make it out, make it back to Sagan Base, warn them. They deserved that much.

But how? He couldn't walk. His legs trembled, shook. His hands and arms, just from the act of moving across his body, ached from exhaustion. How was he going to get back to the others? To warn them?

Kilometers away, on the great plain and low hill country where Sagan Base was established, nearly four thousand colonists prepared for Landfall Day, just as they had every year since landing at their new home. More and more Cryo-sleepers from the Nostradamus were revived, inoculated against the ESH virus, and then added to the surface settlement. The appeal of an open world, full of promise and possibility, had resonated. Earth, while mostly empty, still held the memories of those they had lost. But here, on Zarmina's World, they had a chance at a new life, simpler, with higher gravity, but a place with seemingly limitless potential.

Each Landfall Day built on the last, becoming even more of a celebration with each year that passed. The colonists had let the old traditions, the myriad of holidays they had celebrated in their respective countries, die away. There were still birthdays and anniversaries to celebrate, but Landfall Day had become more and more important. A symbol of the life they had now, versus the one lost forever. The siblings, friends, classmates and more who had been left behind - most were dead. Zarmina's World was a new start, a hope that life would continue on, that humanity was not out of the cosmic game yet, and that it would flourish on this vast new world.

Festive flags and pennants, in a dozen colors, hung from poles along the sides of buildings. The 3D printers had been kept busy, creating biodegradable glitter and garland. Daniel's children ran, shrieking, in groups with their other age mates, watched over by Kit Tanner and several other parents. As Daniel helped Sam set more tables out in what had become Sagan Base's town square, he couldn't help thinking that it looked as if a great giant party monster had barfed up a rainbow of decorations.

"Put the moonshine over there on the taller tables, so the kids don't get it." Sam directed a couple of men staggering under the weight of the newly decanted moonshine Fenton Aaronson and Jackson Sebring had brewed up.

The town square was bustling with at least two dozen other colonists. Next to a line of pigs slowly turning on spits, someone placed a booth filled with flower garlands and hand-wrapped flower crowns. The smell of the slow-roasting pigs was absolutely delectable.

Thanks to advances in the artificial wombs, they now had a steady supply of pork and beef. The first had emerged from the wombs and successfully bred further generations. The colonists followed this with cattle, observing the birth of the second and third generations in the last three years, which slowly increased their beef supply. One bull, the first from the artificial wombs, was slaughtered a week before in anticipation of the celebration. The smokers at the northern edge of the town square emitted their own tantalizing odors as Anton Webster oversaw their finish.

Daniel's stomach rumbled. "I think I'm going to pass out with hunger." He said, as he lugged yet another table into place.

In the southern corner, a group of musicians were tuning their instruments. Some of the instruments had come all the way from Earth, others created here using the versatile 3D printers. Maria breezed by, a ukelele in hand with Jacqueline following close behind holding her own smaller version. Maria joined the others on the small stage, tapping at the microphone.

"Mic check, one, two, three, four."

Kevin Edmonds, her partner and Jacqueline's father, was already there, helping Miguel tune his guitar before he scooped up their daughter and waved at Simon, kissing Maria on the cheek before heading toward his son on the far side of the square.

Simon, now twelve, was finishing the assembly of another stall, one that would serve non-alcoholic drinks. He waved back at his dad, calling, "I'm helping the Chief with some rides for the kids next. Grab me a meat stick, please?"

Kevin nodded, hoisted his daughter up on his shoulders and headed to the smoker to grab some of the meat sticks Anton was now placing on the table. Zarmina's World had no equivalent of the housefly, something the colonists were very grateful for. This meant they could put out food with some level of impunity. As long as it wasn't a local plant variety, it didn't risk having insect invaders. The only exception to this was their local honeybee population, which wasn't that local. All the hives were set some twenty klicks away to the south to serve a section of fruit trees and cropland.

The trees weren't much bigger than head-height yet, but the bees had certainly been a boon to the squash and cruciferous vegetable crops. Now in their second hive split, the honey they produced was yet another luxury that the colonists could enjoy today. The stall dispensing small 3D printed jars of honey was close to Anton's.

Sam followed Daniel's gaze. "I hear Anton whipped up a honey barbecue sauce using the honey and is adding it to the smoked meat. I can't wait to try it."

Daniel's stomach gave another twisting complaint. "I can't wait. I'm getting a meat stick."

He strode off, hearing Sam call after him, "Get me one too!"

"Happy Landfall Day, Medry." Anton grinned and handed him several meat sticks. "Get 'em before they're gone."

"Thanks, man." They smelled even more delectable up close and Daniel opened his mouth to bite into one, convinced he was going to salivate like a dog. He tore off a chunk, closed his eyes, and chewed. "Oh God. These are... amazing. I never realized how much I missed meat." The MREs had been a steady diet, but one that grew tiring day in and day out. On board, and on planet, the varieties of fresh vegetables and fruits had certainly helped, but having first the chicken, then pigs, and finally beef, had been life-changing.

"Here, dip it into the sauce." Anton pushed a paper cup of barbecue sauce towards him and Daniel dipped the meat stick into it and groaned again at the next mouthful.

"I gotta get this to Sam. Sorry to eat and run, but that woman of mine needs sustenance, and she's dying to try this sauce."

"Go, go." Anton laughed and turned to a group of women and girls who had just finished with the garlands. He winked at them, pushing a plate of meat sticks in their direction and pointed to the tiny cups of sauce. The crowd had expanded, and Daniel wound his way around dozens, bringing the prized meat sticks to Sam, who sat, wiping her brow, looking tired but satisfied.

She took a bite and groaned, rolling her eyes. "I never thought I'd miss meat this much."

"Right? Tell me about it." Daniel flopped down next to her, extending his hand to Fenton's dog, Dunkin' who was staring up at him with hopeful eyes. The dog licked his hand clean of the sauce and meat juice. "I'm beat, and the party's just starting."

"Nightmares again?"

"Yeah." He frowned. "You know, Carter said the nightmares are likely trauma-based."

"And we all have trauma, so yes, that makes sense."

"Except it doesn't." Daniel replied, frowning.

"Why do you say that?"

"Well, the *kids* keep having nightmares, too. What trauma have they got? Us? Sure, we've all got trauma in spades, but the kids? They know nothing other than this place. Nothing but love and family. So why are they having nightmares?"

Sam's face was thoughtful. "I never thought of that." She frowned. "Nightmares are normal for kids, too. Psychologically speaking, we have nightmares for a variety of reasons - stress, anxiety, life transitions, and they help our brains to cope and deal with daytime stressors. Dr. Carter would tell you that nightmares are common in young children."

"Huh. Well, I'm going to talk to Carter about it at our next session." His voice petered off, his attention turning toward the stage.

A tapping on the microphone and Maria said, "Please welcome Mayor Smart to the stage."

She nodded to Alex Smart, who stepped up on stage among the resounding applause.

"Welcome everyone."

A response rose from the crowd, scattered clapping.

"Okay, so first order of business. Happy Landfall Day, everyone!"

There were cheers and whistles from the crowd and more clapping.

"Thank you for electing me your mayor. I'll do my best to fill the shoes of Jackson Sebring, Martin Phoenix and Captain Aaronson. They all have some rather big shoes to fill and I have a slightly smaller shoe size, but I'll give it a go."

There was scattered laughter and applause.

"We've come a long way in six years. Especially now that we've welcomed just a small portion of the Nostradamus, with many more to come. We've made babies, built houses, and planted crops. There are the mining operations up in the east, along with fishing boats pulling in new species to study and possibly assimilate into our diet besides the slickfish." He grimaced, and the crowd groaned. The fish, while edible and nutritionally adequate, had not tasted good. Not at all. However, nutritionally speaking, they were gold for the soil. The compost they created was stinky, but it helped the Terran plants grow faster than expected.

"And the first cotton crop up north is a success, so we can look forward to some cotton fabric soon. And best of all," he nodded at Anton, "Webster over there is slow-smoking our first bull. So, in case your nose isn't working or your half dead, the delectable smells you've been enjoying are sitting over on sticks with dipping sauce. Get them while you can. If you snooze, you lose."

More laughter and applause.

His face took on a more serious look. "This world is full of mysteries, anomalies. We are still working on how we can help the Mayflower and we continue to monitor the situation. The ship is intact and those in Cryo are safe for now. We still are investigating the Paulownia tree fungus and we will keep you updated when we know more." He paused, took a breath and then continued, "This planet can be our home, is our home, even now. We are laying in place the support and the infrastructure for the tomorrows yet to come. It's hard work, it's backbreaking, but damn it, we are doing it. We are creating a future for ourselves on an alien world and we... will... succeed!"

The crowd roared and applauded.

Alex grinned. "There are rides for the kids, hooch over in the corner, amazing beef and pork, and don't forget your flower crowns. Have fun, everyone. Happy Landfall Day!"

Instead of the last round of whoops and applause that Daniel expected from the crowd, there was instead a growing murmur of alarm and shouts. The crowd's attention turned away from Alex and the stage and instead toward the open northeast corner. A Zarmunicorn stood at the edge of the square. Zarmunicorns were shy, and they wanted nothing to do with humans or their settlements. The presence of one here now was not just unusual, but exceedingly rare.

Crouched on its back, legs dangling on either side of the Zarmunicorn's flank, was something that might have once been human. The creature was bony, its body wasted and weak. Streaks of dark green fungus and yellowed strands of exposed muscle marred its skin. It was naked, mostly. A strip of what might be fabric or fungus covered its groin. Its legs and arms held sickly yellowish-white pustules surrounded by the dark green, sometimes almost gray, fungal growths. Large patches of the growths ran down its limbs like an infection. The intact skin was ghostly white, almost translucent.

The eyes sunken in their sockets. Daniel was reminded of the blind cave fish and their white, translucent flesh and white, unseeing eyes. This creature wasn't blind, and its eyes weren't white and unseeing, but it clearly had impaired vision and it looked very sick. This thing ...this ...*man*... looked familiar. Very familiar. In fact, it looked a lot like a man long lost and declared dead... Nathan Zradce.

Daniel's feet propelled him forward, charging toward Zradce. He'd spent *months* searching for this man. This *murderer*. This religious zealot and psychopath. As the years had passed, he'd accepted that he must be dead, had to be dead. And yet, here he was… alive. After all that he'd done. The agony he'd caused. The fear. His hands clenched into fists as he skidded to a stop a few feet from the Zarmunicorn. It held still. He'd never seen a live one up close like this. They were skittish creatures and avoided the human colonists. This one, however, did not move, not at all.

The creature once known as Nathan Zradce croaked, "I've come to warn you. You aren't safe. No one is safe." And then his eyes closed, and he slumped, tumbling from the Zarmunicorn onto the hard ground.

Not a Man

Date: 02.23.2110

The Zarmunicorn, freed of its unwanted baggage, reared and bolted. Whatever had compelled it to carry this man to Sagan Base, it was now released. It wasted no time. Within seconds, the creature had disappeared from sight, heading for the northwestern edge of the forest.

The response to Nathan Zradce arriving in their midst had been quick. Perry Elkins, recently revived from Cryo on the Nostradamus, and filling in for

Carrie Schrader as head physician at the med center while she was on maternity leave; enlisted several men to help bundle Zradce onto a stretcher. They disappeared into the Med Center with him, and Daniel returned to where Sam stood gaping.

Sam's eyes were wide in shock. "Was that?"

"Nathan Zradce? Yeah. Or what's left of him." Daniel answered grimly. His mind was awhirl. Where had Nathan been? How had he survived? While many of the native plants were edible, Zarmina's fauna and flora remained a small part of their diets. The animal meats tasted off, and the vegetation often had rather severe diuretic effects.

I suppose it's possible *he could have lived off the land.*

Around them, people were murmuring. Those from Nostradamus had never met Zradce, but they had certainly heard of the Cryo sabotage. A group of children, Daniel and Sam's included, ran past, unaware of what had just occurred. They were far too busy playing games and wrestling for treats. They seemed marvelously unaware that the festive energy of the crowd was gone, replaced by fear and anxious glances.

"It just can't be. How could he have survived out there?!" Sam asked. "Did he say anything?"

Daniel nodded, chewing on his lip. "He said he came to warn us. He said we aren't safe."

"What the hell does that mean?"

"I don't know, Sam. I don't know."

Nathan's comm badge beeped, and he tapped it. "Medry here."

Alex's voice came through, "We need you at the Med Center, Daniel. We're calling an Emergency Council meeting."

"Right. On my way." He met Sam's eyes, tried to smile. "Good thing you aren't on the Council anymore." She'd resigned shortly after Luke's birth at the end of 2104. Finding someone to watch the kids every time the Council was called had just been too much. "Right, well, I've got to go. Try to enjoy the festivities."

"Yeah, right." She plastered a smile on her face and added, "I'll do my best." As he turned away, she said, "And Daniel? I hope you get some answers."

A small crowd of people gathered outside of the medical center. Nearly all of them were the original colonists, Nathan Zradce's intended victims. Their once-festive smiles replaced with grim mouths and suspicious anger.

As Daniel approached, the crowd parted the way for him. Even now, six years later, his status as a hero had not diminished. Before he ran for mayor, Alex Smart had asked Daniel why Daniel hadn't tried out for the position. "They'd elect you for life in a hot minute."

Daniel had not been the slightest bit interested in the added responsibility. He had a good life with Sam and the kids. Between designing bespoke houses for newly decanted refugees from the Nostradamus, raising their small little horde of kids, activities with friends who also had kids, and serving on the Council, he barely had time for the hiking and rock climbing he loved so much back on Earth. Life was full. If there was a way to fit any more living into his days, he didn't know how.

Alex Smart was now in his late 20s and seemed happily single. Although from what Daniel had heard from Sam, there were a couple of young women determined to change that. He had a level head on his shoulders, was well spoken, thoughtful, and damned good at handling some of the more difficult colonists. Alex had also spent over two years working with Eric Stryder, who served as Chief of Police. He'd seen the darker underbelly of the human condition and not so much as blinked. Daniel had happily endorsed Alex for mayor.

Alex waited for him just inside the glass doors of the entryway. He tipped his head toward the hallway on the left. "He's this way. They are stabilizing him now."

Daniel nodded, saying nothing, and they headed down the hallway. "You got close to him. Some others said they heard him speak."

"Yeah. He said we aren't safe."

"What the hell does that mean?" Alex asked, frowning.

"The guy is nuts. It might mean nothing," Daniel replied, his words clipped. He wanted to believe it was all bullshit, the ravings of a madman. Nathan Zradce was a psychopath, a murderer, or completely unhinged. And it didn't really matter which it was to Daniel. At the same time as he said it, though, his gut was telling him it was shortsighted to dismiss Zradce out of hand. Daniel had to understand the man's survival and his motives for returning. Somehow, Zradce's reappearance felt key to their future on this planet.

The room was full of medical personnel, and the members of the Council were outside, murmuring to themselves as Daniel approached. Several of the members had changed over the years. Jackson Sebring, after serving as mayor for two years, had pushed for young blood, and asked Alex Smart to take his place on the Council. Later, Anthony Vogt was brought into the Council. After all, it was Anthony's grandfather Steve Vogt who had discovered Zarmina's World.

It had taken half of a year for Daniel to stop being tongue-tied whenever he was in the older man's presence. It had been years since he had sat in the enormous auditorium with thousands of others and watched as Vogt announced the voyage to Zarmina's World, but it felt as if it were just yesterday. That speech had set him on the path, put him here on Zarmina's World. The man was an astronomy legend, after all. And damned if it hadn't left him tongue-tied and moon-eyed every time the man so much as looked at him. One day, Vogt had apparently had enough. He took Daniel to the local cantina, got him drunk as a skunk on moonshine, and they shot pool, with Anthony losing, horribly, to Daniel. After that, the older man was just Steve, not some astronomy god. Just a normal guy.

Carrie Schrader, heavily pregnant with twins, stood by Martin's side. She beckoned Daniel over. Her eyes were dark, troubled.

"He's dying. I can tell you that much. Whatever this fungal infection is, it appears to be everywhere. Throughout his tissues, his blood, organs, everything. I've literally seen nothing like it. It defies scientific reason. Fungus shouldn't be able to survive inside the body, and yet, Zradce's tissues are riddled with it." She rubbed the small of her back. Nearly full-term, her ankles looked swollen.

"Sit down, Doc, take a load off." Perry Elkins emerged from Zradce's room, shaking his head. "Or else those babies will make an appearance tonight."

"Bring it on," she snapped back. "Between the nightmares, backaches and heartburn after I eat, I'm ready for this to be over."

Perry laughed and pointed to a nearby chair. "Rest. He's not going anywhere." He folded his arms over his chest and waited until Carrie sat, then shoved a chair over for her to put her feet up.

"Dr. Schrader has already told you most of what we know. This man is dying. How he is still alive is frankly mystifying. His organs are failing and he moves in and out of consciousness." He turned and locked eyes with Daniel. "He's asked to speak with the Council, as well as his former wife."

"Has anyone relayed that to Jennifer?" Daniel asked.

"Yes." Zach Jenkins replied, his face grim, "I contacted her and relayed the message. She refused." Several sets of eyebrows raised in response. "She said there was nothing she had to say, or hear, from him."

"Fair enough." Fenton said, his voice hard, lips in a thin line. "Can't say I don't feel the same way. I take it personally when someone murders folks on board my ship."

Alex spoke up. "Well, I guess we should get in there. Yeah?"

He looked awful, almost worse than he had outside when Daniel first saw him. Nathan Zradce was shockingly pale, and in the low light, his skin mottled, moist. His breaths were shallow, infrequent, and labored. The fungus that infected him had rotted away patches of his skin in some places and Daniel could see exposed muscles in his jaw and neck, as well as his arms, pus pockets running along them. Daniel suppressed a shudder of revulsion and another emotion, something that felt almost like pity. It faded fast, replaced by a growing anger.

"We lowered the lights. From the paleness of his skin, and his reaction to light, I think he's been somewhere dark." Carrie said quietly, settling into a chair in the corner and groaning slightly as she raised her swollen ankles onto another chair. The rest of them stood in a u-shape, keeping their distance. Whether it was from fear of infection, distaste for the man who had nearly ended the lives of everyone in Cryo, or a combination, Daniel wasn't sure.

"He's not conscious," Martin noted, frowning.

"He slips in and out." Perry answered, shrugging. "We can't do much about it. We put him on IV fluids, an antifungal as well, but it caused issues, so we backed off. That's really the best we can do."

Daniel had certainly heard this before. Hadn't Carrie said he would never wake up? And yet he did. And she'd said he'd never be anything but a vegetable. But not only did the man wake up, he got up and walked away from a medical facility. He'd disappeared into the wilderness on an alien world and somehow survived for nearly six years. As far as he was concerned, this man was capable of damn near anything. He stood, staring at Nathan, waiting for him to wake up. He had been fooled once, but he wouldn't be again.

The man who had been Nathan Zradce stirred. "Jenn..." His voice croaked. It sounded as if he hadn't used it in a long, long time.

"Jennifer isn't coming. She doesn't wish to speak with you." Daniel answered, before anyone else could.

He felt Anthony Vogt's hand on his shoulder and wondered if the older man was trying to ensure Daniel didn't act on his urge to strangle the creature in the hospital bed.

Nathan squinted, his eyes unfocused, bloodshot. "Daniel?"

"Yep." Daniel felt his teeth grind together. A fury was rising inside him. The life he had with Sam, with the kids, his friends, his fellow colonists - this man, this monster, had nearly taken all of that from him. If he hadn't come into Cryo when he did, how many would have died? How many more? The room took on a red hazy hue. He hadn't realized just how much anger was inside him until he saw Zradce in the flesh. All the searching, and finally deciding the bastard had to be dead, only for him to show back up again. This close, however, he had to agree with Carrie's and Doc Elkins assessment. This man would likely not survive the night.

"I'd ask you to forgive me... but... there is no... time. For that. There is... danger." His voice faded away as Nathan slid toward unconsciousness.

"Give him epinephrine or something." Daniel snapped, his almost insignificant medical knowledge rising with his anger and frustration. "If there is danger, we need to know it."

"That could kill him." Carrie interjected from the corner.

"He's already dying." He didn't give a damn if the sonofabitch died sooner and he was surprised anyone else did.

"Meaning he would die before he told us whatever he knows." Elkins added calmly. "Don't you think we need to know?"

Daniel had to concede that the doctors knew best. If there was some danger, and Nathan Zradce truly was trying to warn them, well, it was the least he could do after murdering seven people and attempting to murder far more.

"This world is... occupied. A vast... intel... intelligence. Its name is... Entity. And as... best... as I under... stand. Outro is... Entity's child..." Nathan croaked, struggling to form the words.

All eyes riveted on the dying man and, despite their revulsion, Daniel and the others moved closer as Nathan struggled to form each word.

Hours later, only two remained in the room - Daniel and Nathan Zradce, who was not a man, not anymore, but something else entirely. The others had left, in shock, with the agreement to say nothing until they could discuss the ramifications of it all in a meeting early the next day.

Outside the room in the corridor, stretched over several chairs, lay Perry Elkins. He snored softly.

Daniel sat in the dim room, watching, as Nathan Zradce took increasingly infrequent, labored gasps of air, followed by long seconds where his chest did not rise. Each time he stopped breathing, Daniel felt himself holding his breath alongside him. Nathan had told them everything. It had taken a while for him to get all the words out. To answer the many questions they had. But now they knew. Now, they finally had an answer to all the tiny little mysteries, inconsistencies, and random weird events.

The Paulownia forest succumbing to the weird fungus.

The nightmares.

What had actually killed the crew members of Mayflower.

And how, any day, a change in the solar winds could eliminate their one chance at survival. That

Entity's child, Outro, would take over the planet and declare war on the human colonists. They would die, horribly. Just as those on the ground at Heinlein Base had died on the far side of the planet.

Daniel's gaze never left Nathan. No matter what he knew, or even that the man had begged forgiveness in the end, he would trust nothing less than death before he could walk away. And now, his mind reeled at the thought that even then, they would not be safe. Not even close. Everything they had built, the progress they had made, the children and life they had here, it all had to end. This was not their home. It couldn't be. And Daniel's mind spun with fear and dread at their limited options.

Nathan Zradce gave a slight breathy sigh, which was followed by a soft, wet, almost crackling sound. And then Nathan's chest was still. The vital signs on the monitor to the right of his head flatlined.

"Hey, Doc?"

There was a shuffle of feet, and Perry appeared, rubbing his eyes.

"I need you to call it."

The doctor looked at the screens, then reached for one of Nathan's hands, then his neck, before looking at the time displayed above the bed. "Time of death 0300 hours, on the dot." He pulled a sheet over the body, rubbed his eyes again, his back hunched. "What do you think of what he said? About that Entity and Outro business?"

"I think we are in danger. A lot of danger."

Perry nodded. "I was afraid you were going to say that." He reached out, clapped Daniel on the shoulder, "Get some rest, Medry. You and the rest of the Council have some hard decisions to make tomorrow. And don't worry, my lips are sealed. That's why they pay you all the big bucks. *You* get to tell everyone the bad news, not me."

Daniel winced, "Yeah. Thanks." He stared for a moment at the corpse that remained. "What are you going to do about the remains?"

"I'll autopsy him now. We'll study the shit out of this fungus. Maybe get other options on the table for dealing with this Outro creature."

Daniel nodded and left without another word. Sam was waiting. All he wanted right now was to wrap his arms around her and try to forget what he knew. At least for a couple of hours.

What Now?

Date: 02.24.2110

The five other Council members sat waiting, eyes haunted, faces drawn. They looked up at him as he slipped in the door, a tray of coffee held in one hand, a sack of muffins in the other. Fenton's wife, Joanna, had flagged him down as he walked past the house.

"Take these to the meeting, would you, Daniel? Fenton forgot them." She had said, her face somber.

"Thanks, Joanna. Will do."

As he handed out the coffee cups and the muffins, he looked over at the others. Even though he had stayed while the rest left, he doubted any of them had gotten a decent night's rest.

They sat in silence for a moment, sipping the coffee, numbly eating the muffins. They were on automatic, still processing the news they had received.

Alex swallowed, pushed the nibbled muffin away from him, and cleared his throat. "NARA, please record the following meeting."

"Recording."

"I, Mayor Alex Smart, bring the Sagan Base Governing Council to order. Special session, date February 24th, 2110, to discuss the information and warning brought to us by Nathan Zradce, former crew member of the Calypso and accused saboteur."

He rubbed his eyes, shoulders sagging. "Formalities aside, I'm still processing this. I think I managed an hour of sleep last night." He shook his head, half-laughed, "At least I didn't have any nightmares."

"If there is anything to be thankful for, I guess it would be that." Fenton Aaronson spoke from the far end of the table. "Although, I felt like I was in the same boat. I barely slept."

A small murmur of agreement came from the rest of the group.

Anthony Vogt turned to Daniel, "You stayed then? Until he passed?"

"Yeah. It was, I don't know, after 0300."

"Did he say anything more?"

"No."

Anthony sighed. "Okay, so let's review what we know so far. Two fungal intelligences - Entity and Outro. Entity is the parent of Outro, but does not control it. Outro is in control of the far side of the planet, while Entity handles our side. And it is Outro that killed the crew and anyone revived from Cryo, and it doesn't want us there at all."

"And it also killed another bipedal species, according to Nathan and the reports and images of the ruins we received from Heinlein base before it went dark," Martin Phoenix added.

"Entity seems... if not friendly, at least not antagonistic toward us," Anthony continued.

"Entity destroyed the Paulownia forest in retaliation for us damaging its fields, though." Zach Jenkins argued.

"Yeah, but we're still breathing." Daniel countered. "And we've been here for years. Outro murdered the others in, what, three months?"

"But Nathan says that Entity plans to leave." Zach added. "And when it does, Outro inherits Entity's territory."

Fenton frowned, "And we don't know *when* this will happen?"

"All that Nathan said was 'when the solar winds blow' - whatever the hell that means." Daniel growled, frustrated, eyes burning with exhaustion.

"We have to assume this solar wind thing could happen any time. Although, with this level of intelligence, and how Nathan described Entity and Outro, both creatures are likely older than humankind. What does time mean to something like that?" Fenton added.

"In our need to leave, we cannot forget that there are nearly one hundred thousand innocent people over there. Still alive, according to our reports. We have to get them out of there." Alex said, raking a hand through his hair.

"Not to mention we need to build more Cryo units for the additional numbers we have and ensure that all that we already have are in working order." Fenton replied.

"So, are we leaving? Is that a for sure?" Martin Phoenix asked, the shadows under his eyes prominent.

"I don't see that we have a choice." Anthony answered. "This planet is occupied. It has been occupied all along, and we are trespassing. No matter that we didn't know, that we couldn't have known. We do not belong here. Entity was trying to tell us - through the nightmares it sent - we just weren't able to understand."

The room was quiet. The enormity of the loss struck each member of the Council. Years of their lives, an Earth still in ruins, possibly unlivable, and everything they had done to create a home here in vain.

"We need to tell the others." Daniel's voice felt overly loud in the silent room. "They will need time to process this." Several others nodded. "And I need to talk to Entity myself, see if I can get more details on when the solar winds might come, and..."

"How in the hell are you going to manage that?" Fenton barked, "Nathan was the only one who could communicate. We don't even know how he managed it, and he's dead."

"He told us how," Daniel answered grimly. "Through blood contact."

"And you believe him?" Alex asked.

"Yes, I do. Just as much as we all can see now how Entity and Outro control this world."

"We've seen evidence of it," Martin argued, "But the man was unhinged. And he also said that Entity told him he wasn't human when he obviously is."

"Not according to some of the test results," Daniel countered. His fingers flew across his tablet and moments later, each of the other five Council members' tablets pinged in response. "Dr. Schrader and Dr. Elkins ran extensive tests on his blood samples. Dr. Elkins stayed up and performed the autopsy early this morning. Whoever, or whatever, Nathan Zradce was before, he was not human, at least not quite. The differences are tiny, nearly indistinguishable, but it points to a parallel species. He is *not* Homo sapiens sapiens. Whether the fungal aspects have changed him on a genetic level, or he was always this way, we don't know yet. But he is not like us. And that is how Entity could not only heal his traumatic brain injuries and body enough that he woke up in the first place, it is also how

Zradce survived with a fungal invasion inside of his body for the past six years."

Fenton blinked, "And you want to repeat that... blood contact... in order to speak with Entity?"

"Yes."

"Medry, do you know how insane that sounds?" Fenton asked, a look of horror on his face. "What if this goes wrong? What if you are infected with this fungus like Zradce was? Have you thought of that?"

"I have. And I'm willing to take that chance because it's worth the risk, especially because..." Daniel smiled then, "I want to ask Entity to negotiate a truce between us and Outro. We need to rescue those people in Cryo."

By noon, they had a rough plan of action. By mid-afternoon, over one thousand colonists stood in the square at Sagan Base, the rest scattered throughout the continent listening, as the Council outlined what the shocking arrival of Nathan Zradce had truly meant. It was the end of their time on this planet. And there was the additional urgency of possibly returning to a planet in ruins.

Emotions ran high. Questions, so many, pounded the Council at every turn.

In the end, the town hall meeting had ended. The colonists had dispersed, some heading for the cantina to drown their sorrows, others to their homes. They didn't have all the answers, not yet, but a plan was coalescing, along with a hope that Entity could help negotiate a treaty with Outro and allow them to save the lives of so many people.

"Why you, Daniel?" Sam asked later that evening. They lay in their bed, alone, which was a miracle. Usually, their room was busy with kids coming and going at all hours. Instead, all of their children remained tucked in their own beds, sleeping blissfully, no nightmares, just deep, dreamless snoozing.

Daniel pulled her closer, closed his eyes. He didn't want to talk about it. Not for another instant. That's all they had done all day - talk, try to figure things out, including the town meeting that had broken the dark news to their friends and neighbors. The hits had just kept coming, and his mind and body were exhausted, filled with conflicting emotions over the loss of all that they had worked for, and the unknown of what was to come. Could they extricate the Mayflower from the far side of the planet? Would they have enough materials and space aboard Nostradamus and Calypso for all the children and colonists? Would

Earth even be able to sustain them upon their return? His head ached. So did his heart.

"It began with me. Perhaps it should end with me."

"That's bullshit and you know it," Sam snapped as she flipped around to face him in the gloom. "You walked into that situation on the Cryo deck and miraculously survived it. You didn't *cause* this. It didn't *begin* with you. You *finished* it. That murderous lunatic is dead, and good riddance. Why would you endanger yourself by trying to talk to a creature that doesn't seem to care if we live or die?"

"Because it needs doing. Because I have hope." Daniel replied softly. "Someone needs to step up and try."

He could see her shaking her head. "Okay, but why *you*? Why not someone else? You have children who need you. I need you."

"Everyone at Sagan Base has someone who loves them and needs them." He countered and shrugged. "Why shouldn't it be me?" He reached out, slipped a lock of hair away from her face, and gently kissed her. "I will not go into a cave and hang out with Entity for the next six years. I'm not planning on dying. This is different. I want to negotiate a temporary truce, send a team, and get

Mayflower out of there. It would make the difference between over ninety-five thousand people living or dying. What about what they need, Sam?"

"You aren't some damned white knight, Daniel Medry. You are a father, my partner." Sam said, the heat of her anger fading into sadness, fear. "Promise me you will negotiate and then get the hell out of there, even if you aren't successful. Promise me."

He kissed her again. "I promise."

We Must Save Them

Date: 02.25.2110

The flitter was full. It could hold six, and all six seats were occupied, plus a load of medical supplies crammed into the back. Perry Elkins had handed the reins of power back to Carrie Schrader temporarily and insisted on accompanying the group.

"If something goes wrong, you don't want to wait for two hours for proper medical care."

Zach Jenkins piloted the flitter, and Anthony Vogt, Fenton Aaronson, and Eric Stryder filled the rest of the seats. There had been plenty more who had volunteered at the town hall meeting the day before. By now, all the colonists, whether or not they had been at the town hall, knew that staying on Zarmina's World was no longer a viable option. Whether they had accepted that future was a different question entirely.

Of the group, Eric Stryder looked the worse for wear. As Chief of Police in Sagan Base, he had one lone officer under him. There had been two drunken brawls late in the night, prompting him to not only deal with closing the cantina early but also making sure each of those involved got home safely to sleep it off. The dark circles under his eyes showed just how little sleep he had gotten. When the flitter had shown up outside of his door, Anthony Vogt had raised his eyebrows at the younger man.

"Rough night, eh? You sure you don't want to rest a little longer? Skip the fun?"

Eric shook his head and climbed aboard. "Not a chance, old man. I gotta see this damn fungus for myself."

The ride was quiet. Daniel was thankful for that. His thoughts swirled. The dream of seeing Toby again had taken root in his mind and heart. There was plenty to mourn. Walking away from everything they had worked on for the past six years was hard, incredibly so. But the thought of seeing his son again was a small nugget of joy and hope that had grown in his heart. When Daniel had left Earth, it was with the dream of a pristine planet, a new start. His son had two parents - and Luke and Janine were everything his boy needed. He had believed that Luke was everything that he was not. A parent. A mature adult, although he was older by several years. Luke had always been a person capable of being responsible for another life. Whereas Daniel, even as he found himself responsible for Luke after they became orphans, he still wasn't "dad material" as Janine had so astutely put it.

In the years since, from the Cryo Deck incident to the moments he held each of his newborn children in his arms, he now understood how capable he was. He'd let others tell him who he was and what he was capable of. And he'd let his own fears rule him. Fear of not being enough. Of being *less* than what was needed.

Daniel didn't know what kind of place he could have in Toby's life. But he wanted to at least try to be someone his son could know. In some ways, it felt as if fate was calling him home.

"You really think you can get this Outro to listen?" Zach asked as they raced along the open prairie, heading for the dark expanse of forest in the distance. "To agree to let us get the Mayflower out of there?"

Daniel shrugged. "Treaty or bust, I guess."

Zach snorted. A moment of silence passed, and he said, "Medry, if anyone can do it, you can."

Daniel struggled with what to say before finally managing a gruff, "Thanks, man."

They followed the AGPS coordinates Daniel had logged during his search for Zradce in the colony's first year. The description of the cave that Nathan had given, combined with his own memories of seeing it, heading toward it to check it out, and being interrupted by Luke's birth, had been all that Daniel needed. Nathan had described the cave as a super-node, a place where Entity was strongest in its sensory ability. If he was going to communicate with Entity, it would be there. The forest was immense, and they had been flying over it for a while when a wide gap in the trees appeared.

A moment later, the flitter landed in the large clearing with a small jolt. The ground was uneven here and rocky. The surrounding trees were dense, far too dense for them to fly through.

"This is the last open spot. It's about two klicks to the cave." Daniel told the others as they slipped on packs and slid their water bottles into pockets. "Not too bad of a trek, really."

Two hours later, they found it. The last time he had stood in the spot indicated by the APGS records, he'd searched in vain for the cave he was sure he'd seen. Now it was open, plain as day, the vines no longer obscuring it. It felt as if Entity had opened the curtains and was welcoming them inside.

They stood there, staring. The cave's opening was large, at least three meters in height and width, the darkness inside black as pitch. The entrance of the cave remained covered in fungal growths in a rainbow of colors. Fungus was prevalent on the planet, especially since there was no direct sunlight, but here it was dense, incredibly so. Wherever they looked, on the trees, the rocks, the ground, there was a kaleidoscope of fungal growths.

"This is it. This is the fungal node Nathan described." Daniel muttered, "I was feet away from him and never knew. If I'd just walked forward a couple dozen more feet, I would have seen this entrance, even if it was covered in vines."

"And you would have found him, brought him back, and we would have put him on trial for murder." Fenton added. "Per the guidelines of the RUSA, which the Calypso remained under the purview of, despite its international contingent, his crimes would have earned him a death sentence. We might never have learned about Entity or Outro until it was far too late."

Daniel said nothing. And Fenton continued, "Face it, Medry. The woulda, coulda, shoulda's will be the death of us all. Nothing matters but the here and now."

"True that." Anthony chimed in.

Eric Stryder hit the Comm patch on his shirt. "Sagan Base, Sagan Base, this is Chief Stryder. We have reached the cave and are heading in."

"Roger that, Chief. Stay safe." Eric's comm chirped in return.

Daniel turned to look at Eric and the others. "Perhaps I should go in by myself. Just in case."

"No way, man. You aren't alone in this and you aren't going in without us." Eric frowned. "I'm not going back to Sam with that kind of news. She would not take it well."

"What about three of us go inside and three stay out, in case things go south?" Perry Elkins suggested.

"Fine."

With Perry and Eric directly behind him, Daniel led the way, the three men swallowed into the black of the cave in seconds. Within moments, and a bend in the passageway, and the light from the entrance hole was gone. Their beams darted one way, then another, illuminating rock walls covered in mushrooms, thousands of varieties, in all the colors.

Daniel gaped at them. If he thought that the fungal growths outside had been thick, he'd underestimated just how dense and prolific they could be. The passage had emptied into a vast cavern that ate the light from their flashlights. Daniel ran the light along the floor of the cave, watched as some of the fungus shrank away from it, while other fungi leaned out, moving in ways Daniel had never seen such life move.

The cave was warm, wet, and he could smell the damp scent of rot. He stopped near a low archway of rock and watched the growths along the ground and walls move gently toward him. He suppressed the urge to flee. This cave was alive and he could feel something otherworldly, a presence, pushing against his thoughts. Was it Entity? Would Entity perceive him as a threat? He wasn't sure, but he knew he needed to stop, to do what he had come to do, and hope it was enough.

"What now?" Eric asked, his voice hushed.

"Now I see if I can talk to it." Daniel answered and knelt, sliding his backpack off of his shoulders. He slid a knife out of his pocket and unsheathed it. One deep, calming breath in, and then he slid the sharp blade firmly into the flesh of his left hand. A gush of warm blood followed the burning electric shock sensation. The light from Eric's flashlight focused on Daniel's bloody hand as he pressed it firmly into the fungus growing along the cave floor.

At first, for what seemed like a long time, there was nothing. No sound from the men standing on each side of him, and nothing from the creature Nathan had claimed was there.

Perhaps it was all in his mind. The lunatic ravings of a madman.

Then the sensation he had felt when he first walked into the cave, that of a presence, something not remotely human, flared bright. His thinking, his connection with everything he understood as reality suddenly slipped sideways and fell off a cliff as something enormous brushed against his mind.

human

Oh... shit.

He jerked back. The connection breaking the second his bloodied hand pulled away from the fungal clump, his blood glistening along the frilled edges.

"What happened?" Perry asked, an edge of panic in his gruff voice.

"It's..." Daniel struggled to find the words, "It's there, and it's real. Holy shit, it's real."

He sat back on his haunches, his uninjured hand on the cave floor, steadying his body. He stared up at the two men. "It's so... big."

They stared back, looking both excited and afraid, silent until Eric quirked an eyebrow. "That's what she said."

Perry rolled his eyes. "Biggest discovery of another intelligent lifeform in the cosmos and this guy has to make it raunchy. I'm growing old here. Look, can you talk to it or not?"

Daniel nodded, "Yeah, I think I can." He put his bloody hand back on the mass of fungus and waited for the connection. Nothing. He pulled his hand back and stared at it. "The wound stopped bleeding."

He made a second slice with the knife, deeper this time, and placed it back into the fungus. Seconds ticked by and then he fell off the cliff, deep into the space where this other creature existed in the ether.

human

"Entity."

yes

"My name is Daniel. Daniel Medry."

danielmedry

nathan spoke of you

"Did he?"

yes

danielmedry good man

danielmedry listen

"Yes. I will. I come to ask for your help, Entity."

help how

"Help us negotiate peace. With Outro."

negotiate

"Yes."

outro does not listen

humans do not listen

well matched

If the presence didn't feel so completely alien, Daniel might have suspected an almost dry humor in its response.

"I'm sorry if it seems we did not listen. I promise you, we did not know you were trying to communicate."

nathan explain

human rest state

not conscious

"Yes, Nathan explained to us that you tried to communicate. We have all had nightmares, not realizing it was you trying to reach us, until Nathan told us."

nathan dead

"Yes, Entity. Nathan died."

entity not save

"Nathan told us you tried to save him."

too different

"I hope you might help us save the others. There are many humans still on the far side of the planet. They are in Cryo pods. We must save them."

cryo

"It is like sleep, or a rest state, but we do not age or need sustenance during Cryo. It allows humans to cross long distances and not age too quickly."

rest state

humans live

short lives

a blip

"We have brief lives, I guess. Especially to something like you. Can you help us, Entity?"

outro does not listen

"Could you pass a message along to Outro, perhaps?"

yes

message

"Could you tell Outro we wish to take our people from the ship on the far side of the world and leave?"

yes

There was silence and then an abrupt disconnect. The world came crashing back and Daniel opened his eyes to the all-encompassing dark of the cave, broken only by Eric and Perry's flashlights. He looked down at his hand. Once again, it had stopped bleeding.

He reached for his knife, remembering the parallel cut most suicides don't know about. The one most effective if someone really wants to bleed. He looked up, met Perry's eyes and sliced again, watching the older man's eyes widen with alarm.

"Medry!"

"In for a penny..."

He felt the blood gushing now, a slick river of red running down his wrist, hand, fingers. The world slipped sideways.

what is penny

"Nothing. It's... nothing."

entity ask

outro answer

"Okay."

answer no

Damn it.

"Do you know what we can offer Outro to make it change its mind?"

Daniel felt as if he were at the end of a grueling hike. His head hurt. Occasionally, in small bursts, he could hear Eric and Perry's voices, but they came from far away, as if he had walked away and left them behind.

take ship

ship is

abomination

Daniel felt dizzy, tired. His thoughts were sludge. What about the ship? Why would these creatures think the colonists would leave the ship? He thought about what Nathan had said, how he had described these creatures. They were gardeners. Not just Entity, but Outro as well. And humans had set an enormous ship down in Outro's garden. Oh, shit. No wonder Outro was angry.

"Wait. Outro thought we would leave the ship there? No. We would take it with us. We need it to travel back to our home planet. Its side of the world would be whole again."

how long

"How long would it take?"

yes

"Days. A week at most." He thought for a moment. *"Single rotation of the planet."*

There was a long pause.

acceptable

"Outro will allow it?"

yes

"And those puffball mushrooms Outro sowed. Can it remove them so that we have safe passage?"

yes

four rotations

then rain

then safe

humans remove ship

"Yes. We will remove it. We will send it into orbit and it will never return to the surface again."

humans leave world

"Yes, we will leave this world. We have already begun preparations."

good
danielmedry stop now
dying

"Thank you, Entity."

He felt the presence withdraw. As it did, the sound of voices, and not just Eric and Perry's, but Zach's and Fenton's and Anthony's as well, rushed towards him. He collapsed on the cave floor, cold and shivering, exhausted. Above him, were a sea of faces partially lit by flashlights. Hands held him, lifted him, and carried him back into the light.

Rescue Mission

Date: 03.05.2110

Daniel sat in the Communications Station and watched the screens. He tugged at the bandages on his left hand, wrist, and forearm, eager to remove them. Sam had insisted they stay on after he'd pulled open the skin around the sutures picking up their youngest the other day. And when he'd made the mistake of telling her he wanted to be on the rescue team, she'd glared at him.

"Are you insane?"

"What?"

Her hands perched on her hips, elbows out, her neck gyrating. "You just got out of the hospital! Your wounds haven't even healed and you want to go play the hero again! Enough, Daniel. Leave it to those whose specialties lie in maintaining and operating spacecraft."

He'd known better than to argue. She was right. As it was, he was still moving slow after that stint in the cave. Daniel had certainly had plenty of time to review the conversation he'd had with Entity as he lay in a hospital bed at the medical center. He remembered every word, even if he barely remembered the flight back. Sam had told him Perry gave him an emergency blood transfusion there on the ground outside of the cave. It saved his life, and he was damned lucky to be alive.

The flow of visitors had been constant until Perry put a stop to it.

"The man needs rest, people."

He'd received two more blood transfusions after they flew him back to Sagan Base. And his body had fought the transfusions, causing a fever, itching, and even trouble breathing and nausea. After his release from the med center, if he tried to do anything past sitting or eating, he'd get dizzy, his head aching.

They had sent the D.O.V.E. probes to the far side, much as they had done for the past two years, but now hourly. Alex linked Daniel in via his tablet, and this had kept Daniel occupied as his body healed. It had also kept him in bed, which mostly kept Sam mollified.

He watched the screens, eight of them, all from different viewpoints, and drummed his uninjured fingers on the table. There were five colonists, fully suited, on the ground. Each had cameras set into their helmets. And three drones that provided them with full 360-degree access.

The colonists had been monitoring the Mayflower from space for the past two years, watching as vines grew up the smooth sides of the ship, trying to claim it, cover it, and eradicate it from the surface. They had also received regular updates from Mayflower's NARA that the precious cargo inside was unharmed, safe in Cryo. And NARA had continued to supply them with images from its external sensors that revealed the hull of the ship remained intact, the vines merely a nuisance. The solar panels' advanced design allowed them to withstand the harsh conditions of space and the fiery atmospheric entry. And while the vines had affected their efficiency, it remained enough power, along with the nuclear reactor deep in the ship's heart, to maintain the minimal needs of Cryo for the tens of thousands of people sleeping within.

They had done as Entity said, waiting the four days and through torrential rains before even attempting an approach to the far side of the planet. They had watched from afar as the vines receded, and the strange puffball mushrooms, which had appeared with such abundance, now withered and died.

"It isn't enough that they are dead," Daniel noted, as he recounted his conversation with Entity. "They must also be washed away. Hence the need to wait for the rain."

And it had rained. Torrents and sheets, the winds whipping at the receding and dying vines, until two days later, the clear skies had shown it was go time. They weren't fools though, and unwilling to sacrifice anyone else, just in case Outro still held any malice toward them. They suited up in spacesuits and had lugged chemical showers with them to ensure they didn't track any of the deadly fungus onto Mayflower, the shuttle, or leave with it on their suits. Their planning and execution had to be meticulous.

"Rescue Team in place. No sign of puffball fungus."

"Roger that, Rescue Team. Proceed." He answered through the Comm, wishing he was there, but happy to at least be a part of it on this side.

Daniel watched as they fitted the outside hatch with the chemical shower, clear membrane walls on all sides, the motor and apparatus on the roof of it. Each suited figure entered, received a wash-down, and then proceeded inside once the hatch opened. The drones showed the figures disappear inside one by one. The last figure was Zach Jenkins, and the younger man waved for the camera as he entered the shower and then moved on inside of the massive ship. Inside, the team's suit cameras kept Daniel and the others up to date with visuals, and they watched as the team set up the mobile anti-fungal tanks and sprayers they had brought with them to make sure all surfaces inside were thoroughly decontaminated and safe.

"Rescue Team inside, decontamination protocols enacted."

"Roger that, Rescue Team."

Alex stretched in the chair beside him. "Wish I was there."

"Me too." Daniel muttered, feeling rather useless.

"Buck up, Medry. You're a hero for the second time. The only other person to commune with a planetwide entity is dead and you are still kicking. How many of those nine lives have you got left?"

Daniel opened his mouth to answer, before being interrupted by Wesley Perdue's voice over the comm.

"Rescue Team to NARA Mayflower, systems check."

"Checking all systems," NARA answered. And seconds later, "All systems are within operational capabilities."

"NARA, what are our fuel levels?"

"Sixty-eight point nine two of capacity."

"Sagan Base, we have enough for liftoff and return to Earth with a margin of twenty percent error."

"Roger that, Wesley, err, Rescue Team, prepare the countdown." Daniel turned to Alex. "Outro agreed to give us time, but I'll feel a lot better if we can get Mayflower out of there and back into orbit."

"Agreed." Fenton's voice came over the comm. "Decontamination complete and sealing hatch now."

Alex frowned. "They're leaving the shuttle?"

Daniel shook his head and grinned. "NARA? Please return the shuttle on autopilot. Make sure it's got a good arc in and out of atmosphere." Doing so would ensure the fiery re-entry cleansed the hull.

"Autopilot return enacted."

"NARA will give it time in space and then back through the atmosphere. If anything is on the hull or the landing gear, it'll freeze and then burn. And just to be triple-sure, we'll run it through an automated chemical shower in the hangar."

No one wanted to die like Mayflower's crew members had, and they were taking every step, and then some, to ensure that didn't happen.

The Council debated extensively whether Entity, and especially Outro, could be trusted. Were the creatures capable of deception? They really did not know. Daniel, however, swung the vote.

"I believe Outro will uphold its end of the agreement," he'd said weakly as he linked into the Council meeting via his Comm unit, still recovering in the hospital. "Nothing about Entity felt deceptive. Both beings did their best to communicate with us, through the dreams we were all having, to the destruction of the Paulownia forest two years ago. Entity was more patient, sure, and far less deadly than Outro, but I think Outro will listen to Entity, and allow us to clear its land of Mayflower."

Soon after that, they had voted overwhelmingly in favor of rescuing Mayflower. It was, after all, something they had wanted to do from the start. But the vines rapidly moving in had been a tremendous concern, as had the deadly pathogen released by the puffball mushrooms. It had been hard to wait, to sit by and do nothing for so long, especially when humanity was literally on the brink of extinction.

"So far, so good." Daniel muttered, more to himself than Alex or the others in the room. He'd gotten lightheaded as the team moved over the terrain outside of the massive ship and realized he was holding his breath, terrified something would go wrong.

The men who had accompanied him to the cave were in this room, or part of the team on the far side of the planet. He'd learned that they'd heard nothing on Daniel's side when he contacted Entity.

"I'll admit, man, it was creepy as hell to stand there and do nothing as you bled into that fungus." Eric had told him later. "You stared into the distance like you could see something. Your mouth moved, but no sound came out. Perry kept talking to you, but you didn't respond, not at all. Except those two times you stopped bleeding. I shit you not. I kept wondering if that thing had somehow taken over and possessed you."

"I wish you could have seen and heard what I did," Daniel answered. "It felt like I was touching a tiny corner of it, and it was immense, yet curious."

"Yeah, no. I'll stick to my tiny existence where planet-sized fungal intelligences are left to control a world and I get to go home to Earth. This has been real, and fun, and really fun, but I'm good with going the hell back home." Eric had said in response. He wasn't the only one, either. Even though Daniel had tried to explain that Entity and Outro were like gardeners and scientists, there was a level of fear that ran deep in many. The thought that they had been trampling about in something's garden or science experiment was not reassuring, not at all. And despite their many reasons for coming here in the first place, everyone seemed more than willing to leave, and as soon as humanly possible.

"Sagan Base, countdown to liftoff beginning in twenty-three minutes."

"Roger that, Rescue Team."

The minutes ticked by as the team moved about the inside of the lifeship. They had the fuel; the vines had receded, and the outside and inside had been thoroughly decontaminated. Following a thorough inspection by NARA, and a subsequent double-check by human eyes, the team strapped in for the final ten minutes of the countdown. It was time.

"Sagan Base, counting down to ten, nine, eight, seven, six, five, four, three, two, one, and..."

Daniel could hear the roar of the engines and thrusters over the comm, followed by static and a long silence.

Once again, he held his breath as the seconds ticked by, sucking in oxygen in the overwhelming silence of the room. *Please be a success. Please. We need these people.*

They needed the extra Cryo units to accommodate the additional children born on the planet. But more than that, Earth and humanity's future hung in the balance. Nearly one hundred thousand people lay sleeping, unaware that they had not only crossed the stars, but would now return to a world in ruins, perhaps unlivable. Still, what choice did they have? They were on a world that belonged to someone, something else.

"Sagan Base, we have exited the atmosphere and are establishing orbit."

The room erupted into cheers.

All of Our Tomorrows

Date: 09.07.2111

The house was in shambles. Thousands of things surrounded them they couldn't keep. Couldn't take with them up to Calypso. Art, toys, books made on the surface by the 3D printers, furniture, and so much more. The children were in the meadow, playing when Daniel found Sam clutching one of the kids' old onesies, long since outgrown.

"I can't do it, Daniel. I just... can't." Sam's voice was small, almost childlike. He had never heard her sound so fearful. Sam was brash, down-to-earth, able to handle anything. It was what he loved most about her. Some men might naturally gravitate towards being a knight in shining armor, ready to rescue the helpless female, but he far preferred one who would save his ass in a pinch.

That she sounded so small, so fearful, spoke volumes about how deeply she felt. It was understandable, considering the last time she had been inside one of the Cryo units.

"I know it's scary to get back inside of one of those things, but..." Sam's sniff of disdain cut Daniel's words off.

"Not *me*, numb nuts. I'll be fine. It's not as if someone is going to try to put us on an express train to God this time. It's just that there are *reasons* they don't put kids under five years of age in Cryo."

Ah, that tracked.

"Firelli is less than four months short of the limit. They are putting kids as young as three in. Kevin and Maria's girl is going in."

"It's *dangerous*, Daniel. What if something goes wrong?"

"Nothing is going to go wrong." Daniel felt like a fool. Wasn't this Sam's line? This wasn't like her to be so afraid.

"But what if it does?"

"Would you rather stay here?" Daniel asked.

"I know we can't, Daniel. Entity couldn't tell you when the solar winds would take it away. Besides, Tobias is there. On Earth. He's expecting you. I wouldn't ask you to stay here anymore than I want to put Firelli into Cryo." Sam wailed. "I don't know what to do!"

"We will ask for special dispensation. One of us stays out of Cryo, or we alternate going in and out, so she always has one of us. Calypso's gravity is close enough to Earth that Firelli shouldn't suffer any lasting effects. We can wait until she's five, put her in Cryo, and then she and Lila will grow up together."

Sam snorted at the thought of it. "Those two are like oil and water."

"Sam, you gotta help me out here. I'm running out of solutions." Daniel felt as if his skin and soul were stretched to the limits. Between working with Entity on biofuel options and the additional Cryo unit manufacturing they had to do to ensure everyone had a Cryo unit which was usable and safe, and a host of other things, he was dead tired most days. This was all so unlike Sam, though. She wasn't an overly emotional, psychologically fragile woman. Something was really wrong, but Daniel didn't have a clue what.

He reached out and gave her a powerful hug. "Help me out here, woman. I've got nothing left."

She tensed and then melted into him. Buried her face in his neck and whispered, "I'm pregnant."

"Oh…" He pulled away and stared into her eyes, panicked. "Oh shit, *how?*"

The look she gave him then could wither flowers. "Do I really need to explain this to you, Daniel?"

"I, uh."

"I had the shot of NoProgest. It's over 99% effective. But you know what they say, nothing is for sure. And apparently I hit the pregnancy lottery. Carrie says I've beat some damn one in six hundred thousand odds. How's that for lucky?" She burst into tears. "She says it's early enough that I can make it out of orbit, but I can't go into Cryo. And I absolutely *won't* go into Cryo once he is born, and we are on a skeleton crew, so…"

"So, I can't be awake at the same time." Daniel finished for her.

"I can't end it. I know I probably should, and we could try again back on Earth, but I just... *can't*."

Daniel felt like his brain would explode. Of all the times for the birth control to not work, this was unbelievable. His mind flashed on the six-year journey ahead of them. Sam pregnant and giving birth in the spaceship. Their child, she said it was a boy, raised in corridors and 89% Earth gravity for *years*. How in the hell would that even work?

He pulled her back into his arms. "We'll figure this out, Sam. I promise you we will."

He calmed her and then trudged over to Fenton Aaronson's place. The older man was supervising the last items to be sent up to the Calypso and put in Cryo. They were leaving the farm animals, but there had been such an outcry over leaving the dogs and cats that special Cryo containers were designed for the 30-odd pets scattered throughout the colony. Half of the colony was already in orbit, and most of them were in Cryo. The colony, once thriving and bustling with energy, was now a ghost town.

The older man grinned in surprise. "Medry, you're still here? I figured you and your family would be prepping for Cryo by now." His smile faded at the grim look on Daniel's face. By the time Daniel finished explaining, his face looked as grim as Daniel's.

Fenton reached out and grasped Daniel's arm. "Let me think about this. Okay? You and yours get up into orbit on the shuttle tomorrow and by the time I see you there, I'll have a plan we can all live with."

Daniel didn't know what to think. But he trusted the captain implicitly. The older man had never given him a reason not to. "Yeah, okay." Some part of him felt certain Fenton would find a way that he and Sam hadn't thought of, but for the life of him, he couldn't think of what. They selected the crew months in advance. All necessary skill sets specifically accounted for and the circumstances of the colonists' return were far different from those needed over a decade ago. Daniel agonized over it the entire time they packed and prepared for the shuttle into orbit. The kids kept them hopping. They were sniping and quarreling with each other more than normal. Change was stressful, but they were definitely picking up on Daniel and Sam's emotions as they said goodbye to the only home they had ever known.

The next morning, in orbit high above the meadows and valleys of a planet they had hoped to call home and were now leaving, he stood at the door to the captain's ready room, and knocked. He remembered the last time he'd met with the captain. That fateful day when he and Kevin had told Captain Aaronson about a terrible virus on Earth. It felt like a century ago. Fenton stood up from the wide desk and ushered Daniel in.

"Medry, good to see you. How did Sam do with the g's coming up?"

"Fine. Stressed more about the kids right now, but yeah, she's fine."

"Good. Good. Look, I thought about the situation at hand and I think I have a solution. One that will work well for all involved. From my calculations, I am sure we can accommodate Sam's pregnancy here on board. She can carry your child to term and we will, of course, ensure that Dr. Schrader is available for her birth should she prefer her over Ellie, who will spell her throughout the journey home. And Dr. Schrader assures me that with the nano-tech that Tobias Price and Lenny Snelling of the Mars colony have been collaborating on, there shouldn't be any ill effects to the baby from the lowered gravity field or the meager amounts of space radiation present during the journey. We will find a way for this to work out for the full journey home."

Daniel nodded, some of the pressure he had been feeling for the past day easing from his chest.

"As for you, however, we did not have need of a Comm Tech until later in the voyage, and while you are cross-trained, we have other colonists to consider for maintaining the skeleton crew as well." He sighed then. "I've found this all quite complicated. Even more than the trip here was." He ran his fingers through his graying hair and smiled. "I have a solution, though, that I think you can help me with. A position opening for the first three years of the trip, possibly longer."

"A position opening?" Daniel frowned. "What, a new position?"

"Not a new one. A tried and true one. This one, actually. Mine."

Daniel blinked. "What?"

Fenton laughed. "Daniel, you showed courage and resilience in the face of the greatest adversity our crew, our people, ever experienced on board this ship. If that isn't the making of a leader, of someone with the capabilities to captain this ship, I don't know what is." The older man leaned forward, grasped Daniel's shoulder in his grip. "I talked it over with the rest of the Council. We all agreed. I will resign my position effective immediately. You and Sam will have the captain's quarters. It'll do for the two, well, soon to be three of you. When our scheduled shift change occurs and Martin Phoenix is due to be revived from Cryo, we will revisit it, but he's already made noise about making do with one of the Couples billets since the kids will stay in Cryo until we return to Earth." He leaned back in his chair. "What do you say?"

Daniel gaped at Fenton. "I don't… I don't know what to say."

"Well, you could start by saying 'yes.'"

"I..." He laughed then, relief flooding through him. "Yes. Yes, thank you, Captain."

"I think you can call me Fenton now. Being as you are our new Captain. And that's effective as of 0600 today. Which means," Fenton stood up, "I'm sitting in the wrong chair. And look at that, I've got a date with Cryo."

He pulled Daniel into a hug and clapped him on the back. "You'll do us proud as Captain. I just know it." And before Daniel could thank him, he picked up his rucksack and headed out the door.

Right on cue, NARA's voice sounded over the loudspeakers. "Attention all crewmembers. I will now play a pre-recorded announcement by Captain Fenton Aaronson.”

“Citizens of Zarmina’s World, crewmembers of Calypso, my fellow Terrans. It has been a pleasure to serve as your captain on the long journey here. But it is time for me to step down and dedicate myself to my family and take a much-needed rest in Cryo during our long journey back home. As you make your way to Cryo, and to your Singles billets and positions on board the Calypso, I leave you in the very best of hands. A man who will give his life to project you, one who fought to save every one of those in Cryo as our fates lay in the hands of a madman. The Departure Committee has accepted and approved my nomination of Daniel Medry as Acting Captain of the Calypso Starship on our journey home. I trust I will see all of you there on Earth. All our tomorrows wait for us on the soil of our homeland, the cradle of humanity. Sweet dreams. I’ll see you all on the other side.”

There was a low murmur, and those in the halls within view met Daniel’s eye and nodded. Several clapped him on the shoulder and said, “Congratulations, Captain Medry” as if it were the most normal thing in the world.

Daniel stood there, unsure of what to do until Sam found him, looking as shell-shocked as he was.

Lucas, Lila, and Firelli bobbed and dipped in her wake, the lower gravity still a novel delight to them. Ignoring their parents' silence, they remained unfazed and pushed past to explore the captain's quarters, exclaiming over the difference in space from the individual coffins temporarily assigned to them the night before.

"I can't believe it," Sam whispered.

"Me either."

They both stood there, staring at each other. All that remained was to put the kids in Cryo. Sam had received assurances from Carrie Schrader that even Firelli would be fine. They established the "no children under five" rule out of an abundance of caution, but their youngest, at nearly four years of age, would be just fine to go in now. And together they would wait for the birth of their son. By the time he was old enough to go into Cryo, they would be months from arrival, thanks to the shorter journey home to Earth. It wouldn't be easy raising their youngest on board the Calypso, but it was doable, and that was all that mattered.

Hours later, in Cryo, Daniel held Lucas' hand with Sam on the other side. Tears glimmered in her eyes, but she remained calm, collected. The children had gone in, one by one, youngest to oldest, and Lucas was the last. He lay there, clad in shorts and a tank top, so tiny on the bed meant for a full-grown adult. "Daddy, will I dream?" Lucas asked. He shivered slightly, and his eyelids were heavy, the drugs already pulling him down into sleep.

"Possibly. What would you like to dream about, Son?" Lucas grinned in response, as if he had a secret, then slipped away into sleep before he could form the words.

"All our tomorrows," Daniel whispered. They watched the bots wheel their son, inside the child-sized Cryo chamber, down the line and out of sight. Sam's hand slipped into his, and she leaned against him, sighing heavily. He could see the tears running freely now.

"They will be all right, Sam. I promise. And they will have a sibling to play with when they wake up. I'll bet he gives Lucas a run for his money."

"I know. I'm just really going to miss them." She put her free hand protectively over her still flat stomach. "All our tomorrows. I love that. I really do."

Below their feet, the hum of the engines felt steady and sure. They would accelerate until they reached the edge of the star system where they could engage the warp drive. The rumble was a promise to return to a much-changed home, but a return nonetheless. Daniel would miss the beauty of the untamed world they were leaving behind. But it didn't belong to them and Earth was waiting. His son was waiting.

It was time to go home.

Landfall

Date: 01.16.2117

"Captain, it's time." Daniel looked up to see that David Farnsworth stood at the open door of the captain's suite. Behind him, two others stood in the hallway. The rest of the suite, a large bedroom and bathroom walled off with a closed door behind him, told Daniel that Deeks was giving Sam hell yet again. The time for naps was ending, whether or not his parents were ready for it.

The steady hum of the engines was absent now that they were nearly there. This didn't mean an absence of sound. Far from it, life on board a starship was a constant noise. Pumps, people, the HVAC, all of it made noise. After a while, it simply faded into the background. The engines, though, their absence from the matrix of noise, reminded everyone how close to their destination they were. But after a voyage of five years, four months, one week, and two days, they would achieve orbit around Earth today.

They had dropped out of warp a few months ago, and then the engines had reversed, blasting their speed down to an acceptable level, which now had reduced to intermittent course corrections. The last one had been a week ago, and since, a beautiful green and blue planet swam into view.

Home.

The screens had shown it all. First, a mere blue star in the distance. Then a marble swirled with greens, browns, and blues. Finally, it was Earth. Huge and wondrous, large in their viewscreens, a beauty to behold. From space you could see the pocked and devastated remnants of Ultima Thule upon the surface. The impact points, most of them, remained scars upon their home. The few that had landed in the oceans were invisible, but the data stream from Earth showed the devastation far under the sea was still there, still something that Earth, and its denizens, were recovering from.

They had recovered, though.

The survivors had emerged from underground less than two years ago. As the Calypso made the long journey home, humanity had reclaimed the surface of the planet once again, and begun the long, arduous task of rebuilding.

Once Calypso had dropped out of warp three months earlier, the transmission packets flooded in. The old cities, already in ruins, had actually provided some level of protection to the millions left behind before Impact. Deep in subways, in hillsides, cave systems, even a sinkhole in Guangxi Zhuang region of China - all had become shelters that had saved hundreds of thousands of lives. Every week, new pockets of survivors were being found. And thanks to the massive 3D printers, new cities were rising from the rubble and humanity was once again inching their way across their bruised and battered world.

The loss of human life, both from the ESH virus and the 14-kilometer asteroid, had been devastating. But humanity had survived the most incredible odds. The stories of survival continued to amaze Daniel and the rest of the skeleton crew on board. There was even a temporary world government established. It wasn't without its controversies, of course, and plenty of the survivors left on the surface at the time of Impact had certainly had their resentments, but according to the reports, life was slowly improving surface-side.

Daniel stood, looked over at the closed door, and nodded to David Farnsworth. "I'll meet you there in five minutes."

Sam would want to be included in this and it might just help to have their rowdy, over the top, sleep-deprived and manic son along for the ride. Surely, even Deeks would be impressed by the enormous new planet he would soon inhabit. Daniel grinned at the thought of the boy celebrating his fifth birthday there on Earth. And soon, in just a few days, all of their children would soon be reunited, with space to run and play and just be kids. There were unspoken benefits to being the acting Captain on Calypso. His children were among the first batches of scheduled Cryo revivals. Soon, their quarters on the surface would overrun with children once again.

What will Deeks think of his brother and sisters? And what will they think of Deeks?

Daniel opened the door and narrowly missed being shot with an arrow. The arrows had rubber suction cups on the end, but he'd gotten shot in the eye once with one of the damn things, and could attest that they really hurt at a close distance.

"Sorry, Dad!" Deeks yelled, despite there being less than six feet between them. The boy had three settings - loud, louder, and sound asleep. He did nothing in half measures.

"Deekins Lucas Sydan, if I've told you once, I've told you a thousand times. Use your inside voice. And please put the bow and arrows *down*?" Sam said, emerging from the bathroom, her hair damp as she fought to slide her arms into her shirt, the fabric catching and bunching. Daniel could see she was excited. It had been a long voyage, but they were finally here, finally so very close to returning to the surface of Earth.

"Sorry, Mama." Deeks' voice lowered a decibel and Daniel tried to hide a smile. He felt like bouncing and yelling, too.

Deeks hasn't ever used his voice outside, *but that will soon be remedied.*

"It's time. We're nearly in orbit." Daniel said, excitement surging through him. A splash of fear as well. In a few hours, they would be on the surface.

He would see his eldest son for the first time in eighteen years. His stomach churned, migrating down to his guts.

He wrangled his son into ship shoes while Sam finished getting ready and they were out the door three minutes later, heading for the cafeteria. There, the screens held Earth fully in view. Right now, they showed the world cloaked in darkness. For the first time up close, Daniel could see how many changes the ESH virus and asteroid had wrought. Before, as Calypso had departed Earth over 17 years ago, there had been patches of light glowing in the dark. The cities, often lighting and defining the edges of coastline for much of the continents. Now, there was little, nothing really. It was a shocking change.

Billions of dead and gone.

In less than two decades, Earth had transformed from overcrowded to, well, to the empty land that stretched below them. Daniel had been among the lucky ones. His family had been wealthy, well-off. Their house had been roomy, over 297 square meters of space for him and Luke to grow up in. He knew some colonists had lived their entire lives in vast housing complexes that spanned city blocks and rose as high as skyscrapers, but the individual apartments had been tiny, 46 square meters, sometimes less.

By now, the Esperanza, Masa Depan Bumi, and Vision lifeships had all returned from their temporary orbits around Mars and the Moon. Nostradamus and Mayflower had both beaten the slower Calypso, arriving as the first survivors climbed from their rocky underground fortresses. They hung there above Earth, slowly circling an empty planet, but there were still tens of thousands who remained in Cryo. Most of them were children who had no family left. The last gift their parents could give them had been a spot on the lifeships and a chance at a life on this new, changed Earth. Slowly they were being revived from Cryo and adopted into homes. From the reports that Daniel had read, it would take up to twenty more years to accommodate all the children. It had been that, or stick them into mass orphanages, something that seemed overly cruel after all the trauma the kids had gone through already.

They stood there, the three of them, drinking in the sight of the beautiful blue world turning below them. The sun's rays were peeking over the horizon, and soon they would see the day side. Deeks had quieted, his mouth hanging open at the sight of the world below. A world he had never known, never experienced. His entire existence until now had been of a place with walls, corridors, and weak gravity. He appeared suitably impressed by the enormity of his future home. He reached up and put his small hand inside of Daniel's, as if seeking reassurance.

Daniel took a moment to just absorb the sight, to be there with Sam and Deeks, before returning to the job at hand. He looked over at David Farnsworth and nodded.

Farnsworth hit the comm unit on his ship suit. "NARA, please open a line to the TUPG for Captain Medry, please."

"Connecting now." NARA replied. A series of clicks and then...

"This is Captain Daniel Medry of the Calypso Starship."

"Captain, this is Chairman Ryan Evers of the Terran United Planetary Government."

"Good morning, Chairman. Calypso and crew formally request permission to establish orbit and land on Earth."

The warmth in the Chairman's voice rolled through the connection. "Permission granted, Captain. Welcome home. We all look forward to seeing you and the others again."

"Thank you, Chairman. Calypso out."

An hour later, and a rather bumpy ride down to the surface, Daniel unlatched Deeks' restraints. The boy looked pale, perhaps a little green from the turbulence, and he stood wide-legged and confused at the difference in gravity. It wasn't a lot, but it was noticeable.

The shuttle had landed, and the locks were cycling. Sam held tight to their son and to Daniel as the door opened and fresh, shockingly cold air from outside rushed in. It smelled so different from the canned ship air and Deeks was uncharacteristically silent. His eyes wide as his nostrils flared and he pressed close to his parents. There was a crowd of people outside, but one in particular, close to the front, caught Daniel's eye.

Tobias had said he would be there, if possible, but he told Daniel that Syn, his partner, was expecting another set of twins. "This close to the due date I can't promise anything for sure." That had been his last message. And Daniel had understood. Besides, Tobias didn't owe him anything, not after Daniel had left him behind on Earth. He'd thought about it so often, how a reunion between the two of them might go. He had no right to expect anything from his son. Did he even have the right to the label of father with Tobias? And the communications across the millions and billions of miles had not lent themselves to soul-baring missives.

Once I'm back on Earth, I can focus on creating a relationship with him, if he is willing.

How often had he told himself that? He was afraid to hope. And equally afraid that Tobias would reject his overtures. It was a difficult situation, and one he both dreaded and hoped for.

They walked forward, down the ramp, out the door. The cold air hit them in a rush. It smelled of ozone and evergreen. Daniel squinted in the bright winter sun, held a hand up to shade his eyes from the glare. He hadn't seen sunlight like this, well, not since he'd left Earth. They stepped down, off the ramp, and his gaze fell on a tall man in his mid-20s, with his hair, his eyes, and his face. It hadn't been so obvious when he was young, but now, seeing him here in the flesh, Daniel felt as if he were looking in a mirror.

The younger man's face broke into a wide smile, instantly reminding him of Janine.

There were voices, another man in his 30s, with a shock of red hair and warm blue eyes, introducing himself as Ryan Evers, the current Chairman of the TUPG, who shook his hand, as well as Sam's, and even bent down and shook Deeks's hand. Coats were handed out. They were something they hadn't needed on board and certainly hadn't thought to bring. Daniel slipped it on, operating on automatic, his eyes remaining on Tobias's face.

Protocol be damned.

"I'm sorry. Excuse me for a moment." Daniel said to the Chairman, and abandoned Sam and Deeks, making a beeline for his son. A handful of steps and he was there, standing in front of Tobias with a thousand things he wanted to say, and overwhelmed with emotion.

Tobias was still smiling, but tears glimmered in his eyes. "Hi Dad. Welcome home. I've, uh, I've missed you." And he pulled Daniel close. And Daniel realized two things at the moment. First, all the words he had rehearsed didn't matter. And second, his son was at least two inches taller than him. Seconds later, he felt Sam's hand on his back and Deeks pressing close against his legs. They stood there as the world swirled around them.

"I never should have left you," Daniel choked.

"You are here now." His son said, steadfast, his arms tight around Daniel. "And that is all that matters."

Acknowledgments

This might be a part you skip, but to me, it is essential. Because, just as it takes a village to raise a child, it often takes a village (or at least a good group of friends/readers on Facebook) to write a book. Family and friends, I would love to thank all of you, especially...

My husband Dave, who once said, "I look forward to growing old, stinky, and slow with you." It's important to have someone at your back who loves you and supports you, no matter how many crazy requests you throw his way (p.s. Thanks for the secret doors, my darling, I love them).

My kids, all four of them, especially the littles, who keep me laughing, cussing, and my arms full of sticky hugs and kisses. Danielle, a writer in her own right and an avid reader. I still love you, kid, and always will. Alex, the best friend a mama could ever hope for, I love your heart. Angela, guaranteed to keep me grounded. She calls it like she sees it.

Ethan, my bookend baby, you make me smile every doggone day.

Thanks to James Blevins, for finding a way for me to calculate distances using the handy, dandy, latitude/longitude distance calculator over at the National Hurricane Center. You were a lifesaver!

Suzanne Brown Rebecchi for kindly helping with fraction conversions when my writer's brain was rejecting math. I am so sorry you did not get to read this book. Your kindness lives on in my memories and your family's lives.

Kudos to Rebecca Liberty for showing the math.

Thanks to Dad, who shared his love of sci-fi to begin with. I wish you had gotten to read the entire series, Dad. I think you would have liked it.

And of course, always and forever, to Dori, Kate and Rachel from Independent Learning School - thanks for allowing me to learn grammar on my terms. You may not realize it, but you gave me wings. It took a while for me to get off the ground, but hey, look at me flying now!

Finally, a thanks to Stephen King's *Mr. Mercedes* that I binged near the beginning of my journey to completion on this book. It gave me some ideas to toss about and then make uniquely my own.

Thanks to all of you, I couldn't have done it without you!

Author's Note

Thank you for reading this book!

If you enjoyed this book, I have a small favor to ask.

Reviews are incredibly important for authors like me. They not only help new readers discover my books, but also allow me to keep writing and sharing more stories with you. A few words—what you loved, your favorite character, or even just a star rating—can make a big difference.

Please consider leaving a review on *Goodreads* and your favorite bookselling platform. Your feedback helps others find books they might enjoy and supports the entire reading community.

Thank you for taking a moment to share your thoughts. Your support means the world to me!

With that out of the way, it's time for me to confess. It took me over *seven years* to figure out the ending to the Gliese 581g series.

Okay, to be completely honest, I thought I had ended it with the first book. Readers told me otherwise.

"Oh, my God! 'Nathaniel Zradce opened his eyes'," one reader said. "When is the next book coming out?"

The answer?

"Um, I have no idea."

What can I say? I was a baby author. It was my first sci-fi novel, and I was still learning the ropes.

That was where it stood for three, nearly four years. In early 2020, as the first rumors of COVID circulated, I paid little attention. I was looking forward to traveling out of the country for the 2nd time ever. The first time really didn't count. The first time I had ventured past the confines of the country of my birth was in late 2016 to rescue my very ill father from Panama. But that is a story for another time.

In early March 2020, I was excited to be going to England to attend a writer's conference, then visit the city of Bath after a week in London.

"Are you worried about this COVID virus?" A friend asked me.

"Nah!" I might have said something far more derisive. Worry about a lowly virus? As if! But my oh my, I would soon learn differently.

It was a wonderful trip across the pond. I loved it. I especially loved seeing the Roman baths in the ancient city of Bath. Amazing!

As we returned and landed in the United States, we learned the president had issued an order to close the borders. Overnight, the country, heck, the world, seemed to shut down - restaurants, schools, bars, airports. Life became small, stressful, and dark. As COVID gathered strength in the days following our return, I lost around two-thirds of my income - a cleaning business I had run for 15 years, and most of the bookings in our newly opened short-term rental. The rental recovered a few months later, but losing the cleaning business, well, let's just say it was just the excuse I needed to make a serious change and pivot on how I spent my days.

Instead of cleaning houses and trying to fit in a little writing on the side, I instead spent my days focused on my writing, with the goal of finishing far more than my average of one book every two years. And, despite sales of a book on a killer virus being firmly in the toilet at that point, I realized it was time to return to *Gliese 581g* and the world I had created there.

However, I *still* didn't know what happened after "Nathaniel Zradce opened his eyes." Not a stinking clue! And, rather panicked at the thought of writing a book when I didn't have the answer readily in hand, I wrote *G581: Mars* instead. Because writing just one chapter, *Mars Needs Moms* (yes, the title is a tip of the hat to a sci-fi movie one of my kids loved) was not enough, I wanted to go back and talk more about the colony on Mars! And as I wrote it, I realized I wasn't done with Earth. There were still nearly 15 million people left to kill off! *G581: Mars* was a perfect segue into *G581: Earth* in 2021.

I got sidetracked by a romantic suspense project, *Smoke and Steel*, and then the psychological thriller/horror book *Winter's Child*, which was delayed by the addition of our infant son, who we fostered in late 2021 and adopted near the end of 2022. There was also a business book thrown in the middle of that for good measure, because I seem intent on proving I'm not a one-trick pony and will never stick to just one genre. But as I eyed the beginnings of *G581: Zarmina's World*, I *still* didn't feel ready enough, so I wrote *G581: Plague Tales* in

May 2023. And there was another romantic suspense book after that because of, well, reasons.

I was still no closer to discovering the answer to what happened after Nathaniel Zradce opened his eyes, but I was becoming excellent at procrastination!

Not that I wrote three G581 books solely because of procrastination, but yes, it figured heavily into it. And while I had managed around 8,000 words in *Zarmina's World* well before September 2023, there would be no more procrastinating after that. It was time to figure it all out. But you knew there was another but in there, didn't you? I then decided that 2024 was the "year of the audiobook" and, halfway through, pivoted again and decided I really needed to sell my long-term rental (and first home I ever owned) and that took a solid month. After that, my sights settled on renovating Cottage East, a house we bought in 2017 and hope to use as another short-term rental.

And while I'm confessing all of my many delays, I might mention I went to Europe for nine days with my second-born to celebrate his turning 18 and then an author conference in Vegas in mid-November 2024. And in the middle of those two events, I lost my father, the man who set a love of all things sci-fi into me at an early age.

I am feeling like Doug from Up!

But finally, FINALLY, here it is, for you, the answer to what happened after Nathaniel Zradce opened his eyes.

Thanks again for buying this book and for sticking with me through this series. I truly hope you enjoyed reading it at least half as much as I have enjoyed finally facing my procrastination and, you know, actually writing the book.

- Christine -

p.s. There will be one more book in this series - *G581: Plague Tales II* will be released at the same time as this book.

Easter Eggs

All of my series connect and cross genres in weird, often obscure and tiny ways. I use the term Easter egg, which Wikipedia describes as "a message, image, or feature hidden in software, a video game, a film, or other formats" - to connect my series, even those that cross genres, in some cool and unexpected ways.

I have done this with my Gliese 581g series as well. And if you are interested, and willing to cross genres, then you will enjoy finding the connections I leave lying in wait in other books.

Nathaniel Zradce, for example, is not a normal man. He isn't even human. Instead, he is a Njerez, a race of people who lived on Fyrsta Heim, a world damaged by cataclysm and separated from our own by portals only a few can control. Imagine an onion, with the outer layer patchy and incomplete, separate from the surface. That is how I imagine Fyrsta Heim. A world separate from Earth, yet inextricably linked. The Njerez were able to go back home to their own planet shortly before The Collapse, a period of socioeconomic collapse and civil war in the United States earlier in the 21st century that is documented in the War's End series.

I keep promising to write about the Njerez more. And it is coming. That series, The Chronicles of Liv Rowan, has a dozen stories (possibly books?) that center on a young woman with enormous magical powers. Ones that are unexpected, which unlock 21 years to the day (and moment) of her birth. Liv Rowan finds herself transported to a dimension where magic works and technology does not. Her power can help her save her people from destruction and rebuild their broken world. It is hinted at, and skirted around, in its prequel Fate's Highway.

And if you were to read the War's End series, which is dystopian and set in the day after tomorrow, you would likely recognize some of the surnames. Fenton Aaronson and Julie Lynn Aaronson from Gliese 581g are descendants of the protagonists in The Storm and subsequent books, Jess and Chris Aaronson. The Perdue family in The Storm also have descendants in the Gliese series. Edith Sarah Hainey, also known as Patient Zero, is the granddaughter of Joseph Perdue. And the list goes on.

I lay the blame for this at the feet of Madeleine L'Engle, who wrote series that intersected in quiet, remote ways. I loved her Wrinkle in Time series as well as the Austins.

Perhaps you are a dyed-in-the-wool, do or die, sci-fi addict. I understand, and I wish you well. You won't need the connections from one series to another to understand the books as a whole, it's just me having a little bit of fun and giving my cross-genre readers a little something extra. I'm a nerd, what can I say?!

Meanwhile, happy reading, and thank you for reading this far!

Christine

The Story Behind the Story

Do you ever wonder about the story behind the story? What made an author think of a storyline? An idea?

Well, wonder no more, for here it is...

I had just moved back to Kansas City, Missouri in 1997. My nine-year-old daughter and I were staying with my mom and I was working for a place called Regional Consortium for Technology and Information Exchange, (RCTIE for short). On my lunch break, sitting in the drive-through at a Wendy's, I was suddenly struck with a "what if?" - a snippet of a scene, if you will.

What if a woman drove up to the drive-through, stark naked, ordered ten combo meals, put her car in park there in the lane, and began stuffing her face until her stomach exploded?

Yes, I know, I've got a dark mind. Folks tell me that often. But that snippet of a scene stuck with me. I called it Plague Tales. I was 27, a single mom, struggling to make ends meet, working full-time and attending college part-time. Needless to say, the story didn't go very far. A few pages of typed notes, that was it.

Fast forward to 2010. I had finished writing and publishing my first two books, *Get Organized, Stay Organized*, and *War's End: The Storm* and I was bit by the writing bug hard. Honestly, I had dreamed of being a writer since my teens and I jumped at the chance to write more. I was thinking about Plague Tales, but I also had this other story idea, about a group of scientists and explorers who travel 22 light years away to the Gliese 581 system to explore a newly discovered planet and there is a saboteur on board. Why was there a saboteur on board? I had no idea! I called it Gliese 581g, after the world that Steve Vogt and his team discovered in 2010.

It was a year or two after that when the two stories merged and became one. Finally, I had a reason for a saboteur, and a lot of story to tell. *G581: The Departure* came out in late 2016. I honestly thought I was done. One and DONE. Readers told me otherwise. And here we are, five books, and nine years later.

"And that," as Paul Harvey would say, "is the rest of the story."